SECRETS OF THE BLUE HAND GIRLS

SECRETS OF THE BLUE HAND GIRLS

ROWANA MILLER

Cover design by Emily Mahar
Cover images © Peter Dazeley/Getty Images, Exopixel/Shutterstock, Akkalak/Shutterstock, Old Man Stocker/Shutterstock, Jonathan Knowles/Getty Images, Olena Malik/Getty Images, shephotos/Shutterstock, fusiangkara/Shutterstock
Internal design by Tara Jaggers/Sourcebooks

Published by Sourcebooks Fire, an imprint of Sourcebooks
1935 Brookdale RD, Naperville, IL 60563-2773
(630) 961-3900
sourcebooks.com

Cataloging-in-Publication Data is on file with the Library of Congress.

Printed and bound in Canada.
FR 10 9 8 7 6 5 4 3 2 1

For my parents, especially my mom,
who has read every word of every draft
of every manuscript I've ever written.
Their love for me and belief in my
writing have made this book possible.

CHAPTER 1

I DYE MY HAND BLUE when I'm alone, the way the instructions say.

I buy a box of ballpoint pens on my way to school, and when I get there, I crack open each one into a Tupperware in the second-floor supply closet. Then I press my palm into the Tupperware's base, and when I unstick my hand from the plastic, it comes up indigo, except for the pale web of lines in my skin.

Completely coated, the instructions say.

So I keep rubbing the ink into the lines until my whole palm is blue, my other hand inside a rubber glove so I don't get the ink on it—there will be a penalty for drips—and smooth it into the backs of my fingers, my knuckles, and under my fingernails.

I found the letter in my locker three days ago, when I was desperate for a distraction, my name etched on the folded paper with a fountain pen. I don't know how many times I've reread it. Definitely enough to have it memorized, but I keep it propped on a bottle of Windex as I fill in the last few patches of blue, just in case I've forgotten a step. *Kay,* it starts, *we find you intriguing.*

And, I mean, that was enough.

The air in the supply closet is electric with mildew and ink fumes. I check my watch. Four minutes to first period. I flap my blue hand in the thick air to dry the last of the ink, then graze my blue palm with one gloved fingertip. It comes up clean. I peel off the glove and stick it behind a bottle of Clorox, then fold up the letter again and tuck it into my backpack. Three minutes to first period.

There are two remaining unopened ballpoint pens, and I stick them in my pocket as I run to calculus. It's the Thursday before Halloween, which means that no one wants a pop quiz, so Mr. Holmes is definitely planning a pop quiz. On quiz days, he locks the door the moment the minute hand hits 8:01—he says that the first fifty-nine seconds after 8:00 are his gift to us—and gives zeros to anyone unfortunate enough to miss their train. *New York City's transit system is woefully unpredictable, and you should factor that into your decision about what time to leave for school,* Mr. Holmes wrote in the syllabus.

Mr. Holmes didn't say anything about being late due to following mysterious instructions, but I doubt he would consider that a reasonable excuse, either.

I skid through the door at 7:59 and land in my assigned seat, right underneath Mr. Holmes's framed portrait of Watson and Crick. This is the kind of man Mr. Holmes is: On the first day of class, he told us that he was teaching for the prodigies among us, the Watsons and the Cricks, those who would be discovering the DNA of mathematics. And if the rest of us didn't understand his methodology, well, that said more about us than it did about him, right?

After Mr. Holmes made that announcement, one senior raised her hand and asked him about Rosalind Franklin—the biophysicist whose research Watson and Crick relied upon, the one who died via exposure to radiation in the process of conducting her work, but whom Watson and Crick barely left as a footnote in their scholarship. Mr. Holmes got very red-faced and sputtery at that point and muttered something about only winners being able to stick around. It was almost impressive how ill-suited his response was to a class at an all-girls school. At that moment, I decided that Mr. Holmes was an asshole, and in the two months since then, I've received very little evidence to reconsider that verdict.

My tablemates stare at me through drowsy eyes. Two of them

are here today, but the seat across from me is empty. It's empty most of the time, to be honest. But when she's there Zola—the senior who asked about Rosalind Franklin—fills more than the seat. She's the kind of person who radiates enough to fill the entire room.

After a long moment during which my tablemates pretend they're not looking at my hand, one of them—Priscilla, the school's resident weed dealer, although you would never know it from her signature Prada sunglasses—says, "What's up with the blue?"

It's the greatest number of words she's said to me all year. "Um. Nothing."

She raises her pristinely plucked eyebrows. "Did you do it with Margaret O'Malley?"

So I'm not the only one.

I wonder who else got letters. I wonder if they all followed the instructions.

"Quiz time," says Mr. Holmes, slamming the door shut and twisting the lock with as much panache as possible for a burned-out fortysomething who wishes he were anything but a high school calc teacher. "Clear your desks and take out your No. 2 pencils. There will be no credit if you use a pen."

He says the same sentences and uses the same intonation every time he announces a pop quiz. The emphasis is on the *time,* the *clear,* and the *pen.* I look down at my hand. The ink will stain the page. And when it does, Mr. Holmes will come up with an excuse to dock me points. Even if all my answers are correct, he'll claim that I wasn't showing my work or that I was too careless for him to even know *what* my answers were, which really isn't like me...is it now? And even though I wish I were the kind of person who doesn't care about a few points off a math quiz, I can't stop myself from replaying the motivational speech that runs through my mind at least four times a day: *You need full marks because you need an A in the class, and you need an A in the class to keep your scholarship, and you need your scholarship because colleges lose their minds over Davison High School, and you need colleges to lose their minds over you to get into Northwestern next year and forget that you ever had to suffer through high school in the first place.*

After Mr. Holmes hands me my quiz, I tuck a tissue between the side of my palm and the slip of paper. He raises a silent eyebrow at the blue and moves on.

Despite Mr. Holmes's incomprehensible lectures, my hours per day spent memorizing the textbook have rendered the problems easy and dull. I turn in the quiz after a perfunctory double check. As I return to my table, I notice another blue hand in the room. Not Margaret. Margaret is the reason why this school now offers AP Computer Science. This hand belongs to Vanessa Hargrove, about whom I know exactly two things: 1) her wrists always contain matching stacks of Van Cleef & Arpels and Cartier bracelets, and 2) her hand is currently blue.

"Put down your pencils. The quiz is over. Once again, put down your pencils," says Mr. Holmes. He unlocks the door, and from the other side, Zola strides out of Quiz Jail in a way that makes me feel stupid for being on time. Her long red hair bounces behind her, one stray tendril swinging its way over her shoulder, slashing across the Davison High School crest embroidered on the white polo of her uniform. Mr. Holmes meets her sharp blue eyes with his unreadable black ones. "Thank you for joining us, Miss Wolfe."

"Always a pleasure," Zola says. "Fantastic pocket square, Mr. Holmes."

Today Mr. Holmes's pocket square is red with orange paisley swirls, stark against his plaid olive jacket. It isn't one of his fresher combinations. It's lousy timing for a mismatched outfit, too. In addition to being our calc teacher, he's the director of Davison's famed internship program, so after school today he'll be running this season's internship expo featuring the girls who worked at the most prestigious companies last summer. For the second year that I've been eligible, I'm not one of these girls. The third-floor bathroom has seen a normal number of stress tears from me about this.

"Thank you," Mr. Holmes says stiffly.

Zola nods at him, chin up before down, and folds herself—all six feet of her—into her seat across from me. Her eyes dart to my hand and then to the tissue on my desk, stamped with the side of my palm print. A smirk twitches on her lips. "Your hand is blue, Anderson."

"I've noticed." I try my best to maintain eye contact with her while reaching into my backpack for my calc binder. It doesn't work. I come up with a fistful of crumpled history handouts instead.

"Got a reason for the ink?" Zola's desk is bare except for a single sheet of loose-leaf paper, which I know from experience she's not even going to pretend to use for notes. Her favorite things to doodle are thunderstorms.

"It's an experiment," I tell her.

"Oh?"

"I'm putting aside twenty-five cents every time someone informs me that my hand is blue. Testing the human impulse to point out the obvious."

"Let me pay my share, then." Zola reaches into the pocket of her slacks and pulls out a quarter, which she presses into the center of my blue palm.

When I peel off the coin, the circle it leaves behind is slightly less concentrated with ink than the rest of my hand.

"Um," I say.

"Quiet, Table Four!" says Mr. Holmes.

"Looks like you need a touch-up," Zola says, her voice a shade softer. "If you let it wear away, you won't be able to test for a damn thing."

A few minutes later, the two extra ballpoint pens and I are back in the closet, and I'm massaging the ink into the pale circle.

"Is there a point to your experiment?" Priscilla asks when I get back to the classroom.

I shift the tissue back under my palm to keep my binder page pristine while I take notes. Mr. Holmes collects the binders once a month and kills our participation grades if he doesn't think they're tidy. "If you can figure it out, I'd love to hear it."

• • • • •

There are flickers of blue in the halls today. I don't see who all the hands belong to, but I catch some—the professional model who sports an immaculate face of makeup to school every day, the goalie of the soccer team, the a cappella singer who wears her uniform beneath Chanel jackets sharp enough to slice a cantaloupe. Just on the journey to the library for lunch, I count five blue hands, all on other members of the junior class.

When I give tours of Davison for prospective students and their families during my weekly shifts as a student tour guide, the library is the only room that I don't have to pretend to revere.

The arched ceilings smooth out the sounds of pages turning and laptop keys clacking into a single blanket of atmospheric noise, and a skylight casts a hazy glow onto the stacks of shelves that surround the cluster of armchairs in the center of the space. A few girls are scattered throughout the room—two pressing their heads together over one of the mahogany tables near the doorway, another hooking up her computer to the printer just past the biology section—but unlike in the atrium, where most girls eat lunch, there's no one stage-whispering about the rooftop party on the Upper West Side where someone lit a bottle of peach schnapps on fire.

As I head toward my usual armchair, the one with the gingham patch sewn over a rip in the leather, I see several blue fingers rise over one of the aisles in the NYC history section. The fingers wrap around a fabric volume, then disappear behind the shelf. Maybe the owner of that hand has the right idea. Today, there may be a better use of the library than doing homework.

Before I make it to NYC history, the girl steps out of the aisle. I freeze. Of all the juniors at this school, the only one I'd hoped had nothing to do with this was Aubrey Clarke.

As usual, her dark hair—all bangs and no length—is obscuring too much of her face for me to see her expression. All I can tell is that she's looking straight at me. And then she cocks her head back toward the aisle.

Suddenly, my usual armchair seems like exactly the right place for me to be: right under the skylight and in view of the doorway. I swivel in my path and nestle myself in the chair's familiar embrace. Looking anywhere but the NYC history section, I rustle around in my backpack until my hand connects with a folder, then yank it out and spread it on my lap. Info sheet for spring internship applications? Perfect. It's the only thing in the world that merits my attention at this moment.

The leather of the chair next to mine releases a squeak as a body settles into it. "You shouldn't make it so obvious when you're trying to avoid people."

I don't look up from the internship info sheet, even though it might as well be written in hieroglyphics. "I have homework to do."

"You always do…don't you?" Aubrey reaches over and spreads her blue hand across the surface of the page, leaving a stamp of smudged ink. Fuck.

I plan out what to say next: *I don't know what you want, but I'm not interested in having anything in common with you, so if you don't mind, please go back to reading the Unabomber's manifesto or whatever it is you do for fun.*

But those words vanish as soon as I meet her gaze. "Please—please go away."

"What did you think of the letter?"

My breath snags. "I don't want to talk about it with you."

"Personally, I thought it was quite interesting, especially given who else showed up with blue hands today."

I don't say anything for approximately six of my heartbeats. "Like I said, we're not having this conversation."

"You know, I've always admired you, Kay," Aubrey says, tracing one blue finger down the side of my math worksheet. "You don't compromise."

The blue looks oddly natural on her. A thought occurs to me, and it's probably stupid to give myself away by voicing it, but I can't help myself. "You weren't the one who sent the letter, were you?"

Aubrey laughs. The sound is rough, like an emery board scraped across gravel. "Oh, I wish. Unfortunately, for a change, I'm just as much of a pawn as you are."

"Didn't you have some research to do? On the other side of the library?"

"I was just going back there." Aubrey stands and pats my shoulder, leaving a faint blue stain on my white uniform polo. "You should work on your collaboration skills, you know. Colleges tend to like that."

I press my lips together, resisting the urge to have the last word as she strolls back toward the NYC history section. It occurs to me that this is the second real conversation I've ever had with Aubrey Clarke. I hope it will produce fewer casualties than the first one.

• • • • •

I have to know who sent the letter. That's all I can think about today in AP Physics. If it wasn't Aubrey—and that's assuming I believe her—then who would issue such a strange, seductive challenge? In a school like Davison, of course there are rumors about secret societies, although it isn't clear whether those stem from anything that's actually going on here or whether someone was trying to wish fulfill this place into becoming Yale. Until now I assumed it was the latter, but I've probably been projecting.

Instead of concentrating on the wheeled block I've sent rolling down the ramp on my lab table, I think about the letter.

Kay,

We find you intriguing.

We've been watching you. We know that you sometimes put on smudgy eyeliner in the third-floor bathroom before classes start. We know that your favorite scarf is the striped orange and red hand-me-down that you got from your aunt. We know that at lunch, when you're pretending to study, you're listening to true crime podcasts against the backdrop of the pink noise of the library. (If we may offer a recommendation for a case to look into, we think you would be interested in the Poughkeepsie-based murderer who, upon his arrest, was also discovered to be harboring several millions' worth of Nazi-looted artwork.)

We have a request for you. You don't need to follow it, but you should. We want you to dye your right hand blue three days from now before class. Completely blue—no cracks, no faded patches. And no drips on any other part of your body. We'll be watching closely, and if you violate any of our rules, there will be penalties.

Don't tell anyone about this note, of course. That should go without saying. When people ask about your hand, tell them it was your idea.

If you talk, the penalties will be much worse—and much farther-reaching—than the penalties for dripping.

That's everything we have to tell you. So what's the verdict?

Kay, do you find us intriguing?

My lab groupmate, Ruby, yelps. I realize that I've sent the block careening toward her arm. "Watch yourself, Kay!"

I wince. "Sorry."

"Stop being so fucking dramatic, Rubes," says another one

of our groupmates, Samira, as she slides a metal weight into the divot at the top of the wheeled block. "The block is, like, fifty grams."

Samira is wearing yellow latex gloves, but I noted earlier that her hands are undyed underneath.

"You're one to talk about drama," Ruby says. "Come back to me when you've gotten yourself unbanned from every karaoke spot in Koreatown."

Samira emits a high-pitched giggle. "Oh my gosh. Shut *up.*"

The last member of our lab group, Lee, looks up from their notes, their thick black eyeliner framing a bemused glance at Samira. "Oh, damn, I thought you were still allowed in at least Sing 31. What did you do this time?"

Samira launches into a convoluted explanation involving a forty-dollar mascara, a fake ID, and an underripe banana. I listen as I punch times into the stopwatch next to the ramp, and I laugh at all the right moments. But here's the thing: after physics gets out, Samira will go to practice with her band, Ruby will meet up with her boyfriend at the pier, and Lee will do whatever nonbinary emo stoners do with their friends. And I'll go home. Maybe I'll rewrite my notes for the tours I'll be giving next month as Davison's admissions season intensifies, or maybe I'll prep for tomorrow's tutoring session with the fourth grader who lives in my building so that I have the cash to enable my chai habit this week, or maybe I'll walk around Bedford-Stuyvesant and listen to a true crime podcast, even though the episodes make me feel a little sick after what happened two years ago. Probably, though, I'll do homework that isn't due for another week. Otherwise, how will I stay a week ahead?

"This is so funny, Samira, but could you run the experiment with the hundred-gram block?" I say. "I don't want to have to stay late again to finish the lab. We've all got things to do."

• • • • •

When I get home, my aunt Shell is at the kitchen island, sifting through a stack of papers. She's been living with us for the past year while she pursues her master's in environmental studies at NYU, although she's not around much these days.

It probably doesn't do me any favors to admire the way she dresses—as the queer one between the two of us, it's kind of embarrassing for me—but I can't help myself. Really, it's the way that her clothes fit: her vest nips in right at her waist, and the hems of her jeans overlap just a shade with the tops of her ankle boots. I stick a hand in the pocket of my slacks. No matter how I tuck and cuff my uniform, it'll never look as good on me as the crisp polos and work pants do on the interchangeable skinny white mascs on my TikTok feed. But Aunt Shell has an advantage there: she's not dressing around a Great

Stress Weight Gain of Freshman Year. Grief, and guilt, will do that to you.

"I'd almost forgotten that you lived here," I say. "It's good to see you."

Aunt Shell doesn't look up from her papers. "Yeah, sorry. Lots going on."

"Spending a lot of time on the phone with Carlos?" I ask.

Aunt Shell nods. Carlos, her boyfriend, works at a Tesla plant in rural Pennsylvania. They met a few months ago when he came to the city for a conference and she was protesting outside it. Somehow she was willing to take him at his word that he's motivated by a love of engineering rather than a hatred of democracy.

"How many satellites has he hijacked today?" I ask, slinging my backpack onto the floor and pawing through the cupboard for microwave popcorn.

"Kay, you know that's not what he does." For the first time, Aunt Shell glances up. "What's with your hand?"

My blue hand freezes, stark against the yellow of the popcorn bag, my arm midway in flight to the microwave. "It's...it's for..."

If this had been half a year ago, I wouldn't have hesitated. Even when I was a little kid growing up in Brooklyn and she was a teenager in Iowa, I called her a few times a month to update her on my growing collection of secrets. When I lost the ring that my mother gave me for my fifth birthday, I whispered the truth to Aunt Shell on the phone that night. I told her about my panicked first crush on a boy at eight years old and my even-more-panicked first crush on a girl at eleven. (If I was both queer *and* female, I could *never* be president!) And when my grades plummeted in the middle of freshman year after Emily Hendricks turned up dead, Aunt Shell was the only person who knew the real reason I stopped doing my homework. If she hadn't moved in with us, I don't know if I'd have been able to break through the clouds of horror that clustered around me after that.

But that was all pre-Carlos. Now she has him in a way that is so all-consuming that three days ago, on Emily's birthday, I didn't even see her at home. I had to be alone while I lit a cinnamon candle next to my laptop and reread my two months of texts with Emily. But that was also the day that the letter came. And now I have...*Kay, we find you intriguing.*

"It's a social experiment," I say after too long a pause.

"For class?" she asks.

"No." My throat unsticks itself, and I finally place my popcorn in the microwave. "I...thought Davison was too buttoned up. I want to see how far I can push the dress code."

I brace myself for the inevitable lecture about not squandering my scholarship. After all, Aunt Shell's full ride to a private boarding school was what put her on the path to Northwestern. That's what prompted me to look into private education for myself, too.

Instead, Aunt Shell's lips twist slightly, and she looks down at her papers again.

I set the microwave timer and lean over Aunt Shell's shoulder to read the page on top of the stack. It's a form titled *Lease Agreement*.

I breathe in. "Aunt Shell?"

"Kay, I've wanted to bring this up for a while now," she says. "But I wanted to be sure before I said anything."

Neither of us says anything for a moment. Inside the microwave, the popcorn starts to pop.

"So what is it, then?" I ask.

"You know I never expected things to progress like this with Carlos," Aunt Shell says.

"Stop hedging." My voice comes out harder than I intend.

Aunt Shell takes a breath. "I'm moving to Pennsylvania and finishing my degree remotely."

Her jaw muscles tense. I realize that now she's expecting a lecture. And sure, there's plenty I could say—it's almost too ironic, pursuing environmental studies in a home where Tesla pays half the rent—but nothing will make a difference if she already has the lease.

"I hope he's worth it," I say.

The microwave hasn't stopped yet, but I open the door and take out the bag of popcorn, with the kernels still bursting inside the thin paper, and walk out of the kitchen. I dig my fingernails into my palm, hoping that the sting will trigger some feeling, any feeling.

I close the door to my room and lay the popcorn bag on my desk. There's homework to do. I slip a tissue underneath my blue hand—it's starting to feel like a ritual—and open my history binder to a fresh page. *Marbury v. Madison* is more important than anything else I could have on my mind right now. More important than Aunt Shell, more important than the letter in my locker, and certainly more important than the final text Emily sent me the day preceding the manhole explosion seized her life before it had truly started: *I was right, you know.*

My cinnamon candle is now a corpse, a thin layer of wax forming an exoskeleton around a stubby whisper of a wick, but even if I could burn it forever, I'd never know what she meant.

As I open the left flap of my history binder, a scrap of lined paper falls out of the plastic. The edges of the paper are rough.

Written in blue ink, it says, *Stop using the tissue. We want you to leave a mark.*

I slide the tissue out from under the side of my palm.

When I'm done writing, the page is stamped with my handprints.

CHAPTER 2

When I swing open my locker door the next morning, another scrap of lined paper floats to the ground.

I snatch it up. I don't think anyone saw. The hallway is pretty crowded, which means no one is paying attention. I can feel my heart thudding as I unfold the paper.

We're going to answer your first question before you ask it. No, you can't wash off the ink.

Shit. I didn't wash it off, but I didn't keep it fresh. I didn't know if it was a one-day thing, or a blue-hand-forever thing, or something in between. So when I showered this morning, I put on a rubber glove, but the water still trickled inside, and now you can see the yellowishness of my skin peeking through the indigo. And I've run out of ballpoint pens.

Okay. I have thirteen minutes before class starts—thirteen minutes to locate some blue dye. The library isn't open yet, and it would be too strange to ask someone to borrow a pen for something this...private. Maybe I can snag something from an open backpack?

Down the hall, the AP Bio teacher walks out of her classroom, leather boots clicking on the tile. I take a few steps away from my locker and glance through the open door. Her room is empty, and on her desk is a *World's Best Organism* mug filled with writing utensils.

Behind me, she pulls open the door of the teachers' bathroom and closes it behind her.

I allow my body to weave through a couple of student clusters and slip into the bio classroom, then sift through the pens and pencils in the mug. There are no ballpoints, but there's a blue felt-tipped marker, and it'll have to do. I slip the marker up the sleeve of my maroon quarter-zip, the Davison crest emblazoned on its left side. I feel like I'm turning the school into an accomplice.

After I'm a comfortable few paces out of the bio classroom, I pass the Davison principal, Renée Ellison, striding down the hallway. Despite her status, she wears a modified version of the Davison uniform: immaculately tailored gray suits and a deep red lipstick in the same shade as the Davison maroon. The plastic of the marker feels cold against my skin. I expect Principal Ellison's eyes to be drawn to the slight bulge underneath the cotton of my sleeve, but she passes by me without even making eye contact. Because of course she does. Because she's not expecting anyone to have stolen a marker from a bio classroom—hell, because it's a *marker*. No one should get this sweaty from stealing a marker. And yet.

"Kay!" The voice is coming from behind me. I glance over my shoulder and lock eyes with—shit. Aubrey.

I can't deal with this now, or ever. I duck between student clusters and into the bathroom. It serves her right after what she did freshman year. Doing my best to calm my heartbeat, I close a stall door behind me and recolor my hand, intensifying the blue where it's faded and adding it in where it's gone. The marker doesn't match perfectly, but I hope that the letter-writers—wherever they are—won't notice.

When I leave the stall, Zola is putting on lipstick at the sink. It's emerald green, stark against her pale skin. Her eyes meet mine in the mirror, and I realize that, even though it's counterproductive, I can't leave the bathroom without washing my hands.

Almost drowned out by the sound of the running water, Zola says, "You could be a Renaissance painting."

My hands stop moving in the sink. "What?"

"Look at yourself, Kay. Dark hair, dark eyes, water splashing mournfully over a blue appendage. Maybe it's hypothermia; maybe it's Maybelline."

"Jesus, Zola."

Her eyes trace me, starting with my eyeliner-coated eyes and skimming down past where my hair ends at my collarbone, then traveling along the sweatshirt-padded line of my right arm until her gaze settles on the blue marker that I laid next to the sink. I find myself looking at her the same way, noticing her angular jawline and slender fingers, but I'm drawn back over and over to those explosive blue eyes. She returns her gaze to the mirror and perfects the emerald curve of her cupid's bow. "What? It's a good look for you."

She couldn't be one of the letter writers. It would be too obvious. Right?

In first-period calculus, Mr. Holmes hands back our quizzes from yesterday. Full credit.

.....

Halloween is a Saturday this year, which I'm sure is great for Samira and her crowd—perhaps she'll venture out of K-town in search of new karaoke spots to get banned from—but it doesn't change much for me. Every year I hand out candy on the stoop of my brownstone—even freshman year, although if Aubrey hadn't chosen October 30 to stuff Emily's locker with a bouquet of black roses and an invite to a romantic picnic in a graveyard, maybe I'd have broken my tradition.

Ironically, Halloween is the one night when I don't have to wear any kind of mask. Instead, I can blend into the quiet beauty of Bed-Stuy and barter Snickers bars for the flashes of vicarious joy I can leach from kids who are too young to worry about college admissions or teenage social rituals or the unspoken norms of the wealthy.

I situate myself on the center of the steps, my hand resting on a plastic cauldron of candy bars. It isn't dark yet, but whispers of dusk are starting to streak across the sky from beyond the row of brownstones opposite me. This year, I'm a fortune-teller. The primary elements of my costume are an old black shawl, onto which I've hot glued some gold beads in an order that vaguely resembles a pattern, and a pair of black leather boots. It's basic, not that my audience will be particularly judgmental. I just needed a sort of mysterious character that wouldn't look too out of place with a blue hand.

As I begin the candy distribution, I keep a mental catalog of the kids' costumes: some classic vampires and skeletons, a strawberry, some zombie versions of the politicians du jour, and a live coat hanger sculpture. Around seven o'clock, another fortune-teller saunters up to the stairs. She's probably ten years old, beaded braids jingling as she skips up the steps, a sash of tarot cards draped across her chest.

"You've outdone me," I tell her.

The girl gives me a once-over. I can see her eyes taking in the strings of hot glue littering my shawl.

"Kay?"

I tend to skim over the beleaguered adults trailing behind the kids. Which I guess is why I didn't notice that this isn't a parent. Not even close. This is Chioma Akinde, the Chanel aficionado whose voice makes it worth it to go to Davison's a cappella concerts.

And one of the girls I saw in the halls with a blue hand.

"I didn't know you lived around here," I say after a pause. I have the vague idea that she's from the Upper West Side, somewhere near Davison.

"Ah, well, I don't," Chioma says, her eyes flicking over to me as she shifts in place. The fortune-teller darts up to my cauldron and begins to rifle through it. "But when I have the chance, I like taking my little sister to neighborhoods where there are actual Black people. Present company excepted."

Her sister pouts. "There are no full-size candy bars. *Again.*"

"Amara." Chioma's voice is harsh. "That isn't nice."

"No, it's fine," I say, even though what I want to say is *The Upper West Side surely wouldn't have this problem.*

"It's not," Chioma says. "Amara, no candy from this building. Come on."

As she speaks, she gestures at her sister, and again, I see the ink staining her skin navy.

"Wait," I say. "Your hand."

"Your hand too."

"Are we allowed to talk about it?" I ask. As if she has answers. But all I can see are her goddess braids forming tendrils down her back. And her tweed skirt-suit wrapping around her body like a knight's armor. And the deep, shimmering blue of her fingers. And even if she doesn't know anything more than I do, I'm glad someone is seeing me the same way they see her.

"Definitely not," Chioma says. I feel my stomach deflate. "So it's good that no one else from school is here right now."

She looks right at me, mischief sparkling in her eyes, and my stomach swells back up. "Yeah?"

Chioma sits down next to me on the steps of the brownstone. "Okay, what have they said to you so far?"

"Just to dye it blue and keep it blue."

"Anything else?"

"They slipped me a note saying that I should take out the tissue I was using to protect my binders from the ink. They said that I should, um, leave a mark."

"It sounds like they sent us similar first letters, but different notes. I got a reference to a song in the next a cappella concert. But we don't share the song lists until the performances."

"So you're saying that there must be at least one letter writer in the a cappella group?"

Chioma twirls a braid around one blue finger. "Or one of the drama kids. They hang out in the drama office behind the black box theater while we're rehearsing."

"That sounds pretty good for narrowing the list," I say. "Especially given that we know at least one letter writer has to be in one of my classes, if they saw what I was doing with the tissue."

Chioma shrugs. "It's something. But we don't know how many letter writers there are; there's no reason they would be the same person."

"Fair."

"This is some real psychological-thriller shit, isn't it?"

This is the first time I've spoken to Chioma one-on-one, and I notice that *shit* sounds slightly unnatural coming out of her mouth, cocooned in her deliberate enunciation.

"Hurry *up*," says Amara.

"Hush," says Chioma.

For the first time, I take a look at the tarot cards strung together in Amara's sash. The Hermit, the Fool, the Wheel of Fortune, The Hanged Man.

"Why are you following their instructions?" I ask.

"Why are you?"

A glimmer of light from a streetlamp glances off the glossy surface of the Hermit. "I just...I think I need to."

"Okay. Then that's what I'll say, too."

The real answer may or may not have to do with the letter arriving on Emily's birthday. On second thought, maybe that timing wasn't a coincidence. After all, two years ago, Aubrey's now-blue fingers were intertwined with Emily's.

But unlike me and Aubrey, Chioma didn't know Emily, at least not to my knowledge. I'm sure making up a connection is wishful thinking so I don't have to admit just how powerful I found the *Kay, we find you intriguing.*

"What was the song, at least?" I ask.

"Don't ruin our concert surprise, okay?"

"Of course not."

"'Choke,' by the band I Don't Know How But They Found Me." Suddenly, my fortune-teller shawl is far too thin to protect me from the claws of the evening wind. "And is that, um, a threat?"

Chioma tugs the right flap of her jacket to overlap with the left, the tweed taut over her ribcage. "Isn't that the question of the semester?"

.....

I'm back in my room by 8:30, my shawl hung up in my closet. There's that feeling of deflation you get when something good is over. And that other feeling of deflation you get when you know that it's not over for other people, because when you open Instagram stories, you can see that the drama kids—potential letter writers, I guess—have only just finished doing their makeup before they head out to the Greenwich Village parade, and Lee's emo friends are sword fighting in faux-tattered pirate costumes, and Samira is throw-your-head-back laughing in a crowded room, eyeliner whiskers drawn on her cheeks and a cat-ear headband sweeping her balayage-dotted hair out of her face.

There's a knock at my door. "Kay, can I come in?"

In what can now be described as a typical Aunt Shell move, this is the first time we've crossed paths since our conversation on Thursday.

"Sure," I call, swiveling my desk chair around to face the door. I stick my phone in my pocket but leave my laptop open on my desk behind me. Aunt Shell should know that she's interrupting.

She comes in and perches on the side of my bed, my green velvet comforter creasing around her. "How were the kids tonight?"

"They were fine. Cute. One was a coat hanger sculpture."

Aunt Shell laughs a little too long. "I'm glad."

I suppose I have to actually have the conversation she initiated a few days ago.

"I'm happy for you, you know," I say. "Obviously, Carlos is really something."

"Yeah, I guess I'm lucky," she says.

When I look at Aunt Shell, it's hard not to see the version of her who spent a year and a half dragging me to community gardens and baking lemon-curd cake with me, pouring in new memories to replace the images of Emily's scorched body that permeated every fold in my brain's gray matter. But that version of Aunt Shell had calluses on her palms and flour streaked through her hair. These days, she looks less like the aunt who pulled me out of the abyss and more like a Davison girl: pristine and cold.

"Is that all?" I ask.

Aunt Shell shakes her head. "I'm leaving this Wednesday. I thought you should know."

It should feel like a blow, but my breathing stays even. "Thanks for the heads-up."

An image flashes in my mind: the letter in my locker. I remember the zing of electricity that sparked in my stomach when I first saw the folded paper perched on top of my stack of notebooks. Why did that, and not my aunt's news, make me feel something?

"And I wanted to do something together tonight," she continues, "for old times' sake."

"I'm sorry, Aunt Shell, but I have to apply to internships," I say. It's true. Spring internship applications aren't due until just before the holidays, but I've yet to land one of the prestigious placements even after seven cycles, so I can only assume that the other girls are spending more than a month refining their applications. "So if that's all—"

"I'm not accepting that answer," she says. "Kay, close the computer. We're going to the Village parade."

This is what she did before, no matter how many times I pulled my velvet comforter over my head. Maybe there's a chance that things will feel like they used to. Even though my body feels leaden, I bend down and re-lace my boots.

I follow Aunt Shell through the living room. My parents are hunched over the coffee table, locked in a game of Bananagrams, as is their Saturday night tradition. The loser does the laundry for the week. These games have become increasingly intense since they started working sixty hours each, and neither one of them will cave and just let me do the laundry, even though we all know they work this hard because my scholarship doesn't cover the full cost of tuition. To assuage my conscience, about a quarter of my tutoring money appears in their wallets, even though they'd hate it if they knew the source of the sporadic twenty-dollar bills.

I suppose it works in my favor that they're spread too thin to notice. As we're almost out the door, my dad looks up. "Shell, what are you doing with my one and only daughter?"

"Nothing lethal!" Aunt Shell calls back.

"Bring her back by midnight," my dad says.

Aunt Shell grabs my blue hand and tugs me the three blocks to the C train. I wish I could muster the gratitude I used to associate with that gesture.

After we shove through the drunken parade-goers spilling across the train station's staircase at West Fourth Street, we settle a few rows back from the barricades, surrounded by a crush of costumed bodies and wings and lightsabers as the parade streams by. One pod of performers towers above us on stilts, burnt-rainbow ribbons laced around their waists and streaming behind them like turkey feathers. Another group—about fifteen girls in matching Renaissance dresses, their hands encased in indigo gloves—performs a synchronized, fluid dance behind them. I begin to push through the crowd toward them, aching to ask whether they can tell me why my hand is blue, but they're gone before I can do more than make eye contact with the dancer closest to the railing.

The parade is otherworldly. There's no other way to describe it. The lights are throbbing and the floats are gliding and the people are glittering in their costumes, wild and beautiful in the night. Aunt Shell glitters, too, her face blurred into the crowd, part of a writhing mass in which everyone is special but everyone belongs. Every so often, I look at her, but she never looks back at me. None of them do. And even though I'm enveloped by the bodies just as much as Aunt Shell, somehow I don't feel like I belong, and I certainly don't feel special.

CHAPTER 3

On Monday, I get assigned a surprise history paper due Friday; the temperature plummets and I slip on a frozen-over puddle of dog urine on my way home from school; the fourth grader I tutor finally solves a long division problem by herself; and my hand stays blue.

No new notes appear in my locker.

On Tuesday, I do SAT prep questions at lunch before reading the Wikipedia page for Max Becker, the murderer/Nazi art hoarder the letter writers recommended I look up; Aunt Shell finishes packing for Pennsylvania; the Queer-Straight Alliance announces a mixer at a restaurant I can't afford; and my hand stays blue.

"Any updates?" I ask Chioma when the after-lunch hallway crush squeezes us together on the fifth floor.

"Nothing. You?" she says.

I shake my head as the student tidal wave carries me to Spanish.

On Wednesday, Mr. Holmes gives another pop quiz; Chioma and I exchange the first letters we received in our lockers to fully pool our information; Zola switches out her emerald lipstick for a deep purple; Aubrey lunges at me in the fourth-floor hallway, and I duck into an electrical closet, indulging the sick satisfaction that I'm finally able to repay her for the months she spent avoiding me after Emily's death; and my hand stays blue.

Still—no—note.

That evening, I wait with Aunt Shell outside our brownstone as an Uber comes to take her to the airport. She keeps glancing from the street to my face and then darting her eyes back to the concrete.

A silver sedan pulls up in front of us. The trunk starts to lift, and the driver—a bulbous-nosed man with an argyle scarf and tufts of gray hair sticking out from under a peddler cap—begins to get out of the car.

"No, stay," Aunt Shell says. "Thank you, but we can pack the trunk just fine."

"Strong girls," says the driver in a heavy Russian accent.

Aunt Shell and I lift her suitcase, one of us on each side, and slide it into the trunk.

"Will you be okay without me?" Aunt Shell says quietly.

For the first time in weeks, her words trigger a faint spark in my stomach. I hoist her duffel bag and shove it in next to the suitcase so that I don't have to look at her face. "It's been almost two years since Emily died."

She rests a hand on my shoulder. "That's not what I asked."

I toss in her backpack after the duffel bag and close the trunk. And then I can't do anything besides turn and launch myself into her arms. My fingers grasp at the thick fabric of her trench coat as she hugs me back, the point of her chin pressing into my shoulder. Even while I'm hugging her, though, something unexpected occurs to me: this is the first time I've brought up Emily's death without breaking down crying.

"I'll be fine," I say into her trench coat. "I promise."

And maybe it's even true.

• • • • •

On Thursday, Zola is forty-five minutes late to calc. As soon as she pushes open the door, I can see the sickly purple bags under her eyes. Mr. Holmes doesn't pause in his lecture, just glares at her as he talks through an example problem. I watch her red hair dangle in a limp ponytail down her back as she trudges up to Mr. Holmes's desk and drops a stapled packet onto the top of the stack of math projects due today. "What's Mr. Holmes talking about?" she mutters to me, collapsing in the chair across from mine.

"L'Hôpital's Rule," I whisper back.

"I can't deal with that today." Zola sketches a cactus on today's page of lined paper.

I spend the rest of class watching a tiny desert appear across the bottom of her page. When Mr. Holmes isn't looking, I lean across the table and add a flower to one of the cacti.

When the clock hits 8:58, Mr. Holmes clicks off the projector.

"Dude," I say to Zola as the two of us stuff our papers into our bags and push in our chairs. "What's going on with you?"

"Don't call me 'dude.'"

"Fine. Zola. Are you okay?"

"I tried to pull an all-nighter," she says. She starts weaving through desks toward the door. "You know, there was the calc project, and yesterday I had a psych test, and I have an English paper due today. And I have my own priorities, of course."

I follow her. "Of course."

She glances back at me and smiles. Even in her exhaustion, her smile is like those glittering bodies at the Halloween parade: a little carefree, a little inhuman, a little magic. "I fell asleep around five and woke up ten minutes before class started."

"I'm glad you got the work done, at least."

As Zola reaches for the door handle, Mr. Holmes snaps, "Zola! Stay behind."

She smiles at me. "Clearly, I'm needed here, but you're wrong. I didn't finish all my work. I'll be seeing you in the library for lunch."

I didn't know she paid me enough attention to know where I eat.

• • • • •

Halfway through lunch, I find Zola sunk into my favorite armchair in the library. Somehow the purple under her eyes has gotten darker.

I slide into the seat next to hers, the one Aubrey occupied a week ago, and try to ignore the shiver that shoots up my spine when my back presses into the leather. "How are you doing?"

The clacking of her laptop keys pauses as she emits a low growl. "Mr. Holmes is subhuman garbage."

"For any particular reason?" I ask.

"You wouldn't believe what he says when there's no one else in the room."

I can imagine. "Try me."

"Can't. Have to write. English paper due next period."

I don't want to drop it, but I can take a hint. "You haven't eaten today, have you?"

A shadow passes over her face. "Not a damn thing."

Based on the rumors that Zola's family works in "international business," I have no doubt that she's rich, and with rich girls, food is always the first thing to disappear from the priority list. I hand her a brown paper bag. "Sesame bagel, toasted with cream cheese, and an iced latte."

Her hands hover over her keyboard. "Kay, you got this for me?"

Shit. It was too much. Now she must think that I'm some kind of possessive nut who thinks that her decision to spend lunch in the library has anything to do with me.

When I went out earlier to get the bagel, the security guard scanned my ID twice to make sure I was really an upperclassman. This is the first time I've gone out during lunch this year. While he was scanning, he shoved his stubbly sneer too close to my face and muttered that he knows all the juniors, so am I sure that I'm in the right school?

"Sorry," I say quietly.

"What? Why?" Zola takes the bag. Her fingers brush mine. "Kay, I'm touched."

"Oh. Okay." I hope she doesn't hear the shakiness of my exhale.

"I wasn't expecting it, that's all. People don't usually… Thank you." She opens the bag and sucks down a gulp of the latte.

"You're welcome." I open my laptop, and the screen flashes to the Max Becker article.

She glances over at the Wikipedia page, and her eyebrows sink on her forehead. "What's that?"

"Just, um, some stuff I read in my spare time. True crime."

Her jaw clenches. "I don't know why you'd do that."

I close the window and open up my internship applications. "What do you mean?"

"Isn't life bloody enough without reading someone else's trauma porn?"

I search her face, but her features are tight and empty. "I'm... sorry."

"Oh, no, don't apologize. Enjoy your empty graves."

"Zola, I—"

"Kay, forget it. I'm tired, and I'll regret saying this tomorrow. Just let me focus, okay?"

She smiles at me—a real smile, I think—then turns her eyes back to her screen.

I guess this gives me my answer, then. She isn't one of the letter writers. They wouldn't react with such revulsion to the true crime story they recommended. This makes it easy. Now, when I daydream about what her hand would feel like in mine, I don't have to worry that she's the one turning it blue.

I kind of wish I could.

• • • • •

After school, I park myself on a stone bench outside the black box theater. According to the bulletin board next to the theater doors, the a cappella group is currently finishing a rehearsal, and in four minutes, the drama company will gather for a full-company meeting. Even though there's no guarantee that the letter writer who knows about "I Don't Know How But They Found Me" is the same as the letter writer who's in one of my classes, at least it's an opportunity to catalog the potential letter writers who would have been able to write to Chioma. I pull out my leather notebook from my backpack and ignore my skittering heart.

Samira's manicured hand pushes open the black box door, her head turned behind her. "Are we doing omakase tonight?"

Freya, a sophomore sporting two straw-blond braids and a maroon Davison blazer, follows. "Would it be tradition if we weren't?"

As girls continue to stream by, I scrawl down their names: Samira, Freya, Louise, Kyler. And then Chioma. My throat makes a slight choking sound. Chioma looks down and meets my eyes, and we hold eye contact for a moment. I fight to keep my face expressionless. There's something—quizzical, maybe?—bubbling under her stoic jawline. She gives me a small nod.

As the group begins to round the corner, Freya glances back at Chioma. "Unless, like, omakase is cultural appropriation."

Samira's voice rises by an octave. "Hey, Chioma?"

As far as highly selective private schools go, Davison's racial diversity isn't abysmal, but the school is no paragon of inclusion, either. So many of the parents work in multinational business that a lot of the students have dual citizenship in other countries, and some of those kids are nonwhite, albeit from privileged backgrounds. But Chioma is still one of the few Black girls, and I wonder if she ever finds that exhausting.

Drama kids filter toward the door of the black box, their slicked-back hair and nose rings glinting in the warm light of the hallway. I add their names to the list in my notebook: Alpha Rachel, Beta Rachel, Sydney, Aisha, Bennett. A blue hand glints between performers: Tia, a hummingbird-like girl whose Jimmy Choo stilettos barely raise her to shoulder height with the rest of the group.

"Yo, Kay," says Lee from AP Physics, ambling down the hallway at the tail of the clump. "Are you in the drama company now?"

"Oh, uh, hey." I scribble down their name and snap my notebook shut. "No, I'm just doing homework here. But I, um—I didn't know you were in drama."

"Yeah, co-sound designer," they say. The silver hoop on their left ear peeks out from underneath their close-cropped curls. "I don't go to the meetings most of the time, but my partner is too busy to be here, so she can't cover for me today."

As Lee shuts the door of the black box behind them, I reopen my notebook and trace my fingers down the list of names etched on the thick paper. There are only four people who are in any of my classes: Lee, Alpha Rachel, Beta Rachel, and Kyler.

My instincts scream that Lee isn't involved; frankly, it's difficult for me to imagine the letter writers alternating between fountain pens and weed pens. So it's between Alpha Rachel, Beta Rachel, and Kyler. Either of the two Rachels could be interesting. While I don't think anyone outside my head refers to the two as *Alpha* and *Beta*, well, Alpha Rachel makes the jokes and Beta Rachel laughs at them. I guess they could be orchestrating the operation together, but only Alpha Rachel is a senior, and while there's no requirement that the letter writers be seniors, it would make sense. But then wouldn't Beta Rachel be one of the juniors with a blue hand, on trial for the secret society that includes her overlord of choice?

"It's not them."

My head whips up. Chioma is peering down at my notebook page.

"Jesus." I can feel my heartbeat. "When did you get back?"

"Just now. Kay, you're oblivious. I wasn't trying to sneak up on you." Chioma situates herself on the bench next to me, her row of diamond stud earrings glittering underneath the warm light of the hallway. "Anyway, neither Rachel is sending the letters. I have precalc with them, and I've also been doing the thing with the tissue, but the letter writers haven't called me out on it, so I probably don't have any letter writers in my classes."

"Got it." I draw a line through the two names. "Would you want to, um, add anything else?"

"Sure." Chioma guides my notebook toward her lap. "I doubt Kyler is involved. The notes are delivered before and after school, and Kyler is in one of those intense independent orchestras, which means that she's always rushing in and out of rehearsals. Anyway, how about—no fucking way."

"What?"

"Lee is a sound designer?" Chioma grips my shoulder with her blue hand.

"So?"

"In your letter, there was a reference to pink noise. That's not a common phrase. It refers to one type of background noise—low-frequency sounds, I think," Chioma says. "Most people would just say 'white noise' no matter what, but you know who would be more specific? A sound designer."

Holy shit. I guess I'm not as discerning as I thought.

"Oh. Wow," I say. "But the letters seem very out of character for Lee. Do you follow them on Instagram? It seems like they have a pretty successful business doing art commissions."

"So?"

"Maybe it's too soon to say for certain, but don't you feel like this—whatever *this* is—is at the center of the letter writers' world?"

"You're making a lot of assumptions, Kay."

I take back my notebook and close it. "I guess. I'll watch them more closely. Can you keep an eye on them if you guys cross paths in the drama labyrinth?"

"Of course." Chioma pushes herself up into a standing position. "Head out with me? My SAT tutor will be at my apartment in twenty minutes."

Freshman year is the last time I left school with someone. Emily. Before the incident that showed me that maybe it wasn't a good idea for me to have friends.

• • • • •

Two years and one horror ago, I met Emily Hendricks at freshman orientation. We were sitting next to each other in the auditorium. I didn't notice her at first; I was too busy gaping at the twenty-foot-tall painting along the back of the stage, glowing angels crashing through thunderclouds and tumbling down to lie at the feet of a robed man with a sharp, hard chin and a subtle smirk. I'd never seen a painting so grand—later I'd learn that it was from the Davison founders' private collection of eighteenth-century art—and I certainly hadn't been in a room like this before. Stained-glass windows stretched into arches on either side of the pews, magnificent chandeliers cascaded from the ceiling every ten feet, and gold caulk gleamed between the tiles of the center aisle. This was why I submitted myself to the grueling admissions process, and then the equally grueling scholarship process, to get into a high school like this.

"Close your mouth." The girl sitting next to me, a scrawny brunette whose eyelids were slathered in black eye shadow, flicked my arm. "If they see you gawking, they'll know that you're on scholarship."

I was either too gobsmacked by the school or too impressed by her deduction skills to be particularly offended. "Oh. I guess people shouldn't know that about me."

"Damn right they shouldn't." The girl's fingers, I noticed, never stopped moving, skittering across her thighs like she was writing an invisible manifesto with her pinky. "You should invest in a few pairs of high-quality socks, too. Don't get knock-offs of their jewelry—they'll know. But it's the details, anything that's not built into the uniform, that will show them whether you know their rules. Socks are the least-expensive items you can get the real versions of."

"How do you know all this?" I asked.

"Veteran scholarship kid. I went to a private middle school, too," she said. "I'm Emily, by the way."

For the next few months, we were inseparable. Her grades were just as important to her as mine were to me, so we carved out neighboring spots in the Davison library—a coffee table just wide enough for two stacks of textbooks—where we met up before school to compare biology notes. We applied for the prestigious early-internship program, and when neither of us matched with a company, I held back my own tears and rested my hand on her back while she sniffled into her history binder for a full lunch period. I knew that it hurt her worse than it hurt me; she'd applied to work at Bonum Solutions, a pharmaceutical company working on a low-cost treatment for multiple sclerosis—her dad's disease—whereas my closest tie to the art museum where I'd applied was that I liked their Magritte collection.

A few days later, I showed her a tiny garden I'd found tucked into the side streets of the East Village, where there was a tree house lined with velvet seat cushions. We made a tradition of going there on Friday afternoons, sitting back-to-back, sharing a pair of earbuds and gobbling down true crime podcast episodes about the black widows of 1920s New York and the serial killers who haunted suburban schoolyards in the '70s.

Emily particularly enjoyed narratives in which the podcast host, Aretha Colby, did her research by penetrating the world of the ultrawealthy, going undercover at Hamptons parties or uncovering hidden storage lockers beneath the new apartment complexes in Hudson Yards. So did I. Mostly I was fascinated by how, when these people already had it all, they could be possessed by any desire strong enough to risk trading their Upper East Side mansions for jail cells. Listening to those podcasts, I decided that I wanted to be a criminology professor.

During one of those afternoons in the tree house, Emily turned around abruptly and paused our podcast. That episode, I remember, was about a boarding school in Massachusetts where the English teacher held her students' grades hostage until their parents delivered generous gifts to her bank account. "Do you ever think there's something shady going on at Davison?" Emily asked, grinning.

"You just want a crime to solve," I told her.

"Come on, Kay," she said, her ever-moving fingers shooting out to grab my hands. "Think about it. We must have the top two GPAs in the freshman class; we're exactly the kinds of people the companies in the pre-internship program would want to hire. Don't you think there's some kind of favoritism going on?"

"Em, we'll get in next year," I said. "Besides, on the off

chance that you're right—which you're not—I'd really rather not destroy my ticket to Northwestern."

She laughed. "You're cute when you're wrong."

That shocked me into momentary silence. I looked at her then, really looked at her in a way that I hadn't allowed myself to before, afraid to challenge the peace of our camaraderie. I took in the curve of her bony kneecaps poking out from underneath her maroon uniform skirt, the litheness of her fingers as they interlaced with mine, and the quizzical twist of her lips when she was sure of something, which was almost all the time.

"Cute," I repeated. "Like puppy cute? Or like—"

"Exactly," Emily said. "Like the Pomeranian that Samira's mom is always dragging around at family events."

"Ah," I said, letting myself deflate.

Those memories are irrelevant, though. Soon Emily started dating Aubrey, the dream girlfriend who would be willing to go along with her true crime schemes, and I allowed the ugliest part of myself to ruin it for both of them. Then Emily got expelled, and then she died in a manhole explosion somewhere deep in Queens, although before the local news released the details of her death, the Davison girls whispered that it had to have been murder. Regardless of whether it was an accident, I don't know why she was there, and somehow, no matter what Aunt Shell tells me, it feels like my fault.

• • • • •

The next morning, there's another letter in my locker, written in the same precise blue fountain-penned handwriting. Different instructions. Haunting ones. Instructions that scare me with what they leave unsaid.

Kay,

Congratulations on making it through the first round. We know that it wasn't terribly difficult, but it still takes stamina. That's an asset.

We have some more instructions. By now you've seen the others who've dyed their hands blue. They're your peers, but they're your competition as well. Going to a school like Davison, surely you're more than familiar with this dynamic.

So here's our next task for you: write your own letter to one of the other girls who still sports a blue hand. Give her a compliment.

Write in blue ink—it does wonders for the brand—and make sure to sign your name. On Monday morning, leave the letter in the broken tampon dispenser in the fourth-floor bathroom. We'll deliver it.

One more thing: in your letter, be as specific as possible.

We're sure that the other girls will want to learn just how much you know about them.

Ink is powerful, Kay. Especially blue. Especially us.

CHAPTER 4

I WRENCH MY EYES OPEN. Everything is blurry except the glowing red numbers on my wall clock, cutting through the darkness of my room. It's 2:07 a.m.

My eyelids drift back down, and I press my fingers to my face, pulling my skin to keep my eyelids separated. I can't go back to sleep. I have to write it down before I forget. The blue figure, swirling cerulean behind my eyes, that whirlpool silhouette reaching her hands inside my hands—everything finally connected, and I know who's sending the letters—I watched her hold that fountain pen and fold that notebook paper as she sat at a wooden desk right in the center of the galaxy. My hand flops to my night table and scrabbles for my phone. Text Chioma. That's what I'll do. She'll be so excited that I've made sense of our disjointed evidence.

I only manage to pound out a few words before sleep crushes my eyes. But it's okay. It's enough. I'll remember.

• • • • •

I wake up the next morning to my ringtone. The phone is still in my hand from last night.

I pick up the call. "Hello?"

Chioma's voice cuts through the fog of whatever o'clock it is. "Kay, explain yourself."

"What?"

"The text you sent me last night. Explain. Now."

"What text? I—"

I blink again, and then a wavering memory rises to the top of my brain. I had a dream—I knew who was sending the letters—but now the face is a blur. I pull the phone away from my ear and scroll through my messages.

SENT TO CHIOMA AKINDE, 2:08 A.M.:

The letter writer is me

Ugh. Useless.

"Kay, you know what text I'm talking about. If you were playing me this whole time, and you've been sending those letters, I have a lot to say and none of it is—"

"Sorry." I sit up in bed. "No. That's not it. I had some stupid dream last night. And then I texted you."

The first text I sent her. After we exchanged numbers on the way home after school on Thursday. One text, with the first person in a long time whose phone number I have for a reason other than a group project. Obviously, this isn't as bad as the last time I connected with someone at Davison, but it's still proof that maybe I'm not meant to have relationships.

"Oh. Okay."

"Yeah. Sorry. I'd never do that to you."

"So what was it? An anxiety dream about the new set of instructions?"

"I don't think that's it." *I wish that had been it.* "I think I, um, dreamed that I really had been sending the letters from the beginning."

"Weird."

I don't tell her how powerful it felt to hold the fountain pen.

"So who are you going to write your letter to?" I ask.

There's a pause. "I...don't know if I'm going to write it."

My stomach drops. "What?"

"I don't trust them." She pauses again. "They're not really looking for compliments. They're looking for dirt."

"Yeah, I got that." I bunch my velvet comforter around myself and reach for the new set of instructions. The letter is resting on my night table, where I put it after rereading it I-don't-know-how-many-times last night before going to sleep the first time. "But how is it any different from anything else that happens in this school?"

"I don't know about you, but I don't need to take anyone down to succeed. At this, whatever *this* is, or at anything else."

My stomach turns over. She can't possibly be telling the truth. No matter how wealthy her family is, she has to worry about some things: that another a cappella singer will beat her out for a solo, or that an overachiever from Los Angeles will take her slot at the college of her choice. "That's...honorable."

Chioma clears her throat. "So are you going to follow the instructions?"

"I think so."

"Take care of yourself, Kay. I think I'm done."

When I hang up the phone, my chest feels empty. Clearly, Chioma has secrets that she isn't interested in sharing with me. And, I mean, I get it. Why would she be?

I pick up my leather notebook from my night table, then flip to the page I was writing last night, the one with my first thoughts on potential people to compliment. Chioma is on the list, of course. If I thought that the letter writers were looking for genuine compliment letters, I'd address her. But she's right that they're not. And even if she doesn't want to scheme with me, she doesn't deserve any ill consequences that may come from being the subject of a letter.

I have plenty of other options, though. My blue ballpoint scribbles wriggle enticingly on the lined notebook paper. There are other girls at this school whom I do genuinely respect and would have no trouble lauding, but whom I wouldn't mind humbling a bit, either.

.....

NUMBER UNKNOWN, 3:28 P.M.:

You'll have to talk to me eventually.

When the text flashes on my phone screen, my pencil stops in the middle of the word I'm writing on my AP Physics flash card. I won't be able to ruin the curve on the next test—we've progressed from Newtonian basics to astronomy—without many more hours of studying, but that suddenly feels inconsequential. I push my pile of flash cards to the side of my desk and open my laptop, pulling up the Davison student directory and searching the phone number.

As expected: fucking Aubrey.

My heart starts to palpitate. I force myself to suck in a deep breath. If I ignore the text, maybe she'll leave me alone.

NUMBER UNKNOWN, 3:31 P.M.:

You have read receipts on. I know you're seeing this.

...That was on me, really. If I didn't want psychos to text me thinly veiled threats, I should have chosen different default settings.

I take a gulp from my mug of chamomile tea, wincing at the ring that the mug has left on my desk. Aubrey is right. If she's going to be involved with this blue-hand situation, and I'm going to keep responding to these instructions—which I shouldn't do, clearly, but it's feeling increasingly difficult to pull myself away—I can't keep ignoring her. Even if she's the one who dodged me for months after Emily's death, so I couldn't even bury my pride enough to prostrate myself for any information she might have about what happened that night in Queens, and this has been my one sick opportunity for revenge.

ME:

What do you want?

Aubrey's response comes through immediately.

AUBREY:

Ah, here we go!

AUBREY:

The last letter was awfully interesting, wasn't it?

I freeze. I don't know why it didn't occur to me sooner, but I'm not just writing one of the letters—I'm probably going to receive one. And if there's anyone at this school who knows too much about me, it's Aubrey.

ME:

Like I said, tell me what you want

AUBREY:

Why don't you meet me at the main branch of the NYPL and find out.

The Schwarzman Building is not an easy commute from Bed-Stuy. I suppose she doesn't know where I live—hell, I hope she doesn't know where I live—but I doubt she'd be disappointed to learn that she's inconveniencing me.

But I can't let her tell the letter writers anything about what happened freshman year.

ME:

Give me an hour

• • • • •

"I wasn't sure if you'd really come." Aubrey is splayed out on a curlicued wooden chair in the Rose Reading Room, the pile of books in front of her illuminated by the glow of an ornate metal lamp. It's about to storm, and only cold light is trickling in from the arched windows lining the room. The Davison library is modeled after this place. The familiarity gives me what's probably a false sense of calm.

"You weren't going to stop," I say.

This is the first time I've seen Aubrey in anything other than her school uniform. It occurs to me that she looks like the skinny white mascs on my TikTok feed: unkempt hair, corduroy trucker jacket, keys on a carabiner clipped to black cargo pants. I glance down at my own flannel and loose jeans. The jeans are a few inches too long, and I don't think that the cuffs pass as an intentional styling choice.

"Sit down." Aubrey pulls out the chair beside her.

I fold myself into the chair, slinging off my backpack and laying it at my feet. "Tell me what you want, I'll tell you what I want, and we can both leave."

Aubrey looks at me for a moment, then sighs. "Okay. I'll start with the apology I owe you. I shouldn't have avoided you for so long after Emily died."

Pain shoots through my chest. "That's big of you."

"Hold your comments until I'm finished," Aubrey says. "Then you can have at me all you like."

I dig my fingernails into the denim across my thighs but nod.

"Thank you," Aubrey says, twisting one of the chunky silver rings around her fingers. "I was looking into her death, and I didn't want you in my way, so on occasion I slipped into electrical closets when I saw you heading in my direction. That was immature of me."

"I wanted to know more, too, you know." My voice breaks,

and I try to disguise it as a cough. "We could have worked together."

Aubrey shrugs. "You would have spent your time blaming me. You would have assumed—correctly—that after you told me how badly Emily had violated my privacy, I went to the school administration and got her expelled. And you would have been too distracted by that to collaborate on a damn thing."

My stomach plunges. It's one thing to suspect what she did it's another for Aubrey to confirm it, especially in such a cool, matter-of-fact tone. "This is a shitty apology."

"Let me get through it," Aubrey snaps. "Look. Even though I know I made the right choice to investigate on my own at that point, I should've been honest with you. I'm sorry."

I allow her words to suspend themselves in the thick silence of the Rose Reading Room. Eventually I say, "What do you mean by 'at that point'?"

Aubrey fiddles with another one of her rings. "That's why I've been trying to talk to you. I'm still looking into Emily's death, and I no longer think it's the most prudent decision to keep acting alone."

"Her death—it was a freak accident," I say. "I don't know what you've been doing for two years or why you suddenly want me involved, but—"

Aubrey reaches across the table and grips my wrist with her

blue fingers, the intensity of her stare penetrating even the thick bangs across her forehead. "You don't really think that, do you?"

Her words slice through the two years of scabbing that cocoons my memories of Emily. Her fervor as she argued in favor of one of her schemes, her fingertips skittering across her thighs. The text she sent me after weeks of silence, insisting she was right about something I'll never know. The rumor that she was murdered. The unshakable feeling that, somehow, I caused her death.

"It doesn't fucking matter what I think!" I feel myself gulping air, the volume of my sentiment eliciting a dirty look from an old man reading a newspaper from the 1980s. "The police would have uncovered something, or her parents would have sued someone, or even you would have figured out something conclusive from your little Nancy Drew escapades—"

"I don't even get to be Holmes?" Aubrey removes her hand from my wrist. "I know it's hard to accept—and, honestly, it sounds far-fetched—but I think there's something deeper going on. A conspiracy or something."

I focus on pulling the air into my lungs and expelling it without shaking. "Why?"

"Of course, the timing was part of it," Aubrey says. "It happened too soon after she was expelled. That was why I started investigating. Then that local article came out, and it said that she was right by a storage locker facility. There has to be some reason she was there—she had to have known *something* she shouldn't have known—but all I have is conjecture. And the last reason is that the article is the only thing on the Internet that even mentions Emily's death. Don't you think that was strange? She was a pretty, white scholarship girl destined to make something of herself. That's the kind of story that ABC7 would probably murder her themselves to break."

I stiffen when Aubrey says that Emily was pretty. "That could all be coincidence."

"After so long without learning anything else, I was beginning to think so, too." Aubrey reaches into her back pocket and removes a wad of folded paper. "But then I received the first letter."

She hands me the page, and I unfold it. It has been creased and un-creased so many times that it feels soft and fragile. I skim the page, and I recognize most of the sentences; like in mine, the letter writers tell Aubrey that they find her intriguing. But in the section where they're telling Aubrey some of the things they've witnessed about her, one sentence stands out: *We know you believe that Emily Hendricks gained some illicit knowledge that led to her death.*

My heartbeat speeds up again. "So you think the letter writers had something to do with why she died?"

"I don't know," Aubrey says. "But I don't like that they're taunting me with information about Emily. Clearly, they know something I don't, and they're dangling that to gain power over me. I'd like to work with you to figure out who they are. At the very least, that will take back some of the power."

Despite the panic that swirls around me every time I see Aubrey—panic that, I'm realizing, may have less to do with who she is and more to do with the secret that my subconscious has attached to her—a strange calm spreads across my insides. I'm closer to the truth than I've allowed myself to come in two years.

"Again, why me?" I trace the table's wood grain with my index finger, swirling my hand when I reach a knot.

Aubrey drills her eyes into mine again. "Because I knew you would believe me."

And I suspect that I'll regret it, but I do.

"If I help you figure out the letter writers' identities, you have to promise me something."

"Fine."

"You have to write your compliment letter to someone other than me."

A muscle in Aubrey's jaw tenses up. "If you insist."

"Thank you." I glance at Aubrey's stack of books. Like that day in the Davison library, they're about NYC history, with titles like *Queens of the Upper West Side* and *All the News That's Fit to Hide: The Unsavory Underbelly of the New York Herald*. "Also, if you're going to ask me what I know about the letter writers, I don't just want to give it away; I want us to pool information."

"You're pushing your luck," Aubrey says. I grab the strap of my backpack and lean forward onto the balls of my feet. "No—ugh. Fine. Just—you start. I know you've been skulking around the school. Tell me what you know so far."

I do my best to keep my face even and relay most of the information I've collected: the details in my first note about true crime and smudgy eyeliner, the indication that at least one of the letter writers has a class with me, the way I have my eye on the drama club and the a cappella group.

"Why the theater kids?" Aubrey asks.

"Come on, don't you think that this is something that they would do?" The reference to "I Don't Know How But They Found Me" isn't my piece of evidence to share. Regardless of whether Chioma is going to answer the next challenge, I don't want to betray her confidence, especially to someone as slimy as Aubrey. "Besides, I've done some eavesdropping, and it sounds like they're spending a lot of time grilling Tia about her blue hand."

"Hmm." Aubrey looks unconvinced but doesn't push it.

"Now tell me what you've been thinking."

Aubrey rests her hand on top of her stack of books. "You know what I was saying before about the media being involved in a cover-up?"

"What about it?"

"Mai Ngo has a blue hand." Aubrey pauses as if this is supposed to be significant to me. "Kay, it's like you don't even go to this school. Do you know who her mom is?"

I've never crossed paths with Mai. I know vaguely who she is because her poetry is hung up on the first-floor bulletin board—during my school tours, I tell the salivating families about the national awards she's won—but can't picture her face. "Just tell me."

Aubrey taps the top book on the stack. "The executive editor at the *New York Herald*."

I can't help it—I gasp. The old man with the newspaper glares at me again. "So this media conspiracy...do you think the letter writers are trying to dismantle or perpetuate it?"

"That's the big question," Aubrey says. "You're going to write your compliment letter to Mai, and you're going to do your best to draw her out."

"Giving me orders isn't part of the deal," I say.

Aubrey crosses her arms. "Writing to her is the most logical course of action. I can't write the letter myself, because as soon as I learned about her family background in freshman year, I poked around a little too much. Suffice to say that I'm not Mai's favorite person. It would be unwise for me to raise myself on her radar right now, especially if she's using this blue hand thing to draw out and dispose of anyone who knows too much about Emily."

"That makes sense," I say. "In that case, if I write to her, you should write to Tia. She's the only drama company member with a blue hand. Do the same thing and use the letter to form a connection that will get us more information."

Aubrey nods. "A good plan. Can I trust you to be subtle with Mai?"

I dig my fingernails into my palm. "Don't worry about that."

Aubrey gives me a grim smile. "To our alliance, then."

"To our alliance."

• • • • •

When I get back home, the first thing I do is shower. But even after I'm in clean sweats and tucked underneath a throw blanket at my desk chair, my skin still feels like it's oozing.

There is one other thing that might make me feel better: calling Aunt Shell. Other than a few photos she texted me of the exterior of her new house, a picturesque cottage with a red-shingled roof and a circular window into the attic, we haven't spoken since she left. I forgot what it was like to have to make an active effort to talk to her. It makes me feel strange that I haven't really been making one.

It makes me feel even stranger that she hasn't been, either.

Regardless. I scroll to her contact and hit the Call button.

She picks up on the second ring. "Kay! How's it going?"

I glance at my leather notebook, which is perched next to my laptop on my desk, and then out the window at the empty street. The sun has long since set. "It's been a hell of a week."

"Are you still working on those internship applications? Where are you trying to intern next semester?"

I feel a faint smile lifting the corners of my mouth. I didn't expect her to remember. "Yeah, those will be on the to-do list for a bit. My first choice is the Quinn Center for Justice. They're working on a really interesting research project about preventing corporate monopolies. But I'm trying not to get my hopes up, because they're the ones I applied to work for this semester, and I got beat out by a girl whose mom runs a company that makes smartphones for dogs."

Aunt Shell scoffs. "Why the fuck do dogs need smartphones?"

"If you're rich enough for a dog nanny, you're nuts enough to want a sensor that will call you if your dog makes an unhappy bark, and—" I hear a crash in the background. "Is everything okay?"

"Yeah, sorry—one sec—" Aunt Shell's voice is muffled. "Carlos and I are hanging up some paintings we got at the thrift store today—really stunning, the kind with ornate vintage frames—but I just dropped one, and—"

"Aunt Shell, we can talk later," I say.

"No, no, you've been on speakerphone," Aunt Shell says, her voice coming back into focus. "We can keep talking!"

So Carlos has heard all about my internship failings. I feel my stomach sour.

"You know, I don't want to keep you while you're busy. Bye, Aunt Shell. Bye, Carlos."

I hang up right away.

If I can't distract myself from the letter writers and Aubrey, I might as well try to parse through what I learned today. I open my notebook and reread my section on the letterwriters: first Chioma's and my thoughts on the drama kids, then a page with the names of all the girls I've spotted with blue hands, then my list of potential addressees for the compliment letter. I draw an X over the list, then write Mai's name on the bottom and circle it. Then I flip to a new page and make three columns, one for each of the individuals I'd like to know more about: Mai, Tia, and Lee.

The only resource I have at my disposal right now is social media. It probably won't give me real answers, but it will at least give me a sense of who they are. Aubrey was right when she asked if I even went to Davison. I'm beginning to get the sense that I've been passing through the school like a hologram. I mean, I know I have—that's been a conscious choice—but maybe it hasn't served me as well as I thought.

The first name I type into Instagram is Mai's. Once I see the photos in her grid, I recognize her—her locker is down the hall from mine, but I had no way of connecting her face to the bulletin board of poetry. In her photos, she's wearing tattered black skirts and patent leather platform boots, her sharp bob cutting across backdrops of the simulated grunge of the Lower East Side. One series of shots takes place on a corner I recognize, bright graffiti streaked across a peeling brick wall behind Mai's unsmiling face. That's around where Bed-Stuy meets Bushwick. For a moment, I try to picture my life through her eyes, and suddenly it feels much more romantic that there are two dumpsters visible from my window.

These girls really have no idea what they have, do they?

Tia's profile is exactly what you would expect. She has a photo set dedicated to every musical that Davison has performed since our freshman year, and she's beaming in the center of each cast photo. Her blond ringlets strategically block the face of at least one other cast member per shot. But I don't think it makes sense for someone with a blue hand to be orchestrating any of this, despite Aubrey's suspicions about Mai. I think it's much more likely that Tia was chosen for her main character syndrome and that someone else has been hanging back and observing.

Really, it seems like every girl with a blue hand has some justification for being a main character. Mai has created a gothic universe for herself with her poverty cosplay and mournful poetry; Chioma's solos go viral every time the a cappella group posts a clip of her on their TikTok; Margaret could probably computer-science her way into MIT without bothering to finish out junior year if she felt like it; even Aubrey could spin herself a little underdog/loner/detective storyline if she were the narrator. But then there's me. And I'm not remarkable. I wonder why the letter writers think I belong.

This isn't a helpful train of thought. I look up the last name on my list: Leela Rashid. Lee's Instagram is split between photos of their art commissions—the bottom of a skateboard painted with a colorful kraken, a custom prom-posal sign in the same graffiti-inspired style—and photos of them with other Davison students. Most of Lee's friends are other members of the senior class. When they're out of the school uniforms, almost all of them seem to favor silver waist chains and untucked dress shirts protruding from oversize sweaters. I zoom in to scan the faces in a group shot featuring a sea of grinning Davisonites and notice

Mai's head in the row behind Lee's. Maybe Chioma is right and there's something much more calculating lurking beneath Lee's weed-serene exterior.

It's not a good use of my research time, but I look up one more name. I know I shouldn't. She probably doesn't have anything to do with the letters, regardless of whether I want her to—she wasn't at the drama meeting, and she's nowhere in Aubrey's theory. But as long as I'm letting myself spend too much time on Instagram, I type *Zola Wolfe* into the search bar.

Her profile photo is a backlit silhouette of her face from the side, her upturned nose and sharp lips stark against a light-purple background, her hair flowing off the right side of the image. She looks delicate here, in a way that I don't think I've ever seen her look in real life. Most of her photos are the typical staged Upper East Side shots, with her hand resting on a lamppost as it snows or her body draped across the shallow steps of a granite building. She's alone in all of them. Her captions are almost all quotes from authors I like: a bit of Maya Angelou, a bit of Gertrude Stein, a bit of Oscar Wilde—okay, a lot of Gertrude Stein. I didn't know Zola was so literary. I guess I don't know a lot of things about her.

But I think the quotes told me what I came here for. No straight girl would post that much Gertrude Stein.

• • • • •

A few minutes before class on Monday morning, Chioma slumps against the locker next to mine, a folded piece of paper in her right hand. It's still blue.

"I changed my mind. I wrote the compliment letter."

My own letter feels a little lighter in my back pocket.

I take out my AP Physics binder and slide it into my backpack. "What changed?"

"I don't know," Chioma says. "I felt compelled."

I take a moment to check her body language. Her jaw is clenched, and her hand is jammed into the pocket of her uniform skirt. "Chioma, what would you say if I told you that I know you're lying?"

Her jaw thrusts forward, drawing her skin even tighter across her face. "Can't you pretend that I'm not?"

"I thought we were working together," I say.

Chioma swallows. "Everything has its limits."

Now this feels right. Last week, things were almost too companionable. Too close to freshman year. But the transactional meeting in the library with Aubrey, this exchange of unsaid words—that's the only kind of relationship that's safe in a school like this.

"Well, good luck with...whatever this is," I say. "I hope the letter-writing process went okay for you."

Chioma nods tightly. "The same to you."

Still. I don't regret writing a letter of my own. And even

though Chioma may not be my friend, I'm glad that she's still in this with me.

• • • • •

I can't concentrate in calculus, knowing that my letter is just *there,* in the broken tampon dispenser, for anonymous eyes to read.

It was surprisingly difficult to balance my three agendas: providing a genuine compliment, revealing something new to the letter writers, and drawing Mai out. But I think I managed it. I hope.

Dear Mai,

As a student tour guide, I have to say a lot of things that I don't mean. They have me give a whole spiel about the school's commitment to equity, and then I have to out myself as a scholarship kid, and then I become a prize pig for all the snotty thirteen-year-olds and their Lululemon moms.

But when I get to the bulletin board with your poetry, I don't have to bullshit. You're a real master with words, and it's genuinely a pleasure to get to tell families that I go to school with you. Your poetry gets to the truth of this world. You describe beautiful things in such ugly and powerful ways, and it doesn't feel angsty—it feels raw. I particularly admire how you describe secrets: "For every word on the page / there are three laying eggs inside the writer's fingertips / thick libidinous parasites screaming to be known."

When I first read that line, I thought you were the writer in question. But when I saw that your hand was blue, I started to do more research about you and your family, and I learned what your mom does for a living. That was hard to find, since her last name is different from yours, and your dad is the one who shows up to the Davison family mixers. But being raised by the New York Herald executive editor is really something. Now I wonder if there's another writer with secrets.

But regardless of how high-profile your mother is, you're not like the rest of the Davison girls, who will use their trust funds to go to Bryn Mawr and then marry bankers. You're real. You have a lot more in common with someone like me than someone like them.

Maybe I'll see you around Bed-Stuy some time?

With admiration,
Kay

I try to ignore the guilt wriggling in my stomach. The compliment part was true—I really do think Mai's poetry is great, transcendent even—but even after two years at this school, I don't like being this manipulative. Plus, Mai obviously doesn't want people to know about her mom. At the very least, that would call into question some of Mai's writing talent. At most…Aubrey is right, and there's a very good reason why Mai's mother doesn't want to be tied to this school.

But if that's the case, I shouldn't feel any guilt at all. Emily deserves to be avenged. So it might be morally necessary for me to do this.

"Kay, what's going on with you?" Zola asks at the end of class. "No notes at all today?"

"Huh?" I blink at her a few times, then glance down at the blank page in my binder.

"How are you going to ace the next test?" She leans across the table and swats me lightly. I barely notice the cool of her fingernail against my bare forearm.

"Um," I say. "I've just been…preoccupied."

Something changes in her smile, and I might imagine it, but it seems like she's looking right at my lips, as if she's thinking something I definitely want her to be thinking. Even if it's not exactly what's been preoccupying me. "Oh, I'm sure you have been."

• • • • •

When I open my locker at the end of the day, there's another letter inside. My compliment letter. Already.

Hey Kay,

NGL I spent the first part of freshman year resenting you because you messed up my biology grade. I don't know if you even remember this, but on the first test of the year the average was a C, and Mr. Stevens said that he wasn't going to curve it because someone got an A+. I saw you lunge to cover your paper when he said that, and I knew it was you. And then you kept doing that. So Mr. Stevens never curved the tests by more than a couple of points, until the one test right after Emily died, and he curved that one by 10% or 15% or something insane like that.

At first I thought Mr. Stevens felt bad for us, like, oh, your former classmate just died, so I'll take pity and curve the test scores really high. Then I heard you crying in the fourth floor bathroom later that day, and I looked in the trash can and saw your test sitting on top, crumpled, and you were barely pulling a D+.

When I saw that, I remembered that the two of you always sat next to each other and stuff. I think you were in love with her. You probably don't want to admit it. I feel like girls like you are always ashamed of things they can't control, like having feelings.

I appreciated it, though. Not just because that was the only Bio test I scored above a B- on all year. I wasn't even that mad when the curve started going down again because I knew that it meant you were feeling a little better. I liked knowing that you were a whole person, not just a machine for making the rest of us look bad.

I just read this over, and I realize that you might not see the compliment in this. I really do mean one, though. Part of the compliment is that you're super smart, obviously, and the other part is that you're human, which I feel like you don't get complimented on enough. Partially because you probably don't see that as a good thing, and partially because most people don't know that about you. No offense.

See you around,
Daphne

My stomach sinks lower and lower as I read the letter. Daphne Fillmore is the point guard on the basketball team, and this is definitely some student-athlete nonsense. Is she truly stupid enough to think that this counts as a compliment, or did she understand the letter writers' instructions perfectly and she's leaning into the one-too-many-basketballs-to-the-head persona so that they underestimate her? Or, worse, so that I underestimate her?

All things considered, this isn't as divulgatory as it would have been if Aubrey had written about our freshman year, so I suppose that I should be relieved. But on some level, maybe it's worse. The one thing I can't let the letter writers think is that I'm human.

CHAPTER 5

When I walk into calculus the next morning, Zola is already there, alone at our table with a mottled-wood thermos in front of her. She slides it toward me. "Morning, Anderson."

I take the thermos. It's warm but not hot. "Maintaining the coffee equilibrium?"

"It's better than coffee. Taste it."

I take a sip. It's some kind of cinnamon tea, with a sweet undercurrent that I can't quite identify. "Wow. Thank you."

"No, thanks for getting me lunch last week," she says. "I had to do something in return."

I reach into my bag and rummage around for my binder, hoping that Zola can't see the heat in my cheeks. "No you didn't. That's the point of a gift."

She shrugs. "Well, I figured you'd enjoy this, since it's kind of like chai and I've seen you drinking that. I mixed the blend myself."

As I lift the thermos to take another sip, my fingers brush against a too-smooth patch on the bottom. I look down. Tape. I feel along the base of the thermos and find a scrap of paper. "Zola?" I ask.

"Oh, don't read that yet," she says, smiling. "But I think you'll like what it says."

I feel my heart thumping and try to blink back the déjà vu.

After class, I peel off the note and unfold it as I push through the crowds to get to English. The lined notebook paper seems like a taunt. But when I see the handwriting, my heartbeat slows down. It's not the neat, careful fountain pen. Instead, it's almost illegible. I squint to make sense of the scribble.

Lunch today? Meet me on the roof.

My heartbeat speeds up again.

No matter what's going on between me and Aunt Shell, I can't imagine not telling her about this. As I push through clusters of students to get to English, I text her.

ME:

Omg I think I have a date???

She texts back right away.

AUNT SHELL:

Ahhhh!!!! Later, I want to know EVERYTHING!!

I wonder if she'll share it with Carlos.

• • • • •

A blue hand grabs my shoulder when I'm about ten paces away from my English classroom. A jolt of panic shoots through me, and I wrench my shoulder to shake off the grip.

"Hey, hey, relax!" I turn my head and see Chioma gaping at me. "Kay, what was that?"

I force my breathing to slow. "Sorry, hey. Thought you were someone else."

My mind had already started scrambling for excuses to give Aubrey about why I hadn't learned anything new about Mai yet. Which is ridiculous. Like I told her on Saturday, she doesn't get to give me orders while I quake at her feet.

Chioma twists her lips like she's going to ask me to elaborate, but she doesn't. "I need to talk to you. I have some new ideas about the letter writers."

"Right now?" I glance toward my English classroom.

Chioma nods. "I want to talk through it before I forget anything."

Behind the circular window embedded in the wood of the door, Ms. O'Keefe is starting to hand out copies of the book we'll be reading next: *The Secret History*. Ms. O'Keefe's red plastic glasses glint under the light of the lamp in the entryway as she smiles down at her armful of volumes. I'm 98 percent sure that I'm going to ask her to write one of my college recommendation letters. I shouldn't skip her class.

"Got it," I say. "I know a spot where we can have some privacy."

A moment later, I'm pulling Chioma into the second-floor supply closet where I dye my hand. My Tupperware and box of ballpoint pens are still shelved next to the Clorox. A single light bulb dangles from the ceiling.

Chioma gapes at the closest. "This place has been here the whole time?"

It's incredible how well you can get to know a school building if you're designing your experience to avoid other students. But Chioma doesn't need to know that.

I position my boots so that I'm not standing directly over the vent drilled into the closet floor, where cold air likes to come rushing out at will. "So. What did you want to talk about?"

Chioma places her blue hand on a bucket of mop fluid, as if she's swearing on a Bible. "I'm sorry for not telling you the truth yesterday about why I decided to write the letter. But since then,

I've realized a few things, and I've decided that you're probably the most trustworthy person with a blue hand."

I think about my letter to Mai. "I mean, I'm flattered, but we probably don't know each other well enough for you to say that."

"This. This is exactly why I'm saying it," Chioma says. "How many other girls would actively tell me to be careful, instead of just lapping up whatever secrets I'm about to spill? Besides I don't think you've lied to me...yet."

Maybe it's the high of my lunch plans with Zola, but maybe I was wrong yesterday when I decided that a transactional relationship with Chioma was all I deserved. "All right."

Chioma buries her hand in the pocket of her slacks. "What I'm about to tell you absolutely can't leave this supply closet, okay?"

I nod. It's lucky that I didn't tell Aubrey about the reference to "I Don't Know How But They Found Me."

"Did you know that Vanessa Hargrove has a blue hand?" Chioma asks.

"Yeah, she's in my calculus class," I say. "What about her?"

Chioma pauses. "I don't consider myself a vengeful person, but on Sunday I saw a photo of her with her hand dyed—somehow, I hadn't seen her in the halls over the past few weeks, so I just learned about this—and suddenly I couldn't stop myself from writing a letter to her."

I try to picture Vanessa: Van Cleef bracelets, pristine manicure, and probably a personality, although that last one is unconfirmed. "I don't know much about Vanessa. What do you have against her?"

"Something happened freshman year," Chioma says. "We used to be friends because my dad is the chief medical officer for her dad's pharmaceutical company, and she's—well, I can't really talk about it without exposing myself, too, so I don't want to get into the details, but let's just say that she's willing to do some awful things for gossip."

I don't ask for more information. Regardless of any newfound touchy-feeliness I might be experiencing about connecting with other Davison students, I don't blame her for holding back at least some trust. "And you talked about that in your letter, and by extension, you told the letter writers about it?"

"Yeah." Chioma swallows. "And I don't know if that was smart. But I assumed—and I was right—that she would write to me as well. So, regardless of whether I wrote to her, the letter-writers would know about my part in...a scheme of hers, and I decided that the best thing I could do was make sure that they had all the information about her, too."

This time, I can't stop myself. "How big was your part?"

Chioma stares at the floor of the supply closet. Her face is fully in shadow, the bulb only illuminating her slick mass of braids. "I don't talk to her anymore. That's what matters."

I'm not sure it is, but I can take a hint.

"So what do you think this means about who the letter-writers are?" I ask.

"They have to be motivated by money," Chioma says. "I think they're looking for dirt on the Davison families, and then they'll blackmail us or something."

"No." The word rips itself out of my mouth before I can stop it.

Chioma lifts her head. "Kay, do you know something I don't?"

"No, it's—it's probably stupid of me," I say. "I mean, I don't actually have any evidence to support this, but even if they are looking for dirt, I just don't think it's fair to assume that they're going to use that information to do something especially villainous. They might be looking to report crimes."

"That is some serious brainwashed talk," says Chioma. "Do you hear yourself?"

"Over the weekend I had to speak with Aubrey," I say. I tell her that the letter writers may know something about what happened to Emily. "I guess maybe you're right, and this is another case of trying to find something blackmail-worthy, but it seems a lot more like they want us to...share information with them. Less like they're working against us, and more like they want our help in figuring out the truth. And we both know that an undercurrent of threat is kind of necessary if you want a Davison student to help you out."

Chioma is quiet for a moment. Then she shakes her head. "I think you've completely lost track of who to trust. Come on. Get to your English class."

When I reach my desk after a muttered excuse about period cramps, I leaf through *The Secret History*, but I can't focus on any words on the page. Instead, my mind keeps reshuffling the girls with the dyed hands, trying to rank them in order of trustworthiness. I'd like to think that Chioma is at the top of the list, but do I have any real proof of that? And while Aubrey is a snake with chiseled cheekbones, she's the only one who has gone out of her way to be honest with me. Daphne, maybe Mai, apparently Vanessa—they all seem shady, assuming that Chioma is telling the truth. And while Tia and Margaret are both talented in their own ways, that doesn't give me any insight into their motives when it comes to the secret society; plus, I don't know enough about them to make a judgment.

Or maybe I'm being ridiculous and just spinning about whom I can trust. Because that would imply that I'm in some kind of danger. Which I'm almost definitely not.

• • • • •

Students aren't supposed to go on the roof. But if you take the stairs one flight higher than the sixth-floor landing, the door is unlocked and the roof is empty on Tuesdays and Thursdays between 11:00 a.m. and 2:00 p.m. The art teacher takes her third-period class to spray-paint here, and she doesn't bother to lock the door until she comes back a few hours later to take the canvases inside. I don't know how Zola knows this. The only reason I do is because during freshman year, I learned that I could run away from my panic by climbing stairs until I felt sweat seeping into the armpits of my polos. And the first time my armpits weren't sweaty when I got to the sixth floor, I just… kept going up.

Today the wind is sharp against my face as I step onto the red brick of the rooftop, but the gale settles quickly. It's warm again, just for the day. Drop cloths and canvases are laid out in a spiral mosaic on the plane of the roof. Except for a spot in the center. Instead of a tarp covered in iridescent swirls, there's a picnic blanket, blue-and-white gingham like you'd see in a Southern movie. And sitting cross-legged on the blanket, the wind tossing her red hair around her shoulders, is Zola.

"Sit," she says, her eyes glinting. "I need someone to hold down the other half of the blanket."

I cross the roof, taking care not to step on any of the paintings, and join her. The blanket isn't small, exactly, but there's no way to sit that doesn't involve my knees at least brushing against hers.

Judging by the way her smile widens when I settle, I think that was intentional.

"Zola, is this what I think it is?" I ask.

Zola reaches for the picnic basket that's sitting next to her. She unbuckles its two leather straps and reaches inside, removing a heat-preserving container in the same mottled wood as the thermos she handed me this morning. "Well, what do you think it is, Kay?"

Please don't make me say the word date.

I hesitate. "What if I'm wrong?"

"One of us is going to have to say it," she says, laughing a bit. She unscrews the top of the container and reaches into the basket again, this time emerging with two pewter bowls. She lays one in front of me. "On three. I think we should say it at the same time."

I laugh too. "This is ridiculous."

She cocks her head. "Yeah, but are you going to say it any other way?"

"Okay, fine," I say. I can't control my smile anymore. Or my heartbeat. "One. Two. Three—is this a date?"

At the same time, Zola says, "This is a friendly hangout."

My stomach plummets. Fuck. Fuck. I can feel my face

blazing red, and I press my blue hand to the ground to push myself up, and—

Zola touches my hand. It's only then that I notice how hard she's laughing. "Oh my God, Kay, yes. I was kidding. This is a date."

A laugh-sob bubbles out of my throat. "A date."

She doesn't understand. She doesn't understand that for a moment, I thought that she was another Emily, and I can't deal with another lithe-limbed body in the ground. No matter why Emily turned up dead, I find it difficult to believe that it was completely isolated from her expulsion. And I was the one who tipped the first domino. I may be older now, and I don't think I'd try to take revenge on Zola if I learned that she wasn't interested in me. But I'm not sure what my blue hand might do without my permission.

But that's not relevant. Zola isn't Emily. And she's very, very much taking me on a date.

"I'm sorry, Kay. No, wait, no, I'm not sorry. That was hilarious," she says. "Your *face*, man."

"Don't call me 'man,'" I say, feeling the smile creep back onto my face. "This is a date, remember?"

"Yeah, I know. I planned it," she says. Her fingers have been resting on top of my wrist, and she slides them lower, squeezing the top of my hand. "Speaking of which, I made us lunch. Cottage goulash."

"Sorry, what is that?" I ask. Like I'll remember. Like I can be thinking anything besides *I am on a date with Zola Wolfe.*

Zola lifts her hand off mine and ladles out a thick stew, chunks of beef and onion bobbing in a deep-red broth, into the two bowls. "Goulash. It's a recipe from the old country."

There's something charming about the dish, even more so than the picnic setup. Her Tiffany necklace could pay for a used car, and she still spent time sweating over a stovetop for this. For me. "The old country, huh. Where's your family from?"

Maybe I'm imagining it, but I think I see Zola's hand shake as she slides a slice of spongy bread into one of the bowls, then hands it to me. "Just taste it."

I use the bread to mop up some of the broth, then take a bite. "Damn, Zola. Are you trying to drug me into falling for you?"

Zola winks. "Nah. I'm just a good cook. Food is more effective than drugs, anyway."

The rest of lunch passes in seconds, or maybe in years. It turns out that Zola does almost all the cooking for her family, mostly because she likes science and a little bit because she likes looking for shapes in the oil at the bottoms of frying pans, like Rorschach inkblots. Her grades weren't good enough to get her into AP Physics—she says this with a chuckle, but I think it bothers her—but she has a friend in the class who tells her anything interesting, although the friend isn't especially invested in the subject, so Zola doesn't get to hear much. Her favorite color is indigo. She also does technical theater; electrics, she tells me. When I ask what that means, she wriggles her hand through the air toward me and pantomimes shocking my forearm. I hope she doesn't notice that the touch of her finger leaves the hairs on my arm standing on end. The thing she loves most in the world, she says, is being awake and outside at 2:00 in the morning.

I think that's a pretty magical thing to love, which I tell her. I think I can picture myself loving a person who loves that, but I keep that to myself.

In the last few minutes of the period, we start packing the bowls back into the basket and folding up the blanket. "How did you know the roof would be open?" I say.

She screws the lid onto the mottled-wood thermos. "You used to visit pretty consistently on Tuesdays at lunch."

"You know me better than I thought," I say, handing her the folded-up blanket.

She smiles, her lips twisting crookedly in the right corner. "And something tells me that there's much more to know."

• • • • •

A day passes without event. There's only one thing that unsettles me, which has nothing to do with either the letter writers or Zola. Aunt Shell never texts me to ask about the date. I've decided that, no matter what, I'm not going to send the next text. After all, I told her that I'd be okay without her.

On Wednesday, before I leave school, I find a new letter in my locker. It's sitting on top of my binders, notebook paper crisp, fountain pen neat. As I read, I find myself begging the letterwriters to give me some hint that I'm not an idiot for defending them. I'm not sure if it's there.

Kay,

We appreciate your participation in our second round of instructions. Your compliment letter was strong in some ways, but it did leave some room for improvement. We, too, appreciate Mai's poetry—and it's clear where she gets her talent from, although of course her family background doesn't make her accomplishments any less real. That said, Mai's mother's work is an open secret, and your letter didn't quite reach the level of divulgence that we were seeking in this round. We considered eliminating you after this—we're sure you noticed that some other girls who started out with blue hands are no longer sporting them—but we think you have some more interesting information in you yet.

We also enjoyed reading Daphne's letter about you. We

agree with her that you likely weren't happy to receive it, but we found what we learned to be rather touching. Love is nothing to be embarrassed about, Kay. We know that you must think we're some kind of gargantuan, soulless entity, but no matter how far our shadow extends, we're composed of individuals who are, occasionally, driven by love as well. The heart can be a valuable discerner of truth.

We know you're starting to get very curious about who we are, so we're offering you an opportunity to ask us some of the questions scrawled in your leather notebook. Download the app Clandestine and plug in the referral code "1211." This will take you to a private server where we'll have a chance to interface with you more directly. More instructions await you on the app, if you're intrigued enough to join us.

As Mai might tell you, the first rule of good writing is to show, not tell. So we don't expect you to be convinced when we say that we're on your side. But you deserve to have someone looking out for you, and after two years of punishing yourself, we hope you're ready to believe that.

CHAPTER 6

The app taunts me from the corner of my phone screen, a silver *C* embedded in a digital black abyss. I'm back at my desk, my notebook splayed in front of me, open to the page with the list of questions that the letter writers somehow knew was there. *What's the connection between all the girls who've been selected? Who, or what, is behind the letters? Does this have to do with Emily?*

What is this, whatever "this" is, going to cost me?

My AP Physics test is tomorrow. Astronomy. I should be going over the practice problems that we did in class today. But instead of flipping to my diagram of the star death cycle, I tap the *C* on my phone.

Welcome to Clandestine.

White words clack across the screen letter by letter.

Can you keep a secret?

After I plug in the referral code, the app takes me on a tour of its interface. My server, it tells me, is called BHG. It doesn't elaborate on the initials. Most of the layout is fairly standard: there's a central channel for all members of the server, although it doesn't have any messages yet, and I don't seem to have permission to type into it. There are also several locked channels with their names pixelated out. The design looks like it's modeled after a coding window, all boxes and plain text.

I tap on the Members tab at the side of the screen. As I expected, most of the names belong to the other girls with dyed hands, but like the additional channels, there are eight entries with text that's been pixelated out.

I jab at the top pixelated entry, and a text box appears.

Welcome. Would you like to barter?

The two buttons underneath are *yes* and *no*. Unsurprisingly, there isn't an option for *I'll deal with it.*

After I hit *yes*, the text box spits out a new line.

We'll start with an easy question. What is your name?

Okay. This is fine. In the blank box beneath the question, I type.

Kay Anderson.

The text box disappears, and I watch as the pixels obscuring the top entry unscramble themselves to reveal the words *The Baker.*

I guess it's a code name? Nonetheless. This is my first real piece of information about the identity of the letter writers—at least, my first piece coming from them. I wonder if they know how much I've been able to gather. I wonder if they'll be careless enough to give away anything that will connect the disjointed puzzle pieces in my leather notebook.

I tap the next pixelated entry, and it asks me another question.

When is your birthday?

Honestly, I expected better. This is like going to the DMV.

May 10th.

The next code name on the list is *The Healer*

The next questions are equally basic. My neighborhood, my favorite subject in school, my top-choice college, the name of someone I care about. Bed-Stuy, English, Northwestern, my aunt Shell. (I hesitate for a moment before typing that last one, but they have no way of knowing that. Probably.) *The Priestess,The Cleaner, The Philanthropist, The Confiscator.*

My heart thumps as I type my answers. This feels odd, almost like texting your crush, if you thought that there was a vague chance that your crush might transform into a serpent and gobble you down for snakefast.

To reveal the last two entries on the membership list, I have to give two more names: someone I'd like to get to know better and someone I miss. For a moment, I consider lying. But I don't know what will happen if they catch on, and there are plenty of reasons why it would be in my favor to be honest.

Someone I'd like to get to know better: Zola Wolfe. It's not like she's on the other end.

The Jailer.

Okay, I really don't love that, but one thing has nothing to do with the other.

Someone I miss: Emily Hendricks. They've read Daphne's letter. It would be actively suspicious for me to give any other name.

The Killer.

My stomach plummets so violently that I have to grip the edge of my desk to steady myself. That settles it; there's no way in hell that this is a coincidence. Somehow this is all about Emily.

Now I know for sure that I can't back out of whatever this is. Nothing will reverse her death, but I owe it to her to use this situation to do some justice to her memory—and that applies whether or not the letter writers are on my side. Regardless, the first step to winning, whatever *winning* means, is excelling at any challenge that they hurl at me. No more mishaps like the one in the letter to Mai.

Even though I don't tap anything new on the app, another text box flashes on my screen.

Congratulations! You have completed the introduction to Clandestine. Now the real questioning will begin.

I'm digging my fingers into my desk so hard that the edge dents the skin of my fingertips, but I can't let go.

Below, please select the representative with whom you would like to converse. Please note that, as we promised in the most recent letter in your locker, you'll have a chance to learn about us as well this time. So for every question we ask you, you'll have the opportunity to ask one of us.

At the end of the text box, there's a multiple-choice form listing all the pseudonyms on the membership list. Several of the names are already grayed out, which probably means that each one of the…initiates?…will have to select a different representative, and the unavailable names have already been chosen by other Davison girls. I can't select the Priestess, the Philanthropist, or the Jailer. My bedroom feels a little colder than before as I consider who would volunteer for that last one.

I'm sure that this is part of the test, though, and that girl wanted to show this group that she wasn't afraid. That probably means I shouldn't go for one of the unassuming titles. But I sure won't be going with the Killer, either. I have my limits.

I guess the Confiscator it is.

When I tap the title, the app takes me to a chat with the Confiscator. Within seconds, a message appears at the top of the chat.

THE CONFISCATOR:

Delighted to be speaking with you, Kay, but we'll begin our conversation tomorrow. Don't you have an AP Physics test to study for?

• • • • •

Aubrey is waiting across from my math class the next morning, leaning against the trophy case, the debate team's spoils spilling across all four shelves. A wooden plaque hovers behind Aubrey's crossed arms: *Davison High, 1st Place Negative Team, New York Regionals.*

"You haven't held up your end of our deal," Aubrey says.

I zip my quarter-zip all the way to my chin and bury the bottom of my face in its soft fabric. "Forgive me for being too preoccupied with the digital interrogation to corner Mai."

Aubrey scoffs. "Bullshit. Yesterday you spent lunch fucking around on the roof."

"How do you know about that?"

"Unlike you, I observe the people around me," Aubrey says. "But that doesn't matter. What matters is that you need to talk to Mai. Today. That will impact my strategy in conducting this question exchange."

"Have you looked into the drama club?"

Aubrey rolls her eyes. "Tia is a dead end and also an idiot. Frankly, I have no idea what the letter writers see in her."

I see a familiar flash of red hair emerging from around the corner, and my heart thumps. "Fine, I'll find time to approach Mai today. But I have class now, so please go accost someone else, okay?"

Aubrey follows my eyes to the willowy figure gliding toward us. "I want answers by the end of the day. Don't let anything else get in the way."

Still looking at Zola, Aubrey lifts her blue hand to rest on my upper arm. It's almost a caress. Then she presses a single finger into the maroon fabric of my quarter-zip, leaving a blue smudge on my sleeve and a dull throb beneath my skin.

Aubrey spins around and vanishes into the stairwell. As Zola approaches, I see her eyes focus on the mark that Aubrey left behind. "Stepping out on me already, Anderson?"

"I—I wouldn't dream of it," I say.

I should have known better than to get involved with Aubrey. Lie with snakes, get up with strangle marks on your neck.

Zola laughs. "Hey, I'm just messing with you. Call me arrogant, but I don't find Aubrey to be too much of a threat."

I gape at her for a moment. I have no idea what alternate reality she's living in, where she thinks she's involved in any kind of competition for my affection, as opposed to the other way around. "Well, that's your calculation to make."

Zola wiggles her eyebrows. "Ooh, intriguing."

She has no idea how threatening Aubrey can be.

"But enough about her," I say, taking a step closer to Zola. Fuck Aubrey and her agenda. "I'm, uh, free on Friday. Night. You know. If you are."

"For a date?" she says, reaching over and trailing a finger down the back of my blue hand.

I feel goose bumps appear underneath her fingertip. "Yeah. For a date."

"The kind of date where you wear a tweed jacket and take me somewhere fascinating, and then at the end of the night you kiss me on my doorstep, and I tell you how you've never looked more ravishing than you do in the moonlight?" she whispers, stepping closer to me. I can feel her body heat radiating through her polo.

I try to force my mouth to make words. "Yes? Yes."

She winks. "I'd love to, but I'm busy on Friday night. What about Saturday?"

My heart stutters. "Saturday is great."

Her fingers interlace with mine. I hope none of the ink comes off on her. Actually, I hope some of it does. I'd like her to walk through the Davison hallways wearing a reminder of my hand inside hers.

• • • • •

When my lunch hour hits, I give my physics binder a cursory flip-through while standing in front of my locker before tucking it back between my English notebook and my caddy of miscellany. As horrible as it is to admit that Aubrey has a point, anything I learn from Mai may very well determine how I respond to whatever the Confiscator hurls at me, too.

I weave through the clusters of chattering girls until I reach the stairwell to the atrium. On the first, second, and third floors of the school, the hallways wrap around the vaulted room where most students eat lunch. Usually, I make it a point not to pass through the atrium unless I'm giving a tour, when I invite the families to perch on the cushioned seating around the stone fountain in the center of the room and ask them to picture their daughters at the heart of the Davison experience.

My fingers skim the rough red upholstery of the couch closest to the stairwell as I take inventory of the lunching Davisonites. The athletes claim the shallow bleachers on the other side of the fountain from where I'm standing, their shouts echoing through the tiled room and their muscles flexing through the monogrammed color-block crewnecks that they're allowed to wear in place of the standard quarter-zips, cardigans, or blazers. The art kids gather around the long mahogany table at the right side of the room, their heads forming a dome over what I think is a film camera. Samira, Ruby, and Vanessa's crowd—I suppose you could say that they're popular, although that feels a bit immature in a school where overarching social hierarchies aren't nearly as important as excelling within any given student's area of focus—occupies the fountain itself. Ruby is perched on the rim of its basin, her upper body teetering every time she throws back her head to laugh. Vanessa is sitting next to Ruby, steadying her when she leans too far into the fountain.

After my conversation with Chioma, I did some googling about Vanessa. It didn't tell me what happened between her and Chioma, but it did reveal that her dad runs the pharmaceutical company Argenta. Emily used to rant about how evil they are, since they hold the patents for the majority of the best MS medications on the market but price them to be completely unaffordable for families like Emily's. They made headlines last year after beating Bonum Solutions to releasing a treatment that used microfluidic chips, particularly because Bonum announced that they had planned to make it available for free. Plus, Argenta had a cough syrup recalled back when I was in middle school because its drowsiness side effect was so strong that people were using it as a date rape drug.

Mercifully, Mai is sitting alone. She's reading on a Kindle, and her thin frame is enmeshed in one of the brocade armchairs at the edge of the room, splayed out as if she's trying to fill the chair more completely than her body will allow. A Tupperware with two pieces of banh mi perches on the small mahogany table next to her, chunks of beef and leaves of cilantro poking out from inside the thin baguette. A matching armchair sits empty on the other side of the table. I swallow and do my best impression of a purposeful stride toward the empty chair.

"Mind if I join you?" I don't wait for an answer before sitting down.

"Oh, hey." Mai glances up, rewarding me with a grin that I don't deserve. She's wearing enormous earrings in the shapes of Ouija board planchettes. They bounce underneath her earlobes as she slides her Kindle into a Cambridge Satchel knapsack and buckles its leather straps. "It's good to finally talk."

That is...not how I'd have responded if I were her. "You're not angry?"

Mai shrugs. "I figured that my mom's job would come out sometime. You can't really hide something like that in this school, so I didn't mind the big-reveal portion of the letter. But the compliment part felt real, and that was a lot more important."

"It was real." I press myself into the fabric of the armchair, which pushes back taut against my spine. "Despite all the things that unsettled me about having to write the compliment letter, it was nice to be able to drop the Davison facade of dismissiveness, you know?"

"Oh, for sure," Mai says. "Like, it's super off-brand for me to care about sports, but it was cool to gush about Daphne's basketball skills for a few minutes."

Across the atrium, Daphne guffaws as she locks arms with one of the soccer team's forwards. I hope that Mai's letter was a little more vitriolic than she's letting on.

"So what's your take on this whole thing?" I ask, trying to keep my voice even. "What do you think the letter writers are going for?"

Mai's eyes glitter, and she leans in toward me. "Honestly? I think they're trying to take down a criminal."

A grunt emits from my throat. She wouldn't say that if she, or her mother, were the criminal in question. But then who is?

"Tell me more," I say.

"Think about it. They're gathering information. The

compliment letters and this whole app thing are both ways to wring out what we know; plus, they keep making those comments about watching us." She picks up half her sandwich and takes a bite. "So yeah, I think they know something about us that we don't know. Speaking for myself, of course."

"What? You haven't committed any crimes?" I smile as I say it, as if I'm joking.

Mai smiles too. "If I have, it's news to me."

I have no idea how it's possible for Mai to both confirm and disprove Aubrey's theory so completely. "In that case, do you think we're the suspects, or do you think they're trying to recruit us to help them?"

"I'm still figuring that out." For the first time, the crinkles around Mai's eyes smooth out into an intense stare. "I think it might be both, if that makes any sense."

I shake my head. "I mean, it doesn't, but then again, none of this does."

"Yeah." Mai lets out a half laugh. "Who do you think is behind it?"

I don't know what possesses me, but I remove my leather notebook from my backpack and show her my list of clues. Not the page about Emily, which also mentions Mai's mother—I'm not feeling quite that candid—but the page with the notes about the letter writer being in one of my classes and the reference to "I Don't Know How But They Found Me." I'll have to apologize to Chioma for divulging her message, but some instinct tells me that this is the right thing to do. As I hold up the notebook, my fingers clamping it open to those notes and those notes alone, Mai traces a blue finger down the side of the bullet points.

"Oh, wow." Mai looks up. "Kay, you're like one of those true crime podcasters."

I suppose Emily trained me well, and not just about how to navigate wealth. "I'm just curious. We all are."

"The reference to "I Don't Know How But They Found Me" is similar to a message that they wrote to me," Mai says, almost to herself. "I got a note quoting from a piece that I workshopped in poetry club a few weeks ago, which tells us that there has to be a letter writer in poetry club as well. That didn't help me very much before you showed me your notes, because it's a huge group, but a lot of the same girls are in theater and poetry club, so I don't think it's too much of a stretch to wonder if the poetry letter writer is the same as the theater letter writer."

I nod. "Keep me posted on who you think it might be?"

"That goes without saying!" Mai's eyes crinkle up again. "I wouldn't have any idea of this without you."

Without warning, she leans across the table and gives me a quick one-armed hug. I hesitate for a moment, then hug her back. It's strange. Even though she may be hiding something, I kind of want to see if she's free to hang out.

• • • • •

During my AP Physics test, I can't figure out how many light-years it would take for a certain hypothetical supernova explosion to reach Earth. Still, I'm pretty sure that I've ruined the curve enough that I don't need to admonish myself for ignoring my textbook in favor of Clandestine last night.

Afterward, I meet Mai and Chioma in the second-floor supply closet. They're both already there when I open the door: Mai sifting through the bottles of wood-polishing oil on the bottom shelves and Chioma leaning on a tall ladder propped against the back wall. The closet has just enough free space for me to sidle in between them, although this time I'm stuck over the air vent.

"Chioma, Mai, thank you for joining me here," I say.

Chioma nods, but her eyes are focused on the vent. I suppose that, despite my apology text about sharing our clues with Mai, Chioma still doesn't love that I made a unilateral decision.

Mai straightens up from the bottles. "Yeah, it's cool to have, like, a little sleuth team."

Chioma crosses her arms. "This isn't a game."

"No one said it was," I say. "I just thought that three minds would be better than two."

I considered telling Aubrey to meet us here as well. If I were being fully rational, I would have determined that she most likely has more information than the rest of us, and she would be squeezed into this closet right now. Honestly, it's gnawing at me that I haven't done more to uncover what she knows—about both the letter writers and Emily's death. But there's a limit to what I can coerce myself into swallowing. So I texted her that Mai clearly didn't think she'd done anything shady and was therefore a dead end, and then I didn't respond to Aubrey's subsequent *Are you ABSOLUTELY sure?* text.

"What I'd like to know is the list of people in poetry club and who Mai thinks the letter writer might be," Chioma says.

"I'll pull it up." Mai removes her phone from her pocket and taps it a few times, elbowing me softly as she maneuvers in the closet. Chioma and I crowd over her screen. She was right—this must be a quarter of the school. But after a brief glance at the list of names, I suspect Mai is one of very few talented writers in the group. These aren't girls who strike me as having very much to say.

Chioma mutters names as we scroll. "Martina Chang...Ayo Udegbe...Lee Rashid."

My hand slams against a paint can, the thud reverberating in the closet. At the same time, Chioma collapses against the ladder.

"Is there something wrong?" Mai asks.

Chioma steadies herself. "Lee checks the boxes for both me and Kay."

The poetry club must have been the group featured in that shot on Lee's Instagram. Suddenly, something else occurs to me. "The true crime article that they recommended to me. In my first letter. It was about art theft, and Lee has that art business. If they're interested in true crime, that sounds like the kind of thing they would read."

Mai's eyebrows shoot up. "So it's definitely them."

"Almost definitely," Chioma says. "We still shouldn't jump to conclusions."

"Have either of you started communicating with your society members in Clandestine?" I ask.

Both Chioma and Mai shake their heads.

"Okay," I say. "In that case, we should use the opportunity to test whether Lee is behind any of the aliases."

"As long as we're subtle about it," Chioma says. "I doubt that they'll reveal their identities or the identities of the other members."

The three of us look at each other for a moment, the bare bulb overhead casting languid shadows across Chioma's and Mai's faces.

"Well, then." I clear my throat. "Let's start the conversations."

• • • • •

Once again, I'm at my desk with my leather notebook open in front of me and my Davison binders in an untouched pile next to it. It's almost 11:00, and the fall wind is ripping orange leaves from the branches of the oak outside my window, the tree's disembowelment illuminated by the streetlight in front of my brownstone. After poring through Lee's Instagram again and conducting several Google searches, I'm as prepared as I can be to prod the Confiscator for any hints that Lee is involved with this. It's time for me to stop procrastinating and open Clandestine.

I pull up the message box with the Confiscator, my screen black except for the white text forming the Confiscator's initial note.

THE CONFISCATOR:

Delighted to be speaking with you, Kay, but we'll begin our conversation tomorrow. Don't you have an AP Physics test to study for?

Lee would certainly know that.

ME:

Hello, Confiscator. With the astronomy test complete, I look forward to getting to know you

Three dots appear underneath my message. I feel my heartbeat speed up.

THE CONFISCATOR:

No need to use that Davison pre-professional language with us. We want you to relax!

I hesitate for a moment, then reply.

ME:

This app's interface seems to suggest otherwise

Is it foolish to test them? Probably. But then again, I think there's a high chance that they'll respect the boundary-pushing enough to let down their guard a bit.

THE CONFISCATOR:

LOL. Part of the experience.

Another message pops up.

THE CONFISCATOR:

On with the questioning! Some ground rules: we each get five questions. You can ask anything you'd like, within reason. Might decline to answer anything too overt, though. Your first question: during your freshman year, what did you think of Aubrey Clarke?

Beyond my window, a substantial piece of a tree branch, about two feet long, snaps off underneath the weight of the wind. I shut my eyes. This is exactly the kind of question I expected, but there's no way to prepare for the shock of seeing the text on my phone screen.

ME:

It's complicated. She dated a friend of mine

The three dots appear again.

THE CONFISCATOR:

Give us some more detail than that in order to earn the opportunity to ask us something.

I tilt back my office chair and lean over to grab my white faux-fur throw blanket from the foot of my bed. Wrapping it around my shoulders like a cape, I respond.

ME:

As you know, I was close with Emily Hendricks. She got together with Aubrey midway through the fall

I didn't know Aubrey very well, but I had a few classes with her and didn't think she was good enough for Emily

Aubrey seemed fake to me. I mostly just didn't have that much respect for her, but I'd like to think that I've grown since then

If this is the first question, I have my suspicions about what's to come. I dig my fingers into the polyester of my throw blanket as I wait for a response.

THE CONFISCATOR:

Thank you, Kay. Your turn.

Even though I need to guide the conversation toward Lee, I

don't want them to know that I'm heading there. I should start with something more general.

ME:

Are you all Davison students?

THE CONFISCATOR:

Yes.

I wait a moment for a second message to come through, but no dots flash on my screen. It was stupid of me to ask a yes or no question. I'm pretty sure that, unlike the Confiscator, I don't have the power to mandate elaboration.

After a moment, the next question appears.

THE CONFISCATOR:

Now tell us: why did Aubrey and Emily break up?

Nausea bubbles up in my throat, and I clutch a fistful of the blanket as I will my stomach to settle.

ME:

You have to understand that this is the worst thing I've ever done. I've regretted this since the day I did it, but after a few weeks of them dating, I went to Aubrey and told her that Emily had been obsessed with her

Emily was really into true crime, and I said that she had conducted a full podcast-level investigation into Aubrey

I exaggerated a bit, particularly when I showed Aubrey some photos that Emily had taken outside of Aubrey's locker, even though I knew that Emily's intention had just been to catalog the new 18th-century portraits that the school had hung up nearby

It was mostly true though. Emily liked to be thorough with anyone she let into her life

Aubrey didn't react much when I said any of this. But the next day, Emily told me—well, screamed at me, which I deserved—that Aubrey had broken up with her and that it was my fault

Then Emily got expelled the following week and, according to the rumors, it was because she had stalked another student

I feel my breath getting shallow as I type. But when I send the message, there's a certain relief to it. I didn't even give Aunt Shell all these details.

THE CONFISCATOR:

Appreciate your honesty, Kay. This must be difficult for you.

I guess it's nice for the executioner to admit that the guillotine stings a bit.

ME:

Thanks for that, Confiscator. My next question for you is: what's the significance of the various aliases that you and the other letter writers are using in this app?

This should serve as a useful step toward Lee—still general, but slightly more specific than the question that I wasted last time.

THE CONFISCATOR:

Our organization is inspired by the philosophy of a group that was active during a certain medieval movement.

Each member of the group took on a different role that reflected their own mission.

The aliases are based on these roles.

If this has its roots in medieval times... I picture the group of girls in blue gloves who danced in the Halloween parade. I thought that their dresses were Renaissance garb, but my knowledge of fashion history definitely isn't specific enough to differentiate the fifteenth century from the seventeenth. The Confiscator's answer isn't enough to tell me very much on its own, but coupled with the blue gloves from the parade, I might actually have enough information for a Google search.

I start a new list in my notebook—*What They've Told Us*—and start making notes. Within a few seconds, my phone vibrates again.

THE CONFISCATOR:

Third question: what kind of contact did you have with Emily after she was expelled?

I wonder if they know what their line of questioning is doing to me. I wonder if it's intentional.

ME:

We never spoke again after she confronted me about what I did. I texted her a few times, especially after I heard the news, but she never responded, except for one final message the day before she died, telling me that she was right about something

I didn't know what to say to that, so I waited to respond

And then...you know what happened next

THE CONFISCATOR

Regret is a powerful thing, Kay.

Damn right it is. It's the only reason I'm putting up with you.

ME:

Okay, Confiscator. I'd like to know more about this medieval group that inspired you. Why did you choose to be called the Confiscator?

It will be useful intel no matter what, and as I zoom in on the individual behind the alias, it will give me a good excuse to ask something more specific to Lee.

THE CONFISCATOR:

We're all inspired by that group in different ways, so we've adopted titles for ourselves that reflect that.

What resonates with me most is the act of taking away dangerous items from dangerous people. Suppose I could have also called myself "the Thief," but that implies a degree of wrongdoing that I don't believe is accurate.

More and more, it sounds like I was right when I tried to justify to Chioma why I wanted to stay involved with this group.

Maybe they enjoy a little too much dark panache, maybe they revel in their unconventional approach more than they should, but they do seem to be pursuing something good. Even so, my question to Mai remains unanswered: I don't know whether they see us as an aid or an impediment to doing whatever that *something* is.

THE CONFISCATOR:

Getting close to the end of our conversation, Kay. Brace yourself, because the next thing I'd like you to tell me is what you know about how Emily died.

Now my blanket feels like a sheet of lava smothering my limbs. I rip it off and toss it back onto my bed behind me.

ME:

I don't know what you want me to tell you. I heard about her death when Principal Ellison told us about it in the morning announcements in December of my freshman year. She called it a tragic accident, but I don't think that's true anymore. I'm not sure if I ever did

But I don't have any real information about the truth

Frankly, I'm sure that you know much more than I do

The reply comes right away.

THE CONFISCATOR:

If you're trying to ask a question, Kay, ask it outright.

And I want to. So badly. But I've spent my last three questions working up to one about Lee, and even though all my cells are screaming that I need to know what Emily has to do with whoever the Confiscator is, Davison has taught me nothing if not discipline.

ME:

I'd rather know why you, or whichever member of your group was behind this, recommended the art theft true crime case to me

This time, the Confiscator's reply takes a moment to come through.

THE CONFISCATOR:

Can't speak to that, personally. May surprise you to hear, but most of us aren't particularly interested in true crime—at least not when the crime is so far removed from our reality. But we heard about the case and, based on how well we know you, we thought you might want to hear about it, too.

That's…inconclusive. I'm glad I have another question left so that I can ask the same thing through a different angle.

ME:

Interesting

I watch dots bubble on my screen, awaiting the Confiscator's final question. No matter what, I'm sure it will snap me in half.

THE CONFISCATOR:

Are you still in love with Emily Hendricks?

My heart stops. I stare at the text. Of all the invasive, traumatizing questions that I anticipated, this wasn't one of them.

ME:

No

What I don't say is: after you learn that the girl you love is dead, you can tuck in your feelings as if you're putting a child to sleep, but that isn't the same as getting over her. Even if it was just a youthful crush, death freezes your love like a mosquito trapped in amber.

I wonder what will come next: another order to elaborate, an accusation of dishonesty. But the Confiscator's next message is simple:

THE CONFISCATOR:

This completes my round of questions for you. Kay, your final question for me?

I shouldn't have wasted my line of questioning on Lee. I don't even care who's behind this anymore. All I want to know is what Emily means to them.

But it would be too foolish to squander the conversation.

ME:

I still want to know about how you found out about the art theft case, especially if you're not typically interested in true crime

Two messages arrive in quick succession:

THE CONFISCATOR:

It's the kind of thing that comes up between colleagues.

This concludes the question exchange. Thank you for your participation, and please await further instructions.

With that, my phone screen flashes black. I jab at it, trying to return to the main menu with the general chat, but the app doesn't respond.

I stare out my window, watching the tree branches thrash in the wind. No matter how much they tried to throw me, I have to think rationally about what I've learned. If they were telling the truth, they really did give me quite a bit of new information. There's almost certainly a Davison secret society behind this—a society with a deep history, which is unexpected, considering Davison has been open for only a decade. The society also has some kind of cohesive philosophical code, one that's bringing them to Emily, somehow. And then…there's Lee. I've failed completely when it comes to uncovering their involvement. Even assuming that they're the colleague in question, I don't know whether that means they're in the group or in its periphery.

I pull up Google and search for a few different configurations of *medieval vigilante society blue gloves,* but there's nothing more relevant than an ad for PPE for archaeologists. So much for uncovering the group's historical background.

Flipping through the pages of my notebook, I try to piece together these new hints with the clues I've picked up over the past few weeks. Given the types of girls in the poetry club, I'm not surprised that anyone with a higher purpose is only in there to collect information about their recruits. And I suppose this makes sense with the general sense that they have eyes and ears throughout the school. But what about the reference to pink noise that convinced Chioma that someone in the organization is a sound designer?

Wait. A sound designer.

Suddenly the lashing of the wind and the thundering of my heartbeat slip into a terrible rhythm. I know at least one of the people behind those letters.

Lee isn't the only sound designer in the drama company. They told me they had a codesigner—*a colleague.* And I'm certain I know who it is. It doesn't matter how many red herrings she's sent me. Because there's only one other person who's in my classes, knows technical theater, and definitely finds me intriguing.

I don't breathe as I search up the drama company's website.

This year, the fall musical is *Sweeney Todd*. I scroll through the tech staff, past the director, past the stage manager, to the designer titles, to the name listed next to Lee's under the heading *Sound Designers*.

It's the name I knew would be there, but seeing it still feels like a fist crushing my lungs.

Zola Wolfe.

CHAPTER 7

When I open my locker the next morning and see another note deposited on top of my binders, I'm too numb to be surprised. I unfold the scrap of paper, anyway. This neat fountain pen handwriting is much cleaner than the scrawl of Zola's math notes. Most likely, it means she's not the one holding the pen. At least she's part of a group; I don't think I could take it if I thought that she was the only one behind the past few weeks of unanswered questions. There are two sentence fragments on the page.

The Davison rooftop. Tomorrow night at 8:00.

Now I know why she said she was busy on Friday.

Today Zola's calc seat remains empty for the full class period. Occasionally I make eye contact with the portrait of Watson and Crick that usually hovers behind her. I can't decide whether the scientists' cool black-and-white eyes are a satisfactory substitute for her cunning blue ones.

As I'm walking to English, I remove my phone from the pocket of my slacks and open a new message to Zola. There are a number of texts I'd like to send right now.

Why weren't you in class today?

When were you going to tell me that you're in a secret society with ambiguous morals?

What connection do you have to Emily?

I don't send any of them.

• • • • •

Friday night is one of Davison's famed family mixers. Four or five times a year, Davison sends out invitations stamped with gold leaf, dims the chandeliers in the atrium, and opens its iron doors to the parents of current students. Even though the script that I have to deliver on my school tours has a robust section about the mixers—*in addition to the alumni network that will carry your children toward success after high school, the whole family is invited to share in the wealth of connection that the school provides, from the moment of orientation*—I haven't been to one since back-to-school night in my freshman year. My parents were so proud to come with me that evening. Even though my dad had been asked to stay late at the warehouse that night, he told his boss that he couldn't do it; instead, he came home and changed into the suit he usually reserves for weddings and funerals. When we arrived, all the dads were wearing navy Patagonia vests, and all the moms had almost-imperceptible highlights in their hair.

During the school day, my income status never felt quite that rancid. But out of the school uniform, when my parents and I were surrounded by Wall Street tycoons and tech millionaires, it became very clear that the mixer wasn't meant for us.

I don't know why you bothered going, Emily texted me when my parents and I arrived home. We'd only lasted about half an hour. *I told you not to do that to yourself.*

It's 7:45. Tonight's mixer started at 7:00—I guess Zola and her compatriots wanted to give us a chance to mingle before slipping away for our evening of mystery and intrigue—so when I arrive at the steps of Davison, a din of Chopin and practiced laughter is emanating from behind the lit windows at the front of the building. While I have no intention of participating in the performance, I can't pass through the building without attempting to blend in, so I'm wearing my best impression of formalwear: a thrifted J.Crew blazer that's a little tight on my upper arms, my uniform slacks, and a pair of Dr. Martens oxfords. I try not to think about what the other girls will be wearing when we gather on the roof. I hate being around Davison girls out of uniform.

I push open the iron doors and slip into the stairwell closest to the building entrance, not allowing my gaze to lock on the entrance to the atrium across the lobby. While it's probably not wise to show up with sweat stains on my blazer, I just can't deal with the possibility of being stuck in an elevator with one of the other girls. I climb the stairs carefully, taking even breaths in order to stabilize my heartbeat as much as possible.

When I reach the third-floor landing, I hear a door squeak open several flights beneath me. Shit. I didn't account for this. I quicken my pace, willing the other person to leave at the second floor or at least climb slowly enough that they don't catch up to me. But of course that doesn't happen. Even though I'm moving as quickly as I can without risking the sweat stains, the other person must be scurrying. Their soft footfalls grow louder and louder until I decide that it would look churlish to keep pretending that I don't hear someone who's clearly trying to catch up to me.

When I turn around, I see Margaret O'Malley darting up the flight. I wait on the landing, and she comes to a stop beside me, panting. "I'm glad I caught you," she says.

"Mm, totally," I say.

Margaret is wearing a woven cardigan, white with blush-pink trim, and a long skirt in the same deep blush color. "Whatever this is, I'd rather not go into it alone."

I can't imagine admitting that, particularly to a near stranger. Margaret and I have shared a few classes, but I can't say that I know much about her beyond her reputation as a computer genius. "I get that."

We ascend the next flight in silence. Margaret is tapping the banister with her fingers as she climbs. The jittery movement almost reminds me of Emily, but not quite. Emily's energy was wild, frantic even, but it was never quite nervous. Margaret, on the other hand, punctuates each tap with sharp gulps that I couldn't imagine coming out of Emily's throat.

"Do you have any idea of what will happen tonight?" Margaret asks.

I didn't even tell Chioma or Mai what I realized. In fact, I avoided them after saying that my question exchange was inconclusive. "Your guess is as good as mine."

"I'm not sure about that," Margaret says. "I...I probably shouldn't tell you this, but nothing I tried worked."

We round the corner to the next flight. I've lost count of where we are at this point. "What do you mean?"

Her tongue flicks out to moisten her dry lips. "It's like every part of their communication strategy was designed to block me. Me specifically, I mean. Obviously I couldn't trace the notes in the lockers. Then, when they sent us to the app, I thought I would finally be able to crack them, but I've never seen an encryption system like that. I just couldn't do it."

That's interesting, but not really surprising. "I can imagine that'd be rough."

Margaret swallows. "Look, Kay, we don't know each other very well, but I feel like you get this. It's like I failed a test in my best subject."

I don't like this part of me, but I feel a surge of vindication in my stomach. Margaret is probably the smartest person in our grade. It's nice that my strengths came through when hers didn't. "Well, these people clearly don't operate like school."

"They...sure don't." When we reach the last landing before the one that leads to the roof, Margaret halts, and because I don't see another choice, I stop with her. "Before we go out there, I have to tell you something."

"Yeah?" I say.

"I think I messed up...kind of badly." Her eyes twitch beneath her wire glasses. "Between the compliment letter I received and the questions they asked me in Clandestine, they learned some pretty incriminating stuff about me."

Margaret pauses. I'm not sure if she wants me to ask her

what they know. As I open my mouth without a real plan for what should come out of it, she takes another breath and resumes talking. "I cheated on a few English assignments early in high school. Generative AI. And I don't know what they have planned for us tonight, but I don't think they like us very much, and if they decide to tell the school's administration or, worse, colleges—"

"Hey, hey," I say, extending my undyed hand to rest on her arm through the fabric of her cardigan. I wish I owned sweaters this soft. "I think you'll be okay. Based on what I've gathered over the last few weeks, they're looking for a much more damning secret. You weren't involved with any murders, right?"

Margaret's eyes bulge out so far that, for a moment, I think they're going to press themselves against the lenses of her glasses. "S-seriously? You think that's what's going on?"

I check my watch. "In ninety seconds, we'll find out."

Margaret stares up at the door to the roof. "I guess we will."

One flight of stairs later, the bronze door handle is cold beneath my blue hand. I give it an experimental twist. It's unlocked, and the door swings in.

There are no paintings or picnic blankets on the roof this time. Instead, the red brick is bare, surrounded only by ornate iron railings that cage the rooftop like a wrestling ring. Even though it's an uncharacteristically warm day for November, the wind is strong enough to sting my skin as I step out onto the rooftop. There are seven girls standing in a circle in the center of the flat plane. Six of them have blue hands sticking out from underneath their formal wear: Daphne, Chioma, Aubrey, Tia, Mai, and Vanessa. Almost all are wearing thick knit sweaters or beige Burberry trench coats.

The seventh, with her willowy silhouette stark against the moon, is Zola.

My heart crumples. And then it soars. And then it crumples again.

Her eyes meet mine for just a moment, and then she looks away. She's hugging herself for warmth, her arms covered only in the thin fabric of a gauzy white blouse. "Come join us. Now we can begin."

Margaret and I cross the roof, slotting ourselves between Chioma and Aubrey. I try not to look at either of them.

"I'd like to start by congratulating you all," Zola says. Even the breeze seems to get quiet for her. "It wasn't easy to make it this far. In the beginning, we sent letters to thirty people. Twenty-six followed our first instruction. Then, after the compliment letter and question exchange, respectively, we dismissed the girls who weren't useful to us."

She pauses, and the words seep into my skin.

"What does that even mean?" Mai asks, her voice an octave

higher than I've heard it in the past. As she speaks, she tugs on the gold chain around her neck.

"Let me explain," Zola says, that magnetic smile twitching at the corners of her lips. "I have a whole speech prepared."

She scans us. Her eyes stop at each of our faces, one by one. She looks at me last, and maybe the longest, but not long enough for me to be certain. "I'm a representative from the Davison chapter of a much larger society: the Blue Hand Girls."

Of course. BHG.

"For the sake of preserving as much of our secrecy as possible, I'll be your sole liaison and guide throughout this process," Zola continues. "You'll meet the rest of my colleagues if you pass initiation."

"Wouldn't we already know them, if they go to Davison?" Chioma asks.

Zola shrugs. "Most likely. But you're under strict orders not to approach anyone besides me. Even if you think you know the identities of my fellow BHGs, on the off chance that you're wrong, it would be a very bad look for you."

"Has Davison always had this society?" Daphne asks, leaning into the center of the circle.

Zola shakes her head. "While the organization itself is quite old—ancient, even—the Davison chapter has only been around since last year, when several of us were recruited to investigate a serious infraction of justice. That infraction isn't relevant anymore; we took care of it, and those who contributed most to that success gained full status as members of this organization. Now you all have the opportunity to right another wrong and compete for membership in the process."

Vanessa clears her throat. "What do we gain from membership?"

"Excellent question," Zola says. "There's the usual answer when it comes to secret societies: the Blue Hand Girls alumni network is vast and influential, and you'll want to have it on your side. But, more importantly, being part of this society will give you the power to change something enormous, even before you graduate from high school. And I know you all want that. You have several things in common, and one is that you're dissatisfied with the status quo. You see injustice around you every day at Davison, and you want to fix it."

That's not what I would expect from all these girls. For scholarship kids like me and Aubrey, maybe, but what about a student athlete like Daphne? Is she really out here challenging the system? Still, I glance around the circle, and everyone is nodding as Zola speaks. Perhaps I should be more generous in assuming that people contain multitudes.

Zola shifts. "That hunger for justice is what connected all the girls who received the first letter. Then, as we learned more about each of you, we narrowed down our list to the girls who would be the most ruthless in pursuing what's right, as well as the girls who most needed redemption, particularly when it comes to the specific injustice that you'll be addressing in this initiation process."

A chill shoots down my neck as the rest of the girls scan the circle. I'm doing the same, my gaze lingering on Chioma and Mai. How do they need to be redeemed? How do I?

And why would Zola hold my hand if this is what she thinks of me?

"Go back a moment," Chioma says. "If this chapter appeared at Davison last year, why didn't you have a blue hand last fall?"

"Another excellent question," Zola says. "We have different needs each year. Last year our initiation required a high degree of secrecy, so we were Blue Hand Girls in name only. This time we decided that it would be helpful to stir the rumor mill in order to reveal the information we were seeking, so we took the title literally."

"And did you find the information you were looking for?" Aubrey asks.

Zola smiles again, her white teeth glittering underneath indigo lips. "That will be clear in a moment. Take a seat. We're going to do some storytelling."

She lowers herself to the brick and sits cross-legged on the rooftop. The rest of us follow suit. The rough concrete scrapes my hand as I steady myself on the brick.

"As I'm sure you're all aware by now, your group's initiation focus is the death of Emily Hendricks," Zola says.

I wait for a reaction from the group—a gasp, a murmur of movement—but the most I pick up is the twitch of an expression or two. Clearly the Confiscator wasn't the only representative who had all but revealed the group's intentions.

"My collaborators and I have spoken to each of you about what you know," Zola says. "You do know quite a bit, which is what we're going to put together tonight. But, as you'll discover, there are still several unanswered questions. And in order to pass initiation, you need to figure out why she died and carry out whatever consequence is necessary to make things right."

"That's impossible," I mutter.

"As right as it can be," Zola says, her voice a shade softer. "Unfortunately, for many of our missions, there's no way to reverse the wrongdoing in question. But at least we can put some good into the world to balance out the pain."

Now she's the girl who held my hand again. The dread in my stomach begins to dissipate. Despite this group's—not to mention Zola's—proclivity for drama, it's seeming more and more like there's true nobility behind their motivations. Maybe Mai is right—we're both suspects and investigators.

But it doesn't feel like they're punishing us. Instead, it feels like they picked us for our capacity to correct the wrongdoing with which we're most intimately familiar.

Zola looks at me. I try to focus on her eyes, but it's difficult not to be distracted by the silhouette of her torso underneath the semi-sheer fabric of her blouse. "Kay, I'd like you to begin. Tell us about the conversation you had with Aubrey almost precisely two years ago."

"R-right," I say, hating how quietly the word comes out.

"Thank you, by the way," she says, the hint of tenderness still at the edge of her voice. "I understand that this conversation will be painful for many of you. I'd say that anyone here has the option to leave, but we've gotten to know you well enough to feel certain that no one will take us up on that."

I think back to Margaret's words in the stairwell, and I wonder if Zola thinks we really have a choice. "From what Zola is saying, it sounds like the first step in Emily's death was, um, my fault. She was dating Aubrey at the time, and I...didn't like that. I told Aubrey that Emily had been obsessed with her."

Zola gestures at Aubrey, whose lips are pressed together into a thin line. "Aubrey, pick up from Kay."

"Look. I'm a very private person," Aubrey says. "I liked Emily enough, but I'd already told her everything I wanted her to know about me, and I hadn't signed up for her to pry. So I reported her for stalking. Maybe I played it up a little more than was accurate. In a rare example of administrative competence, Emily was expelled the following week."

I don't want to know what Aubrey was doing two years ago that made her so protective over her privacy.

"Mai, what happened next?" Zola asks.

Mai keeps fidgeting with her chain as she speaks. "I, um, didn't know that this was part of a whole narrative, but a few days after Emily was expelled, I texted her. We had a few classes together, and I thought she might need a friend. We met up for coffee a few times. Whenever we spoke, she asked me these very pointed questions about what was going on at school, but she never seemed satisfied with my answers. Then, after one of our coffee hangouts, she told me that she didn't want to see me anymore, and I thought, you know, that was that."

"Do you have any idea why she cut you off?" Margaret asks.

Mai exhales shakily. "Zola—or, I guess, another Blue Hand Girl, I don't know—asked me the same thing in the Clandestine conversation. I think I must have offended Emily. I asked if there was anything I could do to help her find a new school and said that my family had offered to help as well. That was when she ended the conversation."

I glance at Aubrey. Maybe Mai's mom was up to something, after all. Maybe, given Emily's proclivity for investigating,

Mai's mom determined that Emily would be a potential future journalist and took an interest in her because of it. And then… what? Mai's mom somehow sent Emily on an assignment to Queens, and that was what killed her? That's a pretty astonishing degree of far-fetched. But I guess so is a secret society of teenage vigilantes, and yet here I am.

"Let's go with Mai's explanation for now," Zola says. "We might revisit it later. In the meantime, our timeline puts us at the end of November, two years ago. Now, Mai wasn't the only one to have befriended Emily at this point. Daphne, take it from here."

"Yeah, uh, I don't have a lot to add," Daphne says. She looks uncomfortable. I've been assuming that it's because she doesn't enjoy trading in her basketball uniform for cocktail dresses, like the green garment whose fluted skirt splays out below the hem of her athletic jacket tonight, but maybe she has other reasons. "I had biology with Emily—Kay, you know that, you were in our class, too—so I knew who she was. And, man, her situation sucked. I figured, if it were me who had been expelled, I'd want someone to try to distract me from how bad I felt about myself."

I try not to think about how even Daphne, the human equivalent of a brick wall, was there for Emily. And I wasn't.

"And how did you do that?" Zelda prompts.

Daphne smacks the knuckles of her blue hand into the palm

of her undyed one. "I mostly tried to hype her up. We played ping-pong together a few times, and she was really good at it, because she was so little and fast. I didn't even have to hold back for her to beat me."

I picture Emily zipping around a ping-pong table, whacking the ball low and fast so that it whizzed by Daphne's hulking frame before she even had a chance to move her paddle in defense. It makes perfect sense. But I didn't even know that she played.

I suppose there is…was…a lot I didn't know about Emily.

"And, eventually, you invited her to a party," Zola says.

Daphne nods. "Vanessa's party."

Zola gestures at Vanessa. "And how did you feel about Emily attending?"

"It was fine." Vanessa twirls the belt on her Burberry trench coat. Her glossy chestnut hair, flowing over her shoulders in its perpetual blowout, flutters in the night wind.

"I think it was a little more than fine," Zola says.

Vanessa sighs. "It doesn't make me sound, like, the nicest, but we all wanted to see if the stalking rumors were true. And the only alternative was inviting Aubrey. No offense."

Aubrey smirks. "I had more enjoyable plans for that night, like bathing my eyeballs in acid."

"We don't have time for high school drama," Zola says sharply. "The Blue Hand Girls aren't fucking around."

For a moment, it's silent except for the rushing of cars on the street outside the school. Aubrey and Vanessa look anywhere but at each other.

"Now, then," Zola continues. "Chioma, I believe that you and Vanessa used to be close. Remind me how your friend group interrogated Emily that night?"

Chioma looks down as she picks at a loose thread under one of the gold buttons on her Chanel jacket. "You all have to understand that this is the worst thing I've ever done. I would never do anything like it today. It—it haunts me."

That sounds much too familiar.

"Stop being so dramatic," Vanessa says. "It's not that deep."

"Of course it fucking is! She had no idea what she was drinking!" Chioma says, her head jerking up. Her eyes sift wildly through the faces in our circle until they land on mine. "We could tell that Emily wasn't very used to alcohol, so we gave her a Long Island Iced Tea and said that it was practically a mocktail."

Horror drips down my insides. This isn't the Chioma I've been getting to know. Or, worse, maybe it is.

"It didn't get us anywhere, though," Vanessa says. "We thought it would be, like, a truth serum—you know, because it would lower her inhibitions—but she just got super drunk. Even after one drink, she couldn't tell us anything because she was slurring her words so much."

No wonder Chioma has been inconsistent with how much she's willing to tell me. If I had done something like that, I would panic every time it threatened to come up, too. At least she's properly ashamed of it.

But no matter the words coming out from between Vanessa's glossy lips, she must feel some degree of guilt. Otherwise, why would she be here?

"Margaret, pick up the story," Zola says.

Margaret pushes up her glasses on her nose. "I was also at the party, and when I saw how drunk Emily was, I took her downstairs and put her in a cab."

"Did she tell you anything interesting?" Vanessa asks.

Chioma chokes out an exhale. "Really, Vanessa?"

"She sounded paranoid," Margaret says. "I was worried, to be honest. The only thing I really understood was that she thought someone was coming after her."

And she was right. I can't believe I tipped the first domino in all this. I can't believe I wasn't there to at least help her out of the cab when she got back to Brooklyn that night.

"Back to Kay for a moment," Zola says. "About a week after the party, Emily sent you a text. What did it say?"

I shut my eyes. "That she was right about something. But I have no idea what."

Zola nods. "And we all know what happened next: We heard

in the morning announcements that Emily had died in a freak accident, something about a manhole explosion. There was an article about it on *Kew Gardens Online*, but it didn't add much, except that the manhole was by a complex of storage lockers, and one of the lockers was destroyed in the explosion."

I've pictured that moment thousands of times. Emily crossing the manhole, probably without even noticing it underneath her shoes. The heavy bronze cover shooting into the air, dust and fire rushing out of the tunnel below the sidewalk. Emily slamming against the concrete from the force of the blast, choking on smoke, her skull cracking upon impact.

"Nothing that anyone has said tonight indicates that Emily's death was something other than an accident," Vanessa says. "So what if she got expelled and got all weird and paranoid after that?"

Aubrey shakes her head. "There are still too many missing pieces. Why did the school react so quickly when I reported Emily for stalking? What did Emily mean when she told Margaret that someone was after her, or when she told Kay that she was right about something? Most importantly, why was Emily at that storage locker facility?"

Zola smiles. "Excellent questions, Aubrey. I have one more to add: What about Tia?"

Tia nods, her ringlets bouncing with the motion of her head. "Yeah, I, uh, don't really know why I'm here?"

"My peers and I think that your freshman-year incident may be the key to some of the missing pieces," Zola says. "Tell the group what happened in December."

Tia's tiny body looks even more fragile next to Daphne's hulking frame. "My brother came home from college to see me in the fall musical? In case you don't remember, I played Cinderella in *Into the Woods*. It was the first time Davison had ever cast a freshman as a lead in a Sondheim? Usually, the best a freshman can do is a part like Little Red Riding Hood? So I was super humbled, obviously—"

"Tia." Zola clears her throat. "The morning after the performance. Also the day after Emily's death."

"I was getting to that," Tia says. "My point is that my brother was home, and we were in our Fieldston house that weekend, so he wanted to take a drive the day after the show? And it had been a while since I'd seen him, so I made him take me, even though I think he would have preferred to be alone. But he crashed the car? He lost control and hit a tree? He was okay, but I broke two ribs and had to miss school until after New Year's. I was lucky that our concierge doctor could take care of me from home, because I would have hated to be in the hospital for so long? And the car was completely wrecked, obviously. It was nothing super fancy, just our older Cadillac, but my brother was really upset about the whole thing."

Aubrey looks at Zola. "So you think that the car crash has to do with Emily?"

"The timing is too close," Zola says. "What are the odds that one Davison girl—well, ex-Davison girl—dies and the next day another is in a devastating car crash?"

"But the second one actually was an accident," I say. What I don't add is: *if her brother—or anyone else—had been orchestrating the crash, they would have tried harder to finish the job.*

"I don't know what the connection is, but there has to be one," Zola says. "It's part of your arsenal of clues. So, until you figure out why Tia was in that situation, we have to keep her around."

I can't decide whether there's an apologetic undertone to Zola's voice. Then she glances over at me, the corners of her lip twitching like she's fighting them from pulling upward. Yeah, that was an apology I heard.

"What's next, then?" Aubrey asks.

"What's next is that you'll all rejoin your families downstairs," Zola says. "I've already kept you too long. Meanwhile, I'll report back to my peers with some new insights based on our conversation today, and you'll take the weekend to process everything you've learned. Next week, keep an eye on Clandestine for further instructions."

And I guess that's it. We all begin to stand. My back is sore from the slouching that I didn't realize I was doing, and I twist my torso from side to side in order to roll out the ache. One by one, the rest of the girls shuffle back toward the entrance to the rooftop, some of them murmuring to each other.

Mai follows toward the tail of the pack. "Are you coming?" she whispers to me.

I shake my head. "I want to talk to Zola."

"Do you know her outside of this?"

"I…thought I did."

"Good luck." Mai touches my shoulder, then disappears into the stairwell.

Now Zola and I are the only ones left on the rooftop. She rushes up to me, her arms outstretched. All the stiffness of before rushes out of her body. "Kay—"

"What the fuck, Zola?" I say, pushing her hands away from me.

Her voice is higher than I've ever heard it. "I'm sorry—it wasn't part of my plan to take you on a date this week—but you brought me the bagel, and—"

"And what? You were going to summon me to the roof with all the rest of them, force me through your initiation—which I don't even know if I'll pass—and *then* tell me you thought I was cute?"

"No, I—I guess—" She gulps in a breath. Her face is so close to mine that I can see her lips tremble as she inhales. "I didn't think it through. You were on the Blue Hand Girls' list even before I realized I had feelings for you, and then when I did, I didn't know how to adapt. And I fucked it up. Seeing you here, having to treat you like everyone else—it felt so wrong."

"How can I believe any of this?" My chest heaves. "How do I know this isn't some twisted technique to wring more secrets out of me?"

"What kind of a person do you think I am?" Zola spits. "If this were for the Blue Hand Girls, do you think I would—do you think I would—"

She kisses me.

Her lips tender on mine, her hair brushing against my cheeks, her hands pulling my waist forward to meet hers, she kisses me. I can feel all of her. I can even feel the swirl of her fingertips on the strip of bare skin on my back, where my shirt has lifted, exposing me to the gnawing of the wind. But she is warm. Even wearing this thin blouse, she radiates, the way I've felt her radiating across the math table, but now I know what it's like to feed myself to the sun.

After a moment I pull away, my heart slamming hard enough to break my rib cage.

"That was my first kiss," I whisper. I think it's more for my sake than hers.

She kissed me. Zola Wolfe kissed me.

Now her glow surrounds my heart.

“Mine too.” Her eyes dart from the red brick beneath us to the black sky above our heads—anywhere but meeting mine.

I didn’t expect that. I’d have expected her to have kissed a lot of girls. I don’t know why she’s chosen me.

But she has.

CHAPTER 8

The next morning, I wake up to a notification from Clandestine. The message, situated at the top of the general chat, reads:

THE HEALER:

We invite you all to explore the app while you await your next instructions!

While there's nothing particularly menacing about the message—honestly, it's one of the most welcoming things I've heard from anyone involved with this society—reading it makes me shudder. Or maybe I just haven't stopped shaking since last night.

Clutching my comforter around me, I prod at the home page

of the app. It seems like the general chat is unlocked now, but I refuse to be the first initiate to send a message. The member list, too, is unlocked; whereas before I couldn't chat with anyone but the Confiscator, now I can contact any of the other initiates or alias-obscured members of the society. I don't have anything to say to them, except for Zola, and I don't know which name she's hidden behind.

I grip the comforter a little harder, contemplating the options. I'd like to think that she's the Baker, or maybe the Priestess—that would suit her, I think—but of course it's just as likely that she's the Killer. Or maybe she's the Confiscator, lying by omission as she pressed me about whether I was still in love with Emily. That would be the worst option of them all.

Somehow, I think I still have a date with her tonight.

I brush a finger across my lips. I can still feel the softness of her kiss. But if she's the Confiscator, I should call off the date. My dignity is more powerful than the memory of her tongue tracing her name inside my mouth.

Before I can decide against it, I message the Confiscator.

ME:

I have some more questions for you, based on last night. Will you have time to message this evening?

Nausea bubbles in my stomach as I hit Send. It's not foolproof—of course, the Confiscator could have other plans tonight that don't involve going on a date with me—but if she's free, I'll be certain that she isn't Zola.

The Confiscator's three dots appear almost immediately.

THE CONFISCATOR:

Can't promise I'll be able to give you all the information you seek, but you can ask me anything you'd like tonight. I'll be there to answer.

A shuddering exhale rips itself out of me.

ME:

Thanks, Confiscator

In that case, I have about eight hours to sort out my thoughts from last night, draft an essay for history, and travel to the Upper East Side to pick up the most mysterious redhead at Davison.

• • • • •

Seven hours and fifty-two minutes later, I've filled in my leather notebook with all the new information about the Blue Hand Girls; outlined and collected the majority of my evidence for an essay arguing that philanthropy is a secular, modern-day version of the Catholic Church's indulgences; ignored three texts from Aubrey, pointedly not sent through Clandestine, hounding me about needing to talk; and taken the hour-long train ride to Eighty-Sixth Street. Zola's building is almost on

Central Park. I need to look less than half a block to see a crown of bare branches scraping against the night sky. Meanwhile, six Corinthian columns guard the shallow steps leading up to Zola's building. As I shift my weight from side to side and wait for her to come downstairs, the doorman opens the building's heavy wooden door for an old woman and her poodle.

Maybe even more than around Davison, I know that I don't belong in this neighborhood. I pull at the hem of my peacoat. It's an approximation of the Thom Browne men's coats that crossed the runway during the last fashion week, and you don't need to see the polyester lining to know that it's not the real thing. Underneath I'm wearing a navy-and-dark-green argyle sweater over a white button-down. It's not a tweed jacket, but Zola will have to make her peace with not being able to puppeteer this particular element of my life.

As I contemplate whether it would make a better first sight for me to keep my coat open or closed, Zola emerges at the top of the stoop. She nods to the doorman as he closes the door behind her. Then her eyes fall on me, and for a second, I can't breathe. She's radiant. Her red hair tumbles over her shoulders like a cape, its brightness stark against a black leather jacket and black jumpsuit.

"You look stunning," I say.

She descends the steps. "I could say the same about you."

My heart leaps. When I watch those perfect lips curve as she speaks, I remember again how they felt on mine.

"So," I say, eyeing the door behind her, "are you going to invite me inside? Introduce me to the parents?"

Zola's face freezes.

"I'm sorry," I say before she has a chance to respond. I can't decide whether it's a point against her that she doesn't want her family to see her with a poor or a point in her favor that she's going out with me anyway.

"Don't worry about it," Zola says, her face relaxing again. She grabs my blue hand, and I feel a jolt in my fingertips. "I'm ready to see where you take me."

I smile at her and try to shake off the discomfort that comes with both the wealth and the membership in the Blue Hand Girls. I didn't know what she'd count as *somewhere fascinating,* but I did spend several hours on Google searching for the best date spots in NYC and trying not to think about how I, a person who grew up here, had to take recommendations from the NYU freshmen who move here from Milwaukee, layer two skirts, and then deem themselves New Yorkers. I give her hand a squeeze. "You'll love it."

I ignore the whisper in my mind suggesting that, in retrospect, her description of the date she wanted me to take her on sounds like one of the letter writers' challenges.

About half an hour later, I'm pushing aside a beaded curtain blocking off the doorway to the second floor of a Greenwich Village walk-up. The NYU student newspaper called it a "hidden New York gem," which I hope means that it'll be a new experience even for Zola. Smoke from clove cigarettes fills the dim room, its walls lined with framed George O. Frink prints and its floors crammed with rows of leather couches in almost the same shade of maroon as the Davison uniforms. I glance over at Zola, whose eyes are lapping up the space, lingering on the exposed wooden beams of the ceiling. "What is this place?" she asks, her arm brushing against my waist.

Thank goodness. "Dorothy's. It was a queer speakeasy in the '50s. Now it's a restaurant."

"Damn, Kay," Zola says. "You're full of surprises."

Well, I certainly won't correct her. I grab her hand and weave through the couches and faded mahogany tables until we reach an empty corner. Most of the tables are taken by middle-aged couples in faded suits and gaggles of college students with rows of jingling ear piercings and mesh gloves. I hear a high-pitched giggle coming from a few tables over and glance behind me, expecting to see another teenage couple, but the sound is coming from a fortysomething butch with a head of shaggy salt-and-pepper hair and a red Mr. Rogers sweater. Matching wedding rings gleam on her hand and the hand of the stately femme across her table, the femme's black-and-gray cheetah-print dress draped against the red leather couch like the restaurant was designed to display her. I look back at Zola, and her gaze is pointed at the couple as well. To my surprise, Zola's chin is trembling.

"Hey," I say softly. "What is it?"

She sniffs. "Sorry. Gay marriage still isn't legal in Czechia."

I hesitate for a moment, then scoot toward her and put an arm around her shoulders. This must be the old country she mentioned on our first date. I'm not sure if she's doing it consciously, but I like that she's bringing herself into focus for me. "It makes me happy to see them, too."

She sniffs again, and I pull her tighter against me. Even though I don't want to get ahead of myself, a part of me wonders if Zola will wear cheetah-print dresses in thirty years.

A waiter with an impressive mullet squeezes between couches and heads toward our table. As they approach, I spring back from Zola, my heart beating. I don't know what you're supposed to do on a date. Are you allowed to touch if there's someone else paying attention?

"I'm Knox." The waiter slides two leather menus onto our table. "Can I start you off with some water?"

I nod, and they disappear into the back of the restaurant. Zola's knee touches mine underneath the table. "So how many girls have you seduced here before?"

I snort. "How many do you think?"

"Hmm," she says. "Do group-project meetings count?"

I swat her. "Not funny."

"If that were true, you wouldn't be on a date with me," Zola says. Then her grin turns into a probing twist of her lips. "Seriously, there's a lot I'd like to know about you, Kay. I've been seeing you in the hallways for years now, organizing your locker and conducting your admissions tours, but it seems like something has changed recently. Like you were in black and white, and now you're in color."

I glance down at my blue hand. "I think you're just noticing the obvious."

Zola follows my eyes. "No, it's not just that. Why have you been so guarded until recently?"

"That's a bit intrusive, isn't it?" The words fly out of my mouth. "But I guess your expectation of me—and the other initiates, I guess—is that we tell you everything about us. And you don't tell us anything about yourself."

She shuts her eyes. "Kay, that's not what I meant."

Suddenly, everything I've been pressing down feels like it's going to spill out of my throat like bile. "Isn't it, though? I—I think you're fantastic. But I don't like the power dynamics of this whole situation."

"No, Kay—" Zola takes a gulping breath. "Let me explain."

I should stack my menu on top of hers and walk out. Instead, I say, "Go on."

"I think you're overestimating how much power I have over you," she says. "Yes, I have some degree of control over your admission to the Blue Hand Girls—I won't deny that. But your mission is the same as mine: figuring out what happened to Emily. And, as of last night, you know everything I know."

"Maybe," I say. "But we're on our second date, and you've been lying to me since before our first—"

"I never lied." Zola presses her lips into a line. "Not to you."

"Fine, maybe not technically, but being behind my blue hand is a pretty sizable thing to omit. As we get further into this—this induction process, it's impossible for you not to learn certain things before I do, either about my odds of getting into the Blue Hand Girls or about Emily."

"What do you want me to do, Kay?"

I consider her for a moment: her elegant fingers pressed against the table, her blue eyes feverish. "Honestly? I want you to tell me a secret."

Zola recoils, the leather of the couch straining against her back. "Me?"

"You know about *my* biggest regret," I say. "Frankly, it's the least you can do."

Her pale face gets paler, but she nods. "Fine."

"Come on, then." I wonder why I think she'll tell me the truth.

"The day that I pulled an all-nighter, it wasn't because of homework. I thought I'd figured out how to find my father." Zola's chin trembles again. "He left about two years ago, and he made it very clear that he didn't want to be found. But I've been monitoring certain Reddit pages, and I was almost sure that I'd found his account. I've been tracking that account for months, waiting for them to mention anything about a location and, finally, they said that they'd be in—well, it doesn't matter except for being incredibly inconvenient, but they said they'd be at a certain poker hall in Atlantic City."

"Oh." I wasn't expecting something sad.

Zola shuts her eyes. "Needless to say, he wasn't in Atlantic City, and let me tell you, the Uber ride back was astronomical."

Maybe I don't know Zola at all. What kind of Central Park family worries about the cost of an Uber, even a cross-state one? What kind of secret society power player would admit to having an absent father? I've made plenty of assumptions, but as far as hard evidence goes, the only stars in her constellation are thunderstorms on loose-leaf paper, goulash in a mottled-wood thermos, and a father who likely has a gambling problem and definitely has a host of other shortcomings. I wonder what's obscured by the clouds in her night sky.

It takes me too long to figure out what to say, and it's probably wrong, anyway. "You know I want you to be okay."

I reach underneath the table and lay my blue hand on her knee. She smiles at me, something somber twitching at the corners of her eyes. "There's one more thing you should know about me."

I squeeze her kneecap. "Yeah?"

"I worry that I'm too much like my father."

Her skin glints gold underneath the chandeliers. She is a deity. Maybe she's a trickster god, or maybe she's a nymph. Either way, by showing herself to me, she makes me want her even more. "You know, if you're worried about it, then you'll probably be able to make sure it won't happen."

"Do you think I'm a good person, Kay?"

Suddenly, she looks several years younger, and I almost forget that last night she was a warrior atop her chariot.

"I...think I want to be with you," I say. "Is that enough?"

• • • • •

Hours later, we're on the corner of her block, tucked inside the shadow cast by a tangle of bare trees. Our hands haven't let go of each other for more than a moment since leaving the restaurant, and even then it was just to get through the train station's turnstiles.

I pull her in for another kiss. I don't know how many times

I've kissed her tonight. I've forgotten what it's like for the wind to be the only thing brushing against my lips.

When we untangle, I catch my breath quickly enough to pant out, "Zola—will you—will you be my girlfriend?"

She kisses me again, quick and strong, then pulls away, still glowing. "Kay, I would be honored."

A laugh bubbles out of me, the kind of laugh I didn't know I could make. "Wow."

She takes a step toward the door of her building, then turns around. "One more thing."

I can't read her face. "Yeah?"

"I don't think we should tell anyone. For your sake," she says.

My heart smacks down onto the cold concrete beneath us. "Why?"

I sound plaintive. I hate it.

"I don't want the other initiates to think I'm giving you preferential treatment," she says, taking my blue hand between her two pale ones. "Just until you finish the initiation tasks and make it into the society. Which I'm sure you will. And then we can be vigilantes together, like Harley Quinn and Poison Ivy."

I nod hollowly. I suppose this is the natural consequence of dating the sun: you have to insulate yourself to avoid being consumed by her flames.

"Good night, Zola," I say, sliding my hand out of hers.

"Good night, Kay," she says, her eyes full of an emotion I can't name. She climbs the two shallow steps to her building, and her doorman pulls open the wooden door. A moment before she crosses the threshold into her abyss of contradictions, she turns back toward me. "As promised: you've never looked more ravishing than you do in the moonlight."

• • • • •

On Monday morning, while I'm on the train to Davison, a message appears at the top of the Clandestine general chat. It's from the Priestess.

THE PRIESTESS:

we were very impressed with this group upon bringing you together on Friday night. despite the fact that only one of the full members joined you on the roof, you can be assured that we're all up to date on your gathering. now that you're fully informed of our mission and purpose, we trust that you've been thinking about how you can best demonstrate your value in our quest to right the wrong committed against Emily Hendricks.

The train rumbles to a stop at Seventy-Second Street. I sling my backpack over my shoulder and muscle through the crowd on my way out of the subway, my eyes still affixed to my phone screen.

DAPHNE:

So do you guys have next steps for us?

THE HEALER:

Really up to you ;) I think you should take a look at the timeline tab.

I tap the menu of chat options, and to my surprise, one of the pixelated-out chats has been revealed. Unlike the general chat and the DMs, this tab isn't a messaging tool; instead, it's an editable document with a timeline tracking all the events leading up to Emily's death, beginning with my conversation with Aubrey. I swallow some nausea when I read that part. Similarly unlike the rest of the app, which only includes black text on a white background, this page includes bright indigo questions interspersed with some of the event descriptions. They're the questions that came up on Friday, plus some others:

Why was the school so quick to expel Emily?

Why did Emily really stop talking to Mai?

Why did Emily come to Vanessa's party?

Who did Emily think was coming after her? Why did she think that?

What was Emily talking about in her 'I was right' text to Kay?

What brought Emily to Kew Gardens on the day that she died?

What does Tia's car crash have to do with any of this?

As I turn onto Davison's block, I glance around at the rest of the girls streaming toward the school's iron doors and tuck my phone screen half-underneath my open peacoat. To my assessment, there are no eyes on my phone, but there's a familiar shock of red hair bobbing in the crowd about ten feet in front of me. My girlfriend. I whisper the words to remind myself that it's real: "My girlfriend."

If only I weren't limited to a whisper. For a moment I picture myself pushing through the mass of Davison girls and grabbing her hand. Then I force my mind's eye to cut to black. This degree of yearning will only make it worse.

MAI:

Oooh that's super helpful. Thanks BHGs!

AUBREY:

So you want us to answer those questions?

THE HEALER:

Unless you have a better idea of how to proceed ;)

I feel a rush of warmth toward the Healer, whether due to a misplaced feeling of allyship due to her less-threatening choice of alias or due to a probably-more-merited appreciation of the slight jab at Aubrey.

"You." I feel a hand clamp around my arm.

Instinctively, I shove my phone into my pocket, my heart pounding. My head whips toward my assailant. Think of the devil; Aubrey is the owner of the blue hand digging into me, the pressure hard even through several layers of fabric.

"Nice to see you," I say. "Would be even nicer if you'd let go of me."

"Absolutely not," Aubrey says. She pulls me toward her. The rest of the girls must think our arms are linked as we approach the school. Horrible. "You're a terrible ally."

"Forgive me if I'm not especially motivated to help you," I say.

Aubrey clenches my arm even harder. "You're fucking over yourself, you know. I'd like to have someone else to pool information with, but it's a nice-to-have. But you? You're utterly helpless without me."

She has no idea who I have on my side. "It's like you think the Blue Hand Girls are out to get us. There's no enemy here, Aubrey."

"Oh my God." Aubrey stops short, then drags me over to the side of the street, pressing us against the rough stone of Davison's exterior. "That's what it is. You've drunk the Kool-Aid."

"So what?"

"So you're an idiot. There are too many inconsistencies in their story. Like if this Davison chapter launched last year, what's the supposed secret injustice that Zola's group addressed? Emily was already dead by then, and nothing at this school could have been a bigger deal than that. There's no good reason why they would wait another year to look into this."

I...didn't think of that. But Aubrey doesn't know the way Zola looked at me on Saturday night, like she was opening up the gates to her soul. "Maybe they needed more time to gather evidence."

"Jesus, Kay. It's like you're in love with them." Then Aubrey's eyes go wide enough that I can see it even underneath the sweep of her hair. Her hand unclamps from my arm, and I stumble back, the stone scraping the side of my coat. "I have to go."

Fuck. Fuck. She knows. I haven't even been able to make it to the start of the school day, and I've already blown the one promise I made to my girlfriend.

Aubrey ducks between girls until she disappears into the Davison entryway, and I force myself to start moving again. Somewhere in front of me, Aubrey is almost certainly talking to Zola. I don't know if she'll reveal her realization right away. I doubt it. She's too clever to waste a piece of information like that. Instead, she'll clutch my secret between her claws, and whenever it would be most devastating for me, she'll release her grip.

In that case, I need to make the most of however much time I have before Aubrey unveils my relationship with Zola. I have to be invaluable enough to the Blue Hand Girls that they can't get rid of me, even for a transgression like that.

I remove my phone from my pocket again and open

Clandestine. There are no new messages in the general chat, but I open a group DM with Mai, Margaret, and—after a half-second of hesitation—Chioma. Aubrey is right that I need allies right now. Unfortunately, they're to protect against her, which rather eliminates her from the running.

ME:

Hi all. The Blue Hand Girls have set up a kind of strange dynamic between us, in which we're supposed to work together to resolve the issue that will gain us admission to the society, but simultaneously we're competing against each other for membership

I'd like to propose something: I don't want to compete with the three of you. Instead, I'd like us all to collab-orate for real during this process, whatever it will be, and make each other look good in front of the BHGs

I type, crossing the threshold into the Davison building. Mai responds right away.

MAI

Oh yeah ofc

MARGARET:

Yeah, I appreciate this

As I begin to climb the stairs on the way to my locker, Chioma responds, too.

CHIOMA:

You trust all three of us?

After hearing her confession on Friday, I don't know if I do. But they all learned something awful about me, too, and I'd like to think that I'm a different person now than I was back when I ruined Emily's relationship and set her en route to her death.

ME:

I think we'll make a good team

• • • • •

Over the next few days, my routine evolves in several directions that I wouldn't have been able to predict a month ago. At the end of every AP Physics period, I cycle through the same series of thoughts about whether I should try to drop any hints to Lee about the Blue Hand Girls in order to gauge their reaction, and then decide against it; the side effect is that I've spent enough time studying their face that I think I've started doing my eyeliner more like theirs. I've also found myself examining seniors as I pass by them in the hallways, taking second looks at the pink-haired girl with the *JAILERS* patch on her backpack (a band name or a hint?) and the winner of Davison's annual charity bake-off (would that be too on the nose for the Baker alias?).

And then there's Zola. Because of her, my leather armchair is no longer my favorite seat in the library; instead, I've graduated to a deep-maroon couch tucked behind the rarely frequented folk art section of the aisles. Zola keeps appearing on that couch a few minutes into our lunch hour, and who am I to resist the beckoning of gravity? And ever since I showed her my hand-dying station in the second-floor supply closet, I keep finding her waiting for me there, holding a fistful of my ballpoint pens high above her head and promising that they can be mine once more for the low, low price of one kiss. After I mentioned to her that I've been subsisting on rotisserie chickens and Trader Joe's mac and cheese since Aunt Shell left—before, when my parents worked late, Aunt Shell and I cooked dinner together, but I just don't have the motivation on my own—thermoses of goulash started appearing in my backpack. Since Aunt Shell still hasn't texted, the goulash fortifies me in sticking to my conviction not to cave.

It's an unspoken agreement that we don't talk about the Blue Hand Girls. Instead, she tells me about the brood of Venus flytraps she's raising on her bedroom windowsill, and I tell her about the latest ways that the Davison applicant families have been throwing themselves at the staff during their school tours. Occasionally, Principal Ellison opens the door of her office to give Wall Street dads the opportunity to simper at her, and this week I'm pretty sure I overheard one of the traders imply that there's some insider information in it for her if brilliant little Ainsleigh secures a seat. Sometimes I think Emily was right to assume shadiness within the Davison administration. While

Principal Ellison laughed off the bribe, I can't help but wonder what happens for families who are smart enough to make their offers when there isn't a nosy scholarship kid a few paces away.

Zola's silence on the blue-hand front is balanced out by a consistent drip of messages in my Clandestine chat with Mai, Margaret, and Chioma. They come to a zenith on Thursday night, as I sit at my desk, thumbing through my leather notebook without adding to my notes for the fourth time in as many days.

MAI:

What do you think they're going for in the main chat right now?

CHIOMA:

I think they know what they want us to do next, and they're trying to see if we'll figure it out

MAI:

Ooh manipulative

CHIOMA:

You think?

MARGARET:

I think we should rock the boat as little as possible—let's give them what they want

ME:

Okay, yes, but do you guys actually know what they want us to say?

MAI:

I'm sure they want us to start filling in the timeline

CHIOMA:

Yeah obv

MARGARET:

Ok yeah obv AND they want us to propose some sort of quest to find answers

ME:

Yeah we should do that. Establishes us as proactive

CHIOMA:

Nice. Let's start with the first question: why the school was so quick to expel Emily

ME:

That also feels more approachable bc that gives us a clear starting place—prob there are answers somewhere within the school

MARGARET:

I've tried to break through Davison's data encryption and it's medium-secure

CHIOMA:

WTF is medium-secure??

MARGARET:

Like it's not that hard to access individual things, like specific people's email accounts, but it's almost impossible to hack the central database with everyone's permanent records

MAI:

Girl why do you know this?

MARGARET:

...not relevant

ME:

No, you're right. We have to get to Emily's permanent record

CHIOMA:

Margaret just said we can't do that

ME:

Yeah...by hacking

MAI:

Wait wait I know what you're saying! The school must have a file room somewhere!!

ME:

Yeah

MARGARET:

Oh lol I forgot about pieces of paper. But I've never actually seen a file room. Are you sure that Davison keeps anything in print?

CHIOMA:

Yeah. There's a back entrance to the file room through one of the corridors behind the black box

MAI:

Not you too? How do YOU know THAT??

CHIOMA:

That was legitimately an accident

MARGARET:

Isn't that what we all say?

After some more back-and-forth to condense our proposal into a coherent paragraph, we copy and paste it into the general chat, one sentence from each of us. I find myself wringing my throw blanket between my hands as I wait for a reaction from any of the aliased BHGs.

This time, it's the Jailer who responds.

THE JAILER:

Excellent plan. You'll all meet in front of Davison tomorrow night at 8:30 p.m. It'll be just the initiates. No members of the BHG will be there. We don't want you to be tempted to ask for help. Don't leave without Emily's permanent record.

CHAPTER 9

"NO," MY MOM SAYS, CROSS-LEGGED on a stool at the kitchen island. "You went out two nights last weekend, and you almost missed your eleven-o'clock curfew last Saturday. You're not going to this sleepover."

"I have to." I tighten the laces on my Docs. I need to leave in the next few minutes if I'm going to make it back to Davison by 8:30. "Come on. Most weekday afternoons, you wouldn't even be home for me to ask permission."

"Then it's good I happen to be here early today." My mom slams down her mug of tea onto the island counter. Some of the brown liquid jumps over the rim and splashes onto the faux marble. "You can't go out all the time and expect to keep your grades where they need to be for your scholarship. And I don't need to tell you that we can't afford—"

"Mom, it's just one sleepover!" Guilt squirms in my stomach as I stand up. I've never lied to her before. "You don't have to worry about my grades. I promise."

"Kay, is there something wrong?" My mom grips the handle of her mug but doesn't pick it up.

"No, Mom," I say quietly. "It's...the opposite of that."

She gestures to the stool across the island. "Tell me."

I sit, pressing the rubber soles of my boots into the rung of the stool. "You remember Emily, right? The girl who came over a few times when I was a freshman and then died a few months into the year?"

My mom's Adam's apple bobs in her throat. "You can't forget a tragedy like that."

She has no idea. "I don't know if I ever really told you this, but after she died, I was afraid to get close with anyone else."

"You never had to say it out loud, honey." My mom reaches across the island and rests a hand on top of my undyed one.

At her touch, I feel another squirm of guilt. "Well, things have changed recently. For the first time since then, I've met some people who are worth the potential heartbreak."

For a moment I let myself believe what I'm saying: that my allies are simply my friends, that my cult representative is uncomplicatedly my girlfriend. I picture the group of us lying in sleeping bags on the white shag carpet of some girl's bedroom, a smuggled beer bottle traveling from hand to hand as we play truth or dare in lowered voices. My sleeping bag would be next to Zola's, and every so often, I'd roll over and kiss her; she'd push me away, laughing and telling me to cut out the PDA, and all the other girls would groan that we should get a room.

"What more could a mother want to hear?" My mom smiles and takes a slow sip of her tea. "Okay. Go. Have fun, my dear."

• • • • •

As I approach Davison's iron door at 8:18, Aubrey and Mai are already leaning against the craggy stone of the building's exterior. A jolt of fear hits me: Aubrey could be telling Mai what she knows about me and Zola. They're talking quietly enough that I can't hear their words over the roar of the mid-November wind, but as I take in their body language, my chest relaxes a bit. Mai seems to be asking Aubrey animated questions, and Aubrey seems to be responding solely via grunt.

I come to a stop next to them. "Thank goodness," Mai says. Then she glances at Aubrey, whose face is almost completely obscured between her signature bangs and a gray knit scarf pulled up over her chin. "I mean, it's great to have a big group for a heist like this."

"I know what you mean," Aubrey says from beneath her scarf.

"Good to see you," I say to Mai. "Do you feel ready for tonight?"

She tilts her head from side to side, her pirate-sword earrings slashing through the air with the motion. "It'll be nice to have some answers. I didn't realize how much Emily's death has been weighing on me over the past few years."

Aubrey snorts.

I know that I shouldn't antagonize her when she has such damning information about me, but I can't stop myself. "Do you have something to say?"

"I prefer to listen," she says.

Over the next few minutes, the rest of the girls arrive: Tia, the clacking of her Jimmy Choos announcing her presence from half a block away; Chioma, her plaid coat so long that it flirts with the sidewalk; Vanessa, jabbing at her phone to finish uploading an Instagram story as she tucks the device into her purse; and Margaret, her wire glasses fogging up as she exhales into a white cowl-necked jacket. Daphne is the last to join our cluster, shrugging off the cold underneath her zip-up athletic sweatshirt, which is emblazoned with the crest of the NYPD. Her father is someone high up—the police commissioner, I think.

"What's up, team?" she says in a voice far louder than the situation requires. I feel a rush of animosity for her, due to either her family background or her omnipresent student-athlete energy. "Are we ready?"

Some of the others mutter a polite "yeah." Tia lets out a little squeal.

Aubrey turns to Vanessa. "Did you bring the cough syrup?"

Vanessa removes an unmarked vial from her purse and hands it to Aubrey. The red liquid glimmers underneath the light of the streetlamps. "I deserve a lot of credit for this. It's not like my dad just has it lying around, especially since it got discontinued."

Of course, I knew this was coming; we made the full plan in the chat. But the shock of seeing the drug in person makes me fight to keep my face unmoving as Aubrey slips the slim glass tube into her coat pocket.

Chioma sucks in air through her teeth. "I still can't believe we're doing this."

"It's the best tool at our disposal," Aubrey says. "Besides, your plan didn't account for getting past the security guard, so you have no right to object."

"We don't have time to argue," I say. "Let's begin. Margaret, are you still good to execute the first step?"

Margaret gives me a small but firm nod, tugs up the zipper on her cowl neck, and pushes open Davison's iron door.

The rest of us stay huddled outside, holding our breath.

We can't hear her through the insulated walls of the school, but she should be approaching the security guard's desk. This is the same guard who asked me a few weeks ago if I was sure I was a Davison student. He's more than likely glaring at her from underneath his overgrown eyebrows while swishing his coffee in his mug as if he's aerating it, which he probably is. If the rumors are true, when this particular guard is assigned to night duty, he rewards himself with an Irish cream latte, heavy on the whiskey.

Hi, I'm so sorry to bother you, but I forgot a binder in my locker, and I really need it to do my homework this weekend," Margaret should be saying right about now. Knowing her, she's probably shaking a little, which will only make it more convincing. "Would you mind unlocking the stairwell for me so I can go get it?

He's groaning a bit, I'm sure, maybe giving her a muttered lecture on responsibility, but he's pushing back his desk chair. Setting down his mug. Following her to the stairwell around the corner.

We wait the two minutes that we've estimated for the first step of the task, and then Daphne bends over to pluck a medium-sized rock from the side of the gutter. She grins at us and stretches her right arm over her left, the muscle in her shoulder cracking, then tugs on the handle of the front door until it's open just wide enough for a clear shot at the security camera trained on the entrance. Then she winds up her arm and pitches the rock. It smacks against the camera lens hard enough that a dense spiderweb of cracks spreads over its surface.

We all freeze as the rock clatters against the lobby's linoleum floor, the echo ricocheting through the high-ceilinged room. But there are no footsteps of the security guard rushing back to his post and no sputtered excuses from Maragaret following behind him. Daphne turns back to the group, extending her blue hand for a high five. Vanessa rolls her eyes but gives Daphne's palm a perfunctory pat.

Margaret's locker is on the sixth floor, and the stairwell is locked at every landing, so the guard will have to accompany her all the way up. That should give us another three minutes, minimum. With the rest of us hanging back, Aubrey runs into the building, the vial of cough syrup tucked into the pocket of her corduroy jacket. I watch through the ajar door as she pours the syrup into the guard's coffee mug and stirs the concoction with one blue finger.

Then the ding of the elevator rings out from the side of the lobby.

We forgot about the elevator.

In the cluster outside, we all stop breathing. I watch Aubrey's finger, too, stop its motion inside the mug. Then, just as we hear the rumble of the elevator doors opening, a dull crash emits from inside it.

"Argh, uh, I'm so sorry!" Margaret's voice, louder and higher than usual, fills the lobby. "I'm not usually this clumsy. Thank you so much for helping me."

I yank open the door all the way as Aubrey bolts back toward us, flinging herself across the threshold between the school and the sidewalk. As soon as the tail of her jacket is on the other side, I whip the door shut, halting its momentum just before it clangs against the latch and pushing it gently for the last inch of its trajectory. Next to me, Aubrey heaves in the cold wind.

A few seconds later, Margaret pushes open the door, clutching a black binder with papers sticking out at several haphazard angles. "Thanks again!" she calls over her shoulder.

As soon as the door shuts again, Aubrey's blue hand shoots out and pulls Margaret forward by her cowl neck. "Why the fuck didn't you warn me?"

Margaret sniffles. "I'm sorry—I couldn't open my phone—he would have seen Clandestine—"

Chioma steps forward and wraps her hand around Aubrey's wrist, pulling it away from Margaret's neck. "That's enough."

Aubrey inhales sharply but releases her grip, leaving behind an ink stain on the white fabric. "She has no idea what kind of risk she took with me."

"He insisted," Margaret says. There's a tear dripping down her right cheek, either from wind or from stress. "I tried to convince him to take the stairs, but he just wouldn't agree, so I hoped that dropping the binder would buy you some time—"

"You did great," Mai says gently. "I promise."

Aubrey spits on the sidewalk, but I'd rather that come out of her mouth than something verbal.

"Yeah," Tia says. "We're still exactly where we need to be? Now we just need to wait for him to drink some of his coffee?"

I turn to Vanessa. "Remind me how long it will take to kick in?"

"Chioma was always more of a chemist than me," Vanessa says, her lips twisting. She traces Chioma's silhouette with her eyes. "Like, remember the time you figured out how to get cross-faded when we only had two bottles of Pabst and—"

"Vanessa." A muscle flexes in Chioma's jaw.

Vanessa smirks. "About seven minutes."

I wish I understood why Vanessa is here. Generously speaking, maybe she wants more for herself than to be the girl steadying Ruby when she threatens to tip into the atrium fountain. If I'm being less generous...maybe it brings her some vicious joy to remind Chioma of who she used to be.

The next few minutes tick by in silence. Eventually, Vanessa says, "He has to be out by now."

"Are you absolutely certain?" Aubrey asks. "We only have the one chance."

"I'm not fucking incompetent," Vanessa says.

"Enough." I take a step toward the door. "I'm going in."

The whine of traffic and crackling of dead leaves rumble together in my eardrums, forming a sheet of white noise that underscores the pounding of my heartbeat. Slowly, I open the door and peer inside the lobby. My heart leaps as the guard comes into my view. His head is slumped against his chest, which swells up and down in a jerking rhythm that matches his apneic snores.

The others file in behind me as I creep closer to his desk. I focus on breathing through my nose, clamping my lips shut to prevent any exhales from rushing out of my mouth, and lay my footfalls from heel to toe until I'm kneeling behind his worn leather office chair. As his gut shudders, a carabiner with a key ring dances on one of his belt loops. I extend one trembling hand to touch the clip's cool metal. When I lift back the clasp, my fingers fumble, and the clip makes a loud click as metal springs back to collide with metal.

His head tilts up. *Fuck.* Northwestern—Emily—Zola—I can feel them all vanishing.

But after a moment his head tilts back down. I try a second time. My hands are still unsteady, but I manage to pull back the clip and unhook it from the loop. I keep the keys as separated as possible to keep them from jingling as I straighten, holding them over my head like a prize. Chioma gives me a thumbs-up.

Now we're really in.

Daphne leads our group down the length of the hallway toward the black box, tossing her rock at each camera before we come into its view and catching the rock on the rebound. The rock lands in her palms every time, albeit with a few lunges and one four-foot slide on her knees across the linoleum, after which she looks at the rest of us as if she expects a cheer, but it takes a few tries for her to hit some of the cameras. I refrain from making any jabs about her accuracy rate; I suspect that, if I did, Daphne might confuse my head for one of the lenses.

When we reach the black box, Chioma lays a hand on Daphne's shoulder. "There are no cameras here."

"Why not?" I think Daphne may be pouting.

"The drama teacher is super paranoid about people stealing footage of our rehearsals?" Tia says, swishing forward and swiping her ID against the black box key fob. "Which, like, kind of makes sense. Last year we would have swept the Jimmys if the Sacred Heart girls hadn't taken our *Book of Mormon* routine and sung it with more 'authenticity' than we did because they believe in Jesus or whatever?"

Dimly, I recall that the fall musical this year is *Sweeney Todd*.

Maybe I'll come watch if Tia gets rolled through the meat grinder.

Chioma sidles through the black box door and flicks on the light. "Come on."

We follow her through the rows of velvet theater chairs and across the empty space in the center of the room, the overhead lights glinting off the black subway tile lining the floor. Then Chioma pulls back a satin curtain lining the back wall of the room, revealing another door. This one leads into a corridor, also painted black on all sides, with doors and hallways branching off every few feet. The only suggestion of color is a black-and-gray Persian rug that muffles our footfalls, even the clacks of Tia's stilettos, as we shuffle down the hallway.

"Are there any more cameras here?" Daphne asks.

"No, the drama department is a safe space," Tia says.

In front of me, Chioma half succeeds at smothering a bark.

She makes a right into one of the hallways, uncovered bulbs dangling down from its ceiling like in the second-floor supply closet. The hallway doors are labeled with ornate silver plaques, the text engraved in aggressive Copperplate: Dressing Room A, Props Storage, Makeup Studio, Costume Shop. I trail a finger across the Costume Shop plaque as we march by it. If we weren't here on a mission, I'd ask Chioma if her ID can unlock any of the doors. I picture overflowing bins of brocade fabrics and wooden tables holding rusted sewing machines. A few years ago, I tried to teach myself to sew—tailoring my own clothes would have been a nice tactic for impersonating wealth—but, like so many other parts of me, that desire drowned in the whirlpool of grief.

After a few more rights and lefts, Chioma stops in front of an unmarked door. "This is it."

Daphne tosses her rock from hand to hand as I sort through the keys, fitting them into the keyhole one at a time. There are at least fifteen keys in the clip. Finally, I find the one that glides into the hole without any resistance. The door creaks open.

"Wait." As I lift one foot to step into the room, an arm swings out in front of me. Mai. "There might be more cameras here."

She holds the door a few inches open and shines her phone flashlight through the crack. It doesn't illuminate much. She tilts the flashlight toward the ceiling, its plaster grainy in the dim light. "I think we're good. A lens would have glinted."

"That's super weird, though," Vanessa says. "Why wouldn't they be keeping an eye on the file room?"

My heartbeat slams again. "Maybe it means that they'd rather not be caught than catch anyone else in here."

"That…would imply that there's something very bad happening in this room." Even in the low light of the hallway, I can see that Margaret's skin has taken on a green hue.

"You guys are wimps." Daphne pushes through the group and shoves open the door, then steps inside and gropes around for a light switch. Suddenly the room is bright, the fluorescence searing against my eyes. "See? It's just a file room."

I blink as my eyes adjust to the light. Daphne is right. The only thing remarkable about the room is how unremarkable it is. Unlike most of Davison, with its abundance of aged mahogany and gold curlicues, the file room makes no effort to pretend that it was constructed before this century. Floor-to-ceiling acrylic cabinets line all the walls except for a small column of white to the left of the doorway, which is blank except for a digital thermostat, and more rows of cabinets divide the interior neatly into aisles.

The rest of us follow Daphne into the room, Margaret pulling the door shut behind her when we're all through. "So...I guess now we start looking."

The hundreds of identical cabinet drawers, which were a relief a moment ago, suddenly look like hydra heads. I glance at the cabinet closest to me. "None of these are labeled."

Chioma slides open a drawer toward the front of one of the aisles, then tugs out a section of papers wedged into the middle of the stack, which doesn't seem to be separated by dividers of any kind. She shuffles the pages. "Transcript of Odessa Worthington, graduated eight years ago...donation record of the family of Katherine Holliday, current student…a bunch of doctor's notes for Saanvi Kumar, graduated two years ago… There's nothing connecting any of this. I don't understand how the school keeps track of anything."

"Actually, that would make sense," Margaret says. "It took them months to fulfill my request for a copy of my freshman year hackathon certificate."

Tia groans. "So, what, we just have to go through these papers one by one?"

"That's not going to work for me," Vanessa says, twirling a section of hair between her blue fingers. "Some of us have plans later."

Chioma's jaw clenches again. "Think about it this way: You're practically at a party. You've already gotten someone blackout drunk."

"Hilarious." Vanessa flings the hair over her shoulder, where it whips against Chioma's face, a few strands sticking to her ChapStick.

Chioma unpeels the strand from her lips but says nothing.

"Okay, well, no use wasting time," I say. "Let's see if we can find this permanent record before the sun comes up."

"Wait." Aubrey unzips her backpack and pulls out a box of disposable rubber gloves. "We don't want to leave any blue fingerprints."

I refuse to be impressed by her forethought as she tosses me a glove. As the others pull on their own gloves, they begin to spread out across the room. Tia lays out her Burberry on the black-grouted tile floor like a picnic blanket and arranges herself in its center, rifling through the bottom drawers on the back wall of the room. Aubrey locates a rolling step stool in one of the aisles and perches on the top rung to reach the drawers closest to the ceiling. I claim a section of drawers close to the entrance and begin to sift.

Like in the first drawer that Chioma opened, I can't find any patterns that explain the documents in here. All of them pertain to students, current or past, but the students don't seem to have anything in common; they're not united by participation in art club or positions on the soccer team, by honor roll placements or spotty attendance records. The only thing they have in common is that they're not Emily.

Half an hour passes. Then an hour. At first, I skim the papers in their entirety—maybe I'll stumble across something helpful hidden in the center of a paragraph—but soon I'm discarding every page as soon as I see that Emily's name isn't at the top. As I read, though, a sense of dread pools in my stomach. None of this makes sense. Why would Davison bother to build a file room, especially a hidden one, if they don't keep it organized enough to find anything in it?

At the three-hour mark, we're all sweating, our coats piled in the corner. The only interesting document I've come across is a note excusing Vanessa from the dodgeball unit in gym due to the risk of popping her lip filler. I take a break to roll my neck and see that down the aisle from me, Chioma is doing the same. At least the commiserating eye contact is nice.

A bang rings out from the back wall. My head whips toward the noise. Daphne is clutching her knuckles, a drawer trembling on its tracks beside her. "This is a fucking waste of time."

A few mutters emit from different points throughout the room. Mai's head emerges from inside a drawer near me. "Yeah, Margaret, are you really sure you can't hack us a digital copy of her permanent record?"

Even from two aisles over, I can hear Margaret's exhale. She punches her drawer in a similar gesture to Daphne's. "If I weren't sure, don't you think—"

"Wait a second." I bolt upright. "Daphne, do that again."

"Do what, hit the drawer?" Daphne asks.

"Yeah."

Daphne gives her knuckles a reluctant final rub and pulls back her fist, then slams it into the metal of one of the cabinets affixed to the back wall. The sound reverberates through the room.

"Okay, Margaret, do the same," I say.

Margaret raises her eyebrows but winds back her arm and punches the drawer closest to her. There's the same crack of knuckles against metal, but the echo is much quieter.

"That...shouldn't happen," I say slowly. "All the drawers are stuffed to the top with papers, so they shouldn't be hollow enough to produce much of an echo. But considering the sounds that they do release, Margaret's drawer is the one that should be louder. Her cabinet is standing on its own, whereas Daphne's is against a wall, which should muffle the sound."

Aubrey gasps. "False wall."

In this moment, even the fact that she's Aubrey doesn't prevent me from grinning at her. "False wall."

We all glance at each other from our slots around the room. Then, as if both the back wall and our rib cages are lined with magnets, we all bolt toward it, scrambling between cabinets and over each other. I yank open the first drawer I can reach, pawing through its pages and pressing my hand against its back. It's smooth—no indication of a handle. Of course. That would be unrealistic.

"Wait, wait, we can do this systematically," Margaret says, panting. "Everyone, back away from the wall."

Sheepishly, I shut the drawer and look over at Margaret, who's scanning the cabinets.

"There's probably one drawer that's a few inches shallower

than the others, and if we take it out, we'll find a doorknob behind it," Margaret continues. "And if I were the engineer, I'd place that drawer somewhere around the height that people are used to finding doorknobs."

Chioma taps a drawer in the third row above the ground. "So you think we should be looking in this row."

In a lucky coincidence, there are eight drawers per row. We each pull open the drawer in front of us and shove a hand toward the back.

"Oh my God," Vanessa says. "I think I found it."

Gingerly, she slides her drawer off its tracks and places it on the floor to her left. We all crowd around the gap in the wall of cabinets. And there it is. In the center of the gray metal sheet is—well, not a doorknob, but a button.

Vanessa reaches into the gap and presses the heel of her palm against the black plastic. I hear a quiet click. And then the middle four cabinets begin to slide backward.

Electricity crackles between the eight of us as we stand in perfect stillness, watching the cabinets reveal another room. It feels like even our heartbeats are in sync. After a moment, the cabinets halt about four feet back, welcoming us to the other side of the portal.

Soon we're all clustered in the second room—or, more accurately, the other half of the first one. This, too, is a file room, but unlike the first, only the walls are lined with filing cabinets, and these reach maybe three quarters of the way to the ceiling. More importantly, its sparseness is complemented by its careful organization: each drawer has a white plastic label on its top right corner, indicating which letter of the alphabet its contents will feature.

"The other room must be a decoy," Aubrey murmurs. "They keep all their inconsequential papers in there, and anything real gets shelved in here."

I wonder what horrible things Davison is cataloging within this room. Once the Blue Hand Girls find out about this, I'm sure they'll have initiation plans for the next decade of Davison inductees.

The left wall runs from *A* to *G*. I walk almost to the end of the room, searching for the drawer that would include *Hendricks*: *Han–Hay. . . Hea–Hel. . . Hem–Hib. . .*

That's it.

My hands shake as I pull open the drawer. Unlike in the last room, this drawer is divided by neat tabs, alternating between gray and maroon. And sure enough, on one of the red tabs, in thick capital letters as if emblazoned on her tombstone, I see *Emily Hendricks*.

I lift out the folder, my heart slamming. The others crowd around me as I unfold the two pieces of cardstock. Something in me says that I should shut my eyes. I was so focused on obtaining the folder that I didn't consider what might be inside it, and now that it's between my hands, it feels dirty, like I'm about to peruse photos that a Peeping Tom snapped between the blinds of her bedroom window.

"Hurry up," Aubrey snaps.

I clench and unclench my eyes before opening the folder flat across my palms. There are only three pieces of paper inside. The first, scribbled in pencil on a sheet of torn-out notebook paper, is a memo.

For Immediate Attention:

Today Aubrey Clarke (9th grade, partial scholarship) reported a concern about Emily Hendricks (9th grade, full scholarship, honors track). Clarke said that Hendricks, influenced by true crime podcasts, seemed to see conspiracy wherever she went. While Clarke's report centered around the claim that Hendricks was stalking her, Clarke also noted, as evidence of Hendricks's overall mental state, that Hendricks believed something sinister was afoot in the Davison administration.

After receiving this complaint, I retrieved Hendricks's search history from her school-issued phone (printout attached). Please advise.

I don't know whether I'm breathing as I flip to the next page in the folder. It's the printout. Most of the phrases are ones that I'd expect: *formula for arc of a circle, treehouse garden location Alphabet City, when is the next season of* Bloody Right Hand *releasing*. But Davison didn't seem to care about those phrases. In a list of about twenty-five rows, four have been struck through with yellow highlighter: *internship program Davison High, Bonum Solutions, how small is a listening bug, Parker Hargrove.*

A chill crawls down my neck. The first two searches don't surprise me, of course. But…Emily thought she was being bugged? And who is—

"Why the fuck was Emily looking up my sister?" Vanessa says.

I turn to the final page. It's another note, this one in red pen, unsigned but identical in handwriting to the evaluations that appear at the top of my calculus tests.

Recommendation: immediate expulsion.

The chill intensifies so much that my hand shoots involuntarily to the back of my neck, as if external warmth will resolve anything.

"Fuck Mr. Holmes." I don't know how I'm going to be able to look at him in Calculus on Monday without strangling him with his paisley necktie.

"This gives us a lot to think about," Chioma says. "But it's late, and I don't know about the rest of you, but I know I'm going to process this more clearly in the morning. I vote that we take photos of these pages, put back the file, and get out of here."

There are a few nods, and I pull my phone out of the back pocket of my jeans.

"Is that school-issued?" Vanessa asks, sniffing.

It isn't. But now that she's suggested it in front of everyone, the truth doesn't matter.

"I've got it." Mai slides the folder out of my hand and lays it on the floor of the room, then spreads out the three pages side by side. She snaps a photo of the spread and pushes her phone back into the pocket of her patchwork skirt.

"Great. Now let's go." Vanessa steps back through the threshold into the decoy side of the file room without turning around to see if anyone is following her. We are, though. Mai is the last to leave, after replacing the folder and pressing the black button to slide the four columns of file cabinets into the false wall. I jiggle the shallow drawer back onto its tracks and push it into place. A buzz of euphoria zips through my limbs as I take in the complete wall of cabinets, the evidence of our exploits fully obscured.

With our coats draped across our arms again and our backpacks hanging from our shoulders, we approach the door leading back into the labyrinth behind the black box. Vanessa twists the handle. It doesn't budge. She slams it with the side of her fist, then twists it again. Then she turns around slowly, horror knitting together her manicured eyebrows. "We're locked in."

CHAPTER 10

"SO THAT'S WHY THERE ARE no cameras," I say, squeezing my eyes shut. "They can ID your corpse at their personal convenience."

"Don't be melodramatic." Aubrey runs a hand through her bangs, squeezing a clump of hair between her blue fingers. "We can—we can find a way out."

Daphne steps forward. "Punching things has already helped once today."

Before anyone can stop her, she launches her fist at the plaster of the door. A moment later, she's doubled over on the tile, clutching her knuckles. The door smirks at us, unchanged.

"Well, how do the Davison administrators come and go?" Mai asks.

I glance around the room. After spending three hours in here, I thought I had it memorized, but maybe I was so fixated on the drawers that I've missed a back door? I'm unsurprised to find that I have not.

My eyes land on the thermostat next to the entrance, though. It's the only distinct item in the room and probably the only one that we haven't already scrutinized tonight. I lift the cover on the pad. "Holy shit. Here's how."

Despite the sun and icicle decals on the cover, the control panel has nothing to do with temperature. It's a security system. A keypad sits underneath a dull green row of boxes, daring me to press its buttons.

Vanessa leans over and jabs the Ok button with one of her French tips. The green boxes light up, and text appears inside them: *Input vocal recognition.*

"Fuck," Aubrey mutters.

"Yeah, um, I'm really trying to stay calm here, but the corpse thing is looking more and more plausible," Margaret says.

I thought it was over. Once I was holding Emily's folder, I thought we had overcome all the challenges of tonight; I thought there was no more risk of letting Zola down, or failing Emily's memory, or renouncing my spot at Northwestern. But I guess that was arrogant. I didn't consider that the biggest thing I was risking was my life.

"How much air is there in here?" Vanessa asks, her voice high-pitched. "Do you think we'll suffocate before we die of dehydration?"

"You guys need to chill?" Tia says. "I've got this."

"You...what?" Aubrey asks.

And for a reason that I couldn't give—even if the Northwestern admissions committee told me that it was the only thing between me and an acceptance letter—Tia's response is to place a finger against her right eardrum and start warbling.

"Ah-ah-ah-AH-ah-ah-ah," she sings. Then she sings it again, a step higher. And again, a step higher than that. And again, a step—

"For the love of God, Tia, now is not the time," Chioma snaps.

Tia flaps her blue hand in Chioma's general direction. "I'm warming up. Trust me."

For a small eternity, Tia continues her scales until her voice is a shrill whistle, then begins singing lower. After she hits what I assume is the bottom of her range—a rather impressive impression of a bullfrog's croak—she stretches her lips in a circle, her tongue smacking against the roof of her mouth. "The lips, the teeth, the tip of the tongue. The tip of the tongue, the lips, the teeth. The lips, the teeth, the tip of the tongue. The tip of the tongue, the lips, the teeth."

I stare at Chioma, whose face is frozen in a wince. If we make it out alive, I'll ask her if these are real vocal warm-ups, or if Tia is just enjoying the irony of getting to call the rest of us dramatic.

I can't believe I'm placing my life in the hands of a soprano.

Finally, Tia stops emitting animal noises. "Testing," she says, her voice several octaves lower than usual. "No. Hm. Testing…" She adds some nasality to her tone. "Testing…" This time, her voice has a hard edge that makes it sound familiar—not like her own but like someone else's, someone whose lectures I hear four times a week. She clears her throat. In her normal voice, she says, "Okay, I'm ready?"

She leans forward and taps the Ok button on the control panel. "Gerald Holmes, confirming identity. System unlock."

I didn't think that this happened outside of books and movies, but I feel my mouth fall open. If I had my eyes closed, I would have thought that Mr. Holmes was trapped in this room with us.

New words flash on the illuminated green squares. *Authorized user detected. Unlocking door.*

"See?" Tia sighs, then twists the handle of the door and sashays out into the corridor.

I feel a flash of shame. If I'm remembering correctly, I'm two for two on encountering Tia and promptly wishing for her demise. Clearly I shouldn't have been so quick to assume my own superiority.

Or maybe getting out of that room has just made me a little sappy.

"That was amazing, Tia," Daphne says as we wind through the hallways.

Tia pivots on her Jimmy Choos. "Obviously."

Since the security guard is almost definitely awake by now—still out of it, Chioma thinks, but we don't know how out of it—we head for one of the side exits, a door that's locked from the outside but that we'll have no problem leaving through. I lay the keys flat on the floor outside the black box after we pass through it. With the trail of smashed camera lenses, there's no use pretending that someone didn't break in. In a best-case scenario, the guard will be so ashamed of drinking on the job—and allowing an intruder to escape—that the administration won't find out about our heist for years. In a worst-case scenario, the guard will let them know that someone got into the black box, and most likely they'll be able to infer that the real target was the file room. But they won't know who; they won't know whether we made it past the false wall; and since there are no files missing, they certainly won't know which one we were after.

I've never been as grateful for a blast of cold night air on my face as I am when we file out of the side exit. Our line pools into a huddle against the exterior of the school, the way we were when the night began.

"Good job, team," Daphne says.

Now that we've escaped, the electricity of earlier begins to vibrate within my limbs again. As backward as it is, tonight I've felt more a part of Davison than I have in any moment I've experienced during the school day. The scholarship committee may have no idea what kind of inclusion it's perpetuating, but at least some of their smugness is well deserved.

Daphne, Tia, and Aubrey drift toward the train station. Vanessa leans against a lamppost and calls an Uber. I pull on my gloves and turn to Margaret, Chioma, and Mai, who are hovering nearby. "I don't know about you guys, but I can't go home tonight. My parents think I'm at a sleepover."

"So do mine," Mai says. "I'm surprised I pulled it off, actually. Asian parents."

"Same. Nigerian parents," Chioma says, raising an arm to accept a high five from Mai. "Anyway, I know a place nearby where we can spend the rest of the night."

"Oh, I know what you're talking about," Margaret says. "That's great. Let's head over to Sixty-Eighth."

The four of us walk south, past brownstones with cats napping inside first-floor apartments and coffee shops with windows featuring flyers for upcoming after-hours jazz shows. Chioma stops in front of an unmarked wooden door, its emerald paint flaking off around the handle. She raps on it three times.

The door swings open to reveal a skinny host with diamond earrings that sparkle even in the low light. "Ah, Misses Akinde *and* O'Malley! What a treat!"

I glance over at Mai, who's gaping at Chioma and Margaret as if she's never seen them before. She leans over to me. "Davison girls, am I right?"

I consider reminding her that she's a Davison girl just as much as they are—no matter how many Bushwick art galleries she frequents, I've never seen her at the scholarship recipient assemblies—but there's no need to alienate the only other person who seems fazed by this.

"Private room for four, please," Chioma says.

The host nods and beckons for us to follow him. Gold-framed paintings of dogs and children pepper the dark green walls of a narrow restaurant, two rows of booths framing a single aisle through the center of the space. Most of the tables, occupied by groups of teenagers in ruffled Chloé blouses and houndstooth headbands, display white teapots with hand-painted flowers wrapping around their bellies. As we reach the end of the aisle, the host gestures to the first door on our right, which reveals a small circular room with a round booth built directly into its perimeter. A chandelier dangles over the table in the center of the cushions.

"Welcome to the New Amsterdam Tea House," the host says, placing a stack of menus on the table. "A waiter will be here soon to take your order."

After we sidle into the booth, the host shuts the doors. I look down at my polyester jacket and remind myself that I was invited here.

"This place started as twentieth-century New York's answer to debutante balls," Margaret says. "Parents sent their kids here to meet potential boyfriends and girlfriends of, you know, an *appropriate* background."

"Segregated. Rich and segregated," Chioma says, shrugging off her Chanel coat. "It's not my favorite place to be, but on some level, coming here is a nice form of protest, which is why I have a tab."

The waiter appears in the doorway. "Are you ready to order?"

I haven't even had a chance to look down at the menu, but Chioma says, "We'll take a kettle of black Darjeeling and a kettle of imperial oolong."

I glance at the menu, and my eyes fall on the price of the oolong: $124 per pot. I try to keep my scream confined to my mind.

"My treat," Chioma says. Thank goodness.

Over the next hour, we order another two pots of tea—Chioma insists, although she can barely hold back her horror when Mai dumps two packets of Splenda into her cup—and a plate of raspberry scones. The periodic doses of sugar and caffeine maintain the steady chug of adrenaline in my limbs, and the words blur together into a conversation that I have no delusion that I'll recall tomorrow. But I don't think it matters if I remember the words. What's important is that I'm laughing harder than I've laughed in years.

The only thing I wish were different is the aching absence of Zola's body in the booth next to me.

Another hour whirls by. We order another pot of tea and a platter of lemon scones, this time with a side of clotted cream at Margaret's insistence. As I'm coming down from the most recent jolt of sugar, Mai says, "Hey, Chioma, what's your story?"

Chioma raises her eyebrows. "If you have a specific question, you should ask it outright."

"Okay," Mai says. "What's it like being rich and Black?"

I stare at Mai, shock cutting through the stupor of the night. That degree of insensitivity is pretty unusual for a Davison girl.

"What do you want me to say? That I...wouldn't recommend it?" Chioma says. "That if Freya from a cappella tells me one more time that the Vikings had dreadlocks, I'm going to cut off her braids myself?"

I stifle a snort.

"But I'm surprised to get that from you, of all people, Mai," Chioma continues, taking a deep sip of her oolong. "I'd think that your Davison experience isn't all that different from mine."

"In some ways," Mai says. "But there are definitely more Asians than Black girls in school. That said, most of you guys are way richer than me."

"Really?" Margaret asks.

"Most of my mom's salary goes toward paying my grandparents' medical expenses and our private school tuition," Mai says. "I share a room with my older sister."

Surreptitiously, I slide my phone under the table and google *NY Herald executive editor salary*. Even though the most recently released number is from more than a decade ago, it's already half a million dollars.

Still, maybe it's the drunkenness of the night, but as I glance around the table at the faces of the girls who have become my coconspirators, it occurs to me that it may not be helpful to list the ways that they're different than I am.

"Are you first-generation?" Chioma asks.

"Second," Mai says. "But my grandparents live with us, which makes me feel like I'm not too far from my heritage."

"I wish my parents did more to make me feel close to Nigeria."

Chioma's hand trembles a little as she brings her teacup to her lips. "It must be nice to have your grandparents at home."

"Sure, until they convinced my mom that a septum piercing would keep me out of Harvard." Mai bites into her scone, maybe a little more viciously than necessary. "Besides, it's two more people to 'hm!' judgmentally every time I do something they consider irresponsible. Like, at the beginning of this school year, I lost a bracelet that my mom gave me when I started my summer internship—granted, it was a nice bracelet—but they went on about it for weeks until I found it in my jewelry box tucked underneath a bunch of tangled necklaces. The fact they even noticed when I stopped wearing it was nuts to me."

"That's so weird," Chioma says. "My mom also gave me a piece of jewelry right before my internship last spring, this gorgeous pendant, and then it also went missing a few months later."

I feel myself straining to refrain from judgment. The only real pendant I own is a pearl drop that my grandmother sent over from Iowa for my thirteenth birthday, and even though it isn't the kind of fashion accessory I'd choose for myself, I'd never allow it to vanish.

Margaret catches my eye. "Personally, I pride myself on my ability to not lose thousands of dollars of jewelry. More broadly, though, it's interesting to learn more about where you two are coming from. I feel like the Davison experience is more varied than I assumed."

"Yeah, about that," Mai says. "It's your turn."

Margaret peers at Mai over the rim of her teacup. "What do you mean?"

"I have a theory," Mai says. "I'm starting to feel like maybe we all followed that first letter because we felt kind of out of place at Davison. Chioma has her first-gen shit, Kay and I have our socioeconomic class discomfort—"

"Hey," I say. "You're making a lot of assumptions about me."

Mai raises her eyebrows. "Are they false?"

I guess I'm in deep enough with these girls that it wouldn't be helpful to pretend. Instead of responding to Mai, I say a silent apology to Emily's memory and hope that the others at this table feel the same undercurrent of connection that I do.

Margaret exhales into her cup of Darjeeling, the steam fogging up her glasses. "Well, what do you want to know about me? Whether I feel a sense of belonging at Davison?"

"If you're comfortable," Mai says.

Margaret takes a sip of tea and slots her cup into the ridge in her saucer. "In all the ways that are important, yes, the school is the right place for me. My family story is the standard Irish Catholic one: stepped off the boat in the early 1900s, made a living building railroad tracks, next few generations joined the police—don't worry, Chioma, I think all cops are bastards, especially my uncle Connor—and now my dad has a good job in the state government. So we're like a lot of other Davison families in that we own the West Village townhome but didn't pay for it with generational wealth."

Chioma's lips twisted at *all cops are bastards* and have yet to untwist. "But?" she asks.

"But..." Margaret pushes her glasses up on her forehead and rubs her eyes with the heel of her undyed hand. "But, oh God, wow, I am so scared. Every day."

I exchange glances with Chioma and Mai. "What do you mean?"

"I can't believe I'm saying this. I've never told anyone this." Margaret's blue hand joins the other to cover her whole face. "I feel like I'm on the edge of a cliff all the time, and any mistake is going to send me over. I know it's irrational, but if I don't get an A on a test, or if I don't make a good impression on people at the family mixers, it feels like the apocalypse will happen."

"Damn," Chioma says. "Is there anything that makes it better?"

Margaret sighs from between her fingers. "That's what I was hoping the Blue Hand Girls would do. Give me a sense of protection. Make me feel like there's a safety net underneath the cliff."

Mai lays a hand on Margaret's back. "Girl, forget the cult. We need to get you a good therapist."

Margaret sniffles. "Don't you think I've tried that?"

From Margaret's other side, I add my hand next to Mai's, laying my palm against the cashmere of Margaret's sweater. "To be completely honest, I don't know yet whether the Blue Hand Girls have our best interests in mind. I hope they do. But no matter what, I think I speak for Chioma and Mai, too, when I say that no matter what, you've got us."

• • • • •

The next morning, I drag myself through the door of my apartment at 10:00. My mom is at the kitchen island again, drinking tea, as if she hasn't moved since last night. "You're back early," she says.

"Stayed up all night…talking. Have to collapse." I rush past her to my room, dump my backpack on the floor, and throw myself into bed before she can ask any questions. It's true. I talked for longer and in more depth than I have in years.

I don't know quite how I feel, except tired. So, so tired.

And maybe almost content.

• • • • •

As I click my locker shut on Monday afternoon, my phone buzzes in the pocket of my uniform slacks.

ZOLA WOLFE, 3:29 P.M.:

Meet me in the lobby?

My heart leaps. Despite our lunches on the library couch and the touching of our knees underneath our calculus table, she's never suggested any kind of public meeting in Davison. Maybe something has changed her mind about the need for secrecy, Blue Hand Girls be damned. She finally wants the school to see me on her arm.

I stuff my physics binder into my backpack and soar down the stairs, almost crashing into a cluster of blazer-clad freshmen. As usual, I don't need to search very hard to locate Zola; even without her height and hair color, she would be a beacon in the crowd, but with those two attributes, she's the kind of figure you can't see without wanting to cast in bronze.

"Hey," I say, coming up behind her and brushing my blue fingers across her waist.

She jolts back from my touch, and my heart sinks.

"S-sorry," I say. I can feel myself blinking rapidly. "I thought—"

"Good to see you, Kay!" Her voice is bright, but there's a warning at its edges. "Since your tours aren't running this week because of Thanksgiving, I was wondering if you were free to walk through Central Park today."

She gives me a platonic pat on the shoulder. Frankly, I would rather she punch me in the gut.

"Just...a walk," I say slowly.

Zola smiles, her eyes glittering. "What else would it be?"

As we walk toward the lobby door, at least six inches between us, Zola takes out her phone and types something. Inside my pocket, my phone buzzes again.

ZOLA WOLFE, 3:33 P.M.:

I'm sorry, baby. I don't like this either :(

I nod at her, trying not to let my face betray me more than it already has.

A block away from the school, we pass a dark-cloaked street vendor hawking a cart of duck-head umbrellas wrapped in cellophane. Gray clouds have begun to thicken in the sky, and my computer is in my backpack. I consider stopping to buy an umbrella, but the markups are more than I can justify. Plus, I have an itching—but probably irrational—fear that if I stop, Zola is going to keep walking.

I clear my throat. "So. I've got a question for you."

A fat raindrop splatters against my nose. I should have bought an umbrella.

"What?" She brings her eyebrows together slightly and shifts to her left, widening the gap between us by another inch.

I can't ask her my real question: what it'll take to change her mind. My brain filters through alternatives, scanning our most recent moments together: brushing hands as we passed each other on the stairs, the blue heart she hid in the corner of this morning's calculus doodle, the photos of Emily's file that Mai added to the Clandestine chat today. I scan the street and determine that we're far enough away from Davison to whisper, "Did you already know that Mr. Holmes was involved with whatever happened to Emily?"

She glances around, too, probably conducting the same evaluation. "I shouldn't be telling you this, but no. Why do you ask?"

"I mean..." A few more raindrops land on my shoulders. "You take such delight in antagonizing him. When I saw the file, I figured that was why."

She laughs, a bark that I've never heard from her before. "I have plenty of other reasons."

"So tell me," I say.

We pass through the cobblestone gateway into Central Park, dead leaves forming a sheet across the gravel. They crumble underneath my Docs as we follow the winding path that will lead us to the lake.

"I don't know how well you know Mr. Holmes," Zola says quietly. "What do you think he is? Maybe a little sexist, maybe a little too eager to get off on his students' mistakes?"

"Yeah." Several more raindrops scatter on top of the leaves, heavier this time, but somehow none of them hit Zola.

"Mr. Holmes is so much worse than you think, Kay," Zola says. "Mr. Holmes is a weak, easily threatened man who can't bear for his students to prioritize anything besides his useless class. And even when his students have very, very good reasons for breaking his arbitrary rules, he'll use it as an excuse to punish them."

"Oh." I wonder if Zola told him that she was late to class a few weeks ago because she had been trying to intercept her father. I wonder how he responded.

"Kay, I am *failing*. I'm failing even though I've gotten a B minus or above on every test we've had so far. This will keep me from getting into college—fuck, it'll keep me from graduating. And if Mr. Holmes is going to do that to me, I might as well make him look like an idiot in front of a class of merciless high schoolers."

We pass underneath a cobblestone bridge, the tunnel amplifying the sounds of her last few words alongside the scraping of my footfalls on concrete. Anger stabs inside my chest. But beneath it, I feel a squirm of doubt. I've seen where Zola lives, and she sure as hell isn't on scholarship. Girls like her don't need perfect grades to get into college. Even so, I respect that she's taking responsibility for developing an application worthy of admission, rather than relying on the power of a hefty donation. "I'm...I'm sorry."

The raindrops are falling faster and harder now, and Zola pulls me over to wait by the side of the tunnel. "Don't you dare pity me, Kay."

"Zola! Passing this way?"

I whip around, and somehow, here in this tunnel is fucking Aubrey.

Zola yanks her hand back from my arm. "Didn't, uh, expect to see you here."

Aubrey strolls up to us. There's something different about her today: a slower, maybe jauntier gait, the crook of her thumb hooking through one of her belt loops. It takes me a second to notice the much more significant change—the rain has coated her hair just enough that when she runs a hand through it, it stays slicked back and off her forehead. Fully exposed, her eyes are black and catlike in a way that, unfortunately, very much complements her smirk.

"I like the park when it's raining," Aubrey says, inserting herself between me and Zola. "The emptiness gives me more room to think. Although if I'm going to have company, you're not bad."

No.

No no no no no no no.

I was wrong. Last week, when Aubrey accused me of being in love with Zola, she didn't actually think I'd gotten the girl. I can hardly fault her for that—as pathetic as it is to admit, I wouldn't believe it, either. So I guess that, in her moment of realization, she assumed I was lusting after Zola from afar, which inspired her to change her information-gathering tactic from harassing me to throwing her own carabiner into the ring with Zola.

I try to focus on my shallow breaths as I watch Aubrey brace her blue hand on the wall of the tunnel, just above Zola's shoulder. "So," Aubrey continues. "You were saying that Mr. Holmes is a sad little man whom we're going to decimate for his role in prematurely ending the life of one of our classmates?"

How dare she bring Emily into this. My head is pulsating from the déjà vu.

"Don't get ahead of yourself," Zola says, twisting one of her curls between her fingers. Her eyes flick toward me for a moment so quick that I'm not sure if I'm imagining it. "Besides, save it for Clandestine. Outside the app, I'm just a senior at your school."

Aubrey winks. "There are worse things to be."

"Hey, uh, look, the rain is lightening up," I say too loudly, tilting my head at the mouth of the tunnel. "So, Aubrey, if you don't mind, we were just leaving—"

"Kay, I know this isn't on your way. We're still close to the west side of the park, so why don't you head back to the C station?" Aubrey says, turning to me for the first time. "As it happens, my train leaves from the east side, so I can make sure Zola is properly...accompanied."

I open my mouth, a barrage of swears loaded in my throat. But then I see Zola staring at me, her head swiveling in an almost-imperceptible no. *Too suspicious,* she mouths. *I'm sorry.*

"How—very—thoughtful," I force out, and deliver my girlfriend into the boa constrictor's embrace.

CHAPTER 11

Zola's texted apologies are sweet and effusive and still not enough. Even so, now that we've uncovered Emily's file, I feel some degree of confidence that the secrecy has a finite duration. Between the file room's design fitting better into a CIA lair than an Upper West Side private school and the way that Emily's suspicion of the school seemed to catalyze her expulsion, it seems like she was right after all: there's something rotten in the state of Davison. For the hundredth time since Friday, I wonder if Emily would still be alive if I'd believed her when she raised that suspicion with me.

That night, with my now-familiar setup laid across my desk—laptop, leather notebook, and cell phone—I scroll through the most recent messages in Clandestine.

THE JAILER:

Nice work uncovering Emily's permanent record. This gives us plenty to work with.

THE HEALER:

Based on what the file shows, they didn't care much about the stalking, if they did at all (sorry, Aubrey—guess you weren't as convincing as you thought :P)

I snort. The Healer may be my new favorite member. If I'm lucky, it's Zola.

THE CONFISCATOR:

Clearly, she was getting too close to learning something important about Davison.

THE PRIESTESS:

in that case, initiates, your next challenge is to figure out what that is...

MAI:

Ok guys, we have a few different places to start. Obv Mr. Holmes is the one who decided to expel Emily, so we can look into him

CHIOMA:

We also have the four highlighted phrases from Emily's search history, so we can try to figure out the connection between them

As I scroll back up in the general chat to reexamine the photos of the file, I notice that another one of the pixelated tabs has been uncovered. This one reads *Documents*. I tap on it, and it reveals a folder containing the photos, each one renamed with a brief description of its contents. Despite any suspicions I have about the Blue Hand Girls, I have to admire their organizational prowess. I open the page with Emily's search history and reread the highlighted lines: *internship program Davison High, Bonum Solutions, how small is a listening bug, Parker Hargrove.*

The general chat buzzes with a message from Aubrey.

AUBREY:

@Chioma @Mai @Vanessa—you all presented at this year's internship expo, right?

I try to ignore the pang of jealousy that leaps in my stomach.

MAI:

Yeah but idk anything that would track back to Emily

With a start, I realize that I actually might.

KAY:

Emily thought there was something going on with how the school decided which girls were accepted into the internship program. She mentioned it to me once in passing. I thought she was joking, but... maybe that's what her 'I was right' text was about.

I try to ignore the gremlin jumping up and down in my head, jabbering about how this might be the only reason I have yet to get accepted to the Quinn Center for Justice.

CHIOMA:

Damn. It's good that you're here, Kay

DAPHNE:

Nice nice nice

AUBREY:

@Vanessa what internships did your sister have before she graduated?

I have to admire Aubrey, really. I don't think I could stomach making the accusation tucked into that message.

VANESSA:

I want to be honest with you all. I talked to Parker as soon as we saw the highlighted searches in the file. If my family is doing something wrong, I don't want to be complicit

I run my hand across the rough wood of my desk to ground myself. Maybe, as with Tia, I've been making assumptions that Vanessa doesn't deserve.

AUBREY:

And?

VANESSA:

She had never even interacted with Emily and was super confused by the whole thing

AUBREY:

What about her internships?

VANESSA:

Banking, mostly. She's at Wharton now

Of course she is.

CHIOMA:

Based on what Kay said, I think that Emily was less interested in what the internships were and more so in how/why the companies decided to hire their Davison students

That's true. If Parker had chosen to work in pharmaceuticals like her father, Emily would have had more of a stake in the internship destinations.

TIA:

Then we have a clear next step!! We have to figure out why different students get assigned to different companies

MAI:

I mean it'll be a while, but we could wait until after the next round of internship apps is due and then try to spy on Mr. Holmes while he sorts them out

AUBREY:

Not aggressive enough.

DAPHNE:

Really?

AUBREY:

We wouldn't be able to start for another month, and I don't want to waste that time. Besides, the school is too well protected for us to collect anything useful from snooping around. We need to target Mr. Holmes directly and force him to give us intel.

MARGARET:

I don't think that's necessary

AUBREY:

Did any of you notice that all the lobby cameras were already fixed by this morning?

I blink at my phone screen. I definitely didn't. Add it to the list of reasons why I'm probably not cut out to be part of a teenage militia, no matter what Zola sees in me. No one else responds for a few seconds either. Of course, Aubrey is the only one who has what the Blue Hand Girls are looking for.

AUBREY:

I'll take that as a no. As far as I'm concerned, that means two things: 1) they know someone is going after them and 2) they've tightened up their security.

Because of #2, I strongly doubt that they'll be careless enough for us to gain access to anything incriminating.

But because of #1, we wouldn't be giving away anything new if we approach Mr. Holmes anonymously and shake him down for info about how he assigned the previous rounds of internships.

ME:

And how do you propose we do that?

AUBREY:

That's for you to figure out. My blue hand isn't large enough to carry all of you.

. . . . .

An hour later, I find myself staring up at the Corinthian columns of Zola's apartment building. I don't remember making the conscious decision to come here. But if this Blue Hand Girls business is going to require me to threaten a teacher—and forget risking Northwestern, that's risking a jail sentence—I'm going to have to trust Zola in a way that I haven't yet been able to muster.

She doesn't know it, but if she can't give me a very good reason to believe the Blue Hand Girls will keep me safe, I'm going to walk away. From achieving justice for Emily, from joining a group that will give me real power in this world, from the vibrating sense of connection that I felt with the other initiates last weekend. I'll even walk away from her.

Zola pushes open the door of her building, the doorman's figure hovering behind her. Black silk pajama pants stick out from underneath her winter coat. "Kay? What is it?"

"Come on," I say. "Walk with me."

Tortoiseshell glasses frame her unflinching blue eyes. I didn't know she wore contacts. Somehow, the glasses make her even more alluring. "It's ten o'clock and forty degrees out."

I exhale, watching my breath form a cloud in front of me. "It won't take long."

"Fine." Zola descends the shallow steps and grabs my undyed hand, her touch sending a jolt of warmth up my arm. "Where to?"

I gesture to the park, its bare trees curling over the stone wall like claws. "We might as well pick up where we left off."

We walk past pine shrubs and piles of acorns until we're

in the maw of the park, streetlights marking the path every ten feet and stretching out our shadows behind us, wind whispering warnings inside my ears. Despite the insulation of Zola's Moncler jacket, she's shivering. I take off my scarf, the striped orange-and-red one from Aunt Shell, and wrap it around her neck.

She smiles at me. And even with the wind biting at the exposed skin of my collarbone, I feel warmer than before.

Zola leads me to a bench directly underneath one of the streetlights at the side of the path and places both my hands between hers. "Kay, you're scaring me. Please. Tell me what's on your mind."

"You shouldn't—you shouldn't have brushed me off for Aubrey earlier today," I say, trying to keep my voice firm.

"And I apologized," Zola says. "Please, baby. You know that I don't like this any more than you do."

"It's not just that. She's trying to manipulate you. She thinks you're hiding things, and if she…seduces you, you'll tell her."

"Well, as you're quite aware, I'm very good at keeping boundaries between my role as a member of the Blue Hand Girls and my role as the girlfriend of the initiate who has succeeded in seducing me. Which, to be clear, Aubrey never could."

"Yeah. About that."

"Yes, baby?"

"You...have to lower those boundaries." I take a shaky breath, the fog in front of my face wavering. "Even though you pretend I'm the same as the other initiates, we both know that's not true. When the other girls see messages in Clandestine—and, by the way, you have no idea what it feels like to wonder with every message whether my girlfriend is the one speaking—they're getting what they need to make an informed decision about how, or whether, they're going to fulfill the society's challenges. And when I see those messages, what I'm seeing is that my girlfriend wants me to do something dangerous. And because of how I feel about her, I'm much more likely to do it."

Zola squeezes my hands. "I don't think that's such a bad thing, baby."

"Of course you don't." I slide my hands out of hers and stick them in the pockets of my polyester-lined coat, which is nowhere near thick enough for this cold. "It gets you what you want."

Pressure builds behind my sinuses as I push myself up from the bench. I don't let myself look at her. If I do, I'll see a chunk of my heart naked and trembling underneath the lamp light.

"Kay!" She's standing, too, hands pawing at my arms, clamping them still and pulling me toward her. "Please. Wait. Please!"

I shut my eyes, trying to hold on to the illusion that my heart is still safely tucked inside my chest. "I can't."

"You have to!" She presses herself against me, the smell of her citrus fabric softener overwhelming my nostrils. "Kay. I—I'm really falling for you."

My eyes snap open. And I see her, shaking in the darkness, branches pointed like lances at her molten core, and even with my scarf cradling her, my heart is still so very cold.

"I'm falling for you, too." The words leap out of my mouth and wrap around her fragile body, and we're kissing, tangled into a single being, like we were on the roof that night, intertwined and connected and whole.

By the time I regain control of my senses, we're back on the bench, her arms around my neck and her legs draped over my lap. She's radiating again, the way she should.

I can't believe I almost let myself lose this otherworldly being.

But. Something twists inside my mind, reminding me why I came here. Panting, I say, "Things have to be different."

"Anything," she whispers into my chest.

I consider asking her to hold my hand in the atrium tomorrow, but I don't want to know whether *anything* has limits.

"I want you to tell me more than you tell the other girls," I say. "If I have you anchoring me to the Blue Hand Girls' challenges, I want to have additional knowledge to balance out your gravitational pull."

"Baby, I keep telling you: I don't know anything about Emily's murder that you don't know," Zola says.

"Not about that," I say. "Tell me about the Blue Hand Girls. Tell me what I think Aubrey is going to try to cajole out of you: your initiation challenge last year."

"Kay," she says, her eyes trained on mine. "You know that, to this point, I've never lied to you."

"And I'd rather you not begin," I say, leaning in to kiss her again. "So tell me."

"You're irresistible." She lifts her lips away from mine, laughing. "Okay. Here's what happened. One of the college guidance counselors was taking bribes from parents to secure their kids' spots on a fictional Davison lacrosse team and get their kids recruited by corrupt athletic coaches at Cornell and Dartmouth. And, judging by the way that those parents' names kept appearing on the donation plaque in the lobby, the school was in on it, too."

An unplaceable feeling throbs in my stomach. "Did anything ever come out about that?"

Zola shrugs. "Maybe. Or maybe not. Unfortunately for the state of college admissions, it's not exactly an uncommon story, so I'm not surprised if it sounds familiar."

She's right—and it's sickening. "So what did you guys do to...take care of the counselor?"

A shadow of a smile crosses Zola's lips. "Have you ever heard of the grappling hook maneuver?"

"I can't say I have."

"Okay, it's this bank account trick where you wire someone money with a virus attached to the code. The virus picks up the bank account's login info and transmits it to the sender," Zola says, her grin widening. "Anyway, our members mixed ourselves in with the rest of the juniors who were sending bribes around that time, and one of us sent the grappling hook wire. That's why we needed to blend in last year—it was imperative that the counselor didn't know who sent the tainted bribe. Once we had the login info, we drained the bank account and donated the money to a college-access charity. Thanks to the generosity of Davison High, ten first-generation Americans went to university last year, and they didn't come close to catching us."

"Oh, that's brilliant." Relief crashes over me. I don't know how much of me believed Aubrey that Zola's story didn't add up or how much of me was worried—for any reason—that the Blue Hand Girls weren't the good guys after all. But this really explains everything. Theirs is a controversial definition of justice, but I'll be damned if it isn't a sweet one.

"So you believe me now?" Zola says. "You don't think I'm sending you to be gobbled up by the forces of evil?"

I caress the side of her face. "It's still a very different initiation this year."

"I know," Zola says. "But the most important difference is that I'll be beside you, holding your hand and keeping you safe."

• • • • •

The two days before Thanksgiving pass in a blur of quiet moments with Zola. In a concession to normalcy, she's agreed to start meeting me before school at Black Diamond Coffee a few blocks south of Davison. Meanwhile, in Clandestine, we're fleshing out a plan to ambush Mr. Holmes. Every time I question whether this is wise, a bigger part of me says how extraordinary it is that I can do right by Emily and Zola at the same time. And how often can the same action be a gift to both girls who have claimed your heart?

The other change in Clandestine is that my group chat with Chioma, Mai, and Margaret has evolved in a direction I didn't expect. It starts when Chioma sends us a selfie from the hallway outside the black box, Lee's face bobbing in the background, captioned *RIP to me, thinking about all my horrible secrets that they may or may not know.* That opens the floodgates of delightful mundaneness: a tag-yourself meme featuring nine different frogs (Margaret is the one wearing the Easter bonnet, and Mai is the one perched on a raccoon like it's a horse), a list of background roles from a Yiddish play about golems that Chioma had to read for her drama elective.

The next time I reopen my spring internship application, instead of going over my essays for a fifth time, I text our group chat to ask whether they think it's worth the effort before we know what's going on with Mr. Holmes.

CHIOMA:

I wouldn't bother. Use the extra time to join me for tea again soon?

As I'm leaving AP Physics at the end of the day on Wednesday, Tia messages the general chat.

TIA:

@Other initiates: come by my locker before you head out. I have our gear for next week!!

Tia's locker is down the hallway from the physics classroom, so I head straight there, passing the water fountain embedded in the shallow vestibule with a mosaic of the Davison crest and ducking between girls debating whether it's better to spend Thanksgiving in Aspen or Boca. I'm wearing a pair of dangle earrings—downward-facing spikes clamped to the ends of silver chains, not quite at the level of Mai's swords or planchettes but definitely a step more interesting than my usual cubic zirconia studs—and I keep getting thrown off by the weight bouncing underneath my earlobes as I move.

Tia is shifting from side to side in front of her open locker. In a change of pace from the Jimmy Choo stilettos, she's wearing sleek black boots that end just below her knees, highlighting the gap between the leather and her maroon uniform skirt.

"Hey," I say, coming up beside her.

Tia jumps, then lets out a giggle. "Sorry? Nervous? Quick, take a bag."

Her locker swings on its hinges. The bottom is lined with a row of notebooks, each one's binding embossed with her initials. Atop them are eight burlap drawstring bags, bulky with a mixture of soft and hard elements, occupying the rest of the space in the locker. I try to quell the jolt of anxiety that arises when I think too hard about what's inside and whether it will set off any alarms as I leave the building.

That's a ridiculous thought, though, because Tia had to get them into Davison this morning, so there can't be anything too illegal inside there. I tug the top one out of the pile. The burlap is scratchy underneath my palms. Glancing around, I loosen the top of the drawstring just enough to peek inside. There's a ski mask squashed against the wall of the bag, its fabric curved around a box labeled *voice modifier*. A pair of night vision goggles sticks out from underneath the box, alongside a digital silver watch that, if Tia has executed the plans we made in Clandestine, should be set in perfect sync with the seven other watches across the bags, down to the seconds that flash across the screen. I don't recognize the watch brand, but I suspect that it's far pricier than necessary.

Tia smacks my hand. "What are you doing? Put it away!"

I stuff the ambush kit into my backpack. "Right, sorry. Thanks for putting these together."

"I've always thought that being the daughter of a CIA agent would come in handy someday?" she says.

I turn to head upstairs to my locker, too aware of the new weight on my back.

"Oh, and Kay?"

My head swivels back in Tia's direction. "Yeah?"

"Cute earrings."

I feel an involuntary smile spread across my face. "Thanks."

• • • • •

When I walk into Black Diamond Coffee the next Monday before school, Zola is already tucked into the table in the corner, gnawing on the paper straw of an iced peppermint latte. Her gloved hands form a barrier between her skin and the condensation leaking out of the plastic cup.

"You know, they make those hot, too," I say, squeezing her shoulder.

"Hot coffee is for heterosexuals," she says.

A few minutes later, I have one hand on her knee under the table and the other wrapped around a steaming cup of chai.

"So, how was your Thanksgiving?" she asks.

"Honestly?" I take a long sip of the chai. It tastes like molten plastic now that I've become spoiled by ninety-five-dollar Darjeeling. "There was only one person I was looking forward to seeing, but she claims to have gotten snowed in."

Zola's eyes scan the coffee shop, flitting over businesswomen with slick eyeliner and Juilliard students with cellos strapped to their backs. Then she scoots her chair around to the same side of the table as mine, our backs to the rest of the coffee shop. "Why do you say it like that?"

I stare at the brocade wallpaper across the table. "She seems to have forgotten that I'm on her Close Friends story, and her definition of 'snowed in' seems to be 'showing up at my boyfriend's parents' house with a tin of blondies and a tinsel bow in my hair.'"

Zola places her hand on the small of my back. I can feel the warmth of her touch even through my jacket. "Your aunt Shell, right? Do you want to talk about it?"

"There's nothing else to say." I take another sip of the drink, focusing on its burning inside my throat. "How about you? How was your long weekend?"

"Oh, fine, great," Zola says, then gnashes her straw so violently that I can see the indents of her molars in the paper.

"You said you were going to be honest with me," I say. "That doesn't just apply to the Blue Hand Girls."

Zola sighs. "You don't want to hear this kind of thing about me."

I put down the cup and take both her hands in mine. "I promise I do."

She inhales shakily. "If I start talking, something horrible might come out."

"That's fine, baby."

She leans closer to me and starts whispering, her mouth against the crown of my head as if she doesn't really want me to hear her. "Okay. You know how I told you that my dad left a few years ago?"

I nod, feeling the friction of her lips against my hair.

"When my father was around, he used to be very grand about Thanksgiving, you know, 'Ah, we're Americans now,'" Zola says. "My parents were so dedicated to assimilation that they didn't even tell me exactly which part of Eastern Europe we were from, until my mom let it slip after my dad left. And every Thanksgiving, my dad would order an enormous turkey from Whole Foods, and even though it was just the three of us and several centuries of colonization, it was one of the few days per year that my family felt big enough to fill our home."

"And now?" I ask.

"And he left two years ago this December, but my mother still gets extra catatonic on major holidays."

I can feel her bracing herself against me, my shoulders supporting her weight. "You can keep going, if you'd like. If that would make it easier."

Her words begin rushing together. "The thing about my mother is that my father's disappearance destroyed her. Because he didn't just leave. He drained all our bank accounts except for the trust with my Davison tuition, which I guess he couldn't touch. My mother hasn't worked since we lived in the old country, and between that and the way that he anchored her in the U.S., she became a shell. For months, she wouldn't eat more than a few bites per day, and she let her hair mat into a stiff clump, and she inhaled Xanax pills like they were Tic Tacs. And she's a little better now, I guess, after I forced her to the hair salon and the stylist forced her to the doctor, but she's not all there, and she definitely wasn't all there this weekend."

Zola leans into my chest. I stroke her hair, doing my best to stay solid for her as it sinks in that, beneath all her grandiosity, my girl is in pain. "I've got you. I've got you, baby."

"I'm doing okay, though," she mutters into my quarter-zip. "My mom gets disability, and I run sound for shitty bands to supplement—that's why I learned tech theater, there's always a gig somewhere, since every frat-bro-turned-finance-bro decides to learn guitar for his quarter-life crisis—and I have the Blue Hand Girls, and I'm okay, okay?"

"Baby, you don't sound okay," I say, pulling her deeper into me.

"I really am." She chokes on the words. I…think she's crying. I sweep out the section of her hair caught in the crook of her neck, and when I pull back my hand, it's wet. "Except for one thing. I've made my peace with knowing that there isn't money for me to go to a fancy college like everyone else at Davison—before you say anything, I've checked, and financial aid will assume that my father is able to pay for me—but at the very least, I thought I could escape somewhere okay, like a state school in New England, based on decent grades and the Davison name. But that's impossible. Because I'm failing—fucking—calculus."

How could I ever have been afraid of the girl who's shuddering in my arms?

"Hey, hey," I whisper into the crown of her head. "It won't be long until we take care of Mr. Holmes. And I'll make sure that, by the time we're done, he's so cowed that he won't dare to keep hurting students. Especially my girl."

"Kay, I—oh, fuck, Kay, I've fucked up," Zola says, her tears bleeding through the fabric of my sweatshirt. "I didn't mean to tell you this. I don't want to be a burden on you."

"You're not a burden," I say. "Let me take care of you. Please."

"Promise?" She chokes again.

"I promise."

I feel the glow of sunlight on my back as the sun begins to extend its tendrils from beyond the midtown skyscrapers. In about ten minutes, I'm almost certain that Mr. Holmes will produce a pop quiz and lock the door of the calculus classroom.

"Stay with me for a while?" Zola says. "I can't deal with him. Not today."

The threatening drumbeat of my daily chant rises to the top of my skull: *Top marks on every quiz, top marks in the class, keep my scholarship, get into Northwestern.* "Okay."

Zola brings her head away from my chest. Her mascara is smeared in the corners of her eyes, but somehow, it only deepens the infinite holograms inside her irises. "I'm very lucky to have you, you know that?"

I lean down and kiss her gently. As I've come to expect, her lips feel like a secret. But for the first time, that secret is that she is completely mine.

• • • • •

Two days later, I'm crouched on a fire escape in Hell's Kitchen, earbuds plugging my ears and a leather-sheathed knife strapped to the inside of my thigh, cursing myself for the degree of bravado I've allowed myself to spew over the past few weeks.

Chioma's voice emits from my earbud. "Everyone in position?"

We're all connected to Clandestine's voice-call feature, even the Blue Hand Girls, although they don't have a role in the choreography. Zola has assured us that she's listening in from a nearby coffee shop—to evaluate and, if absolutely necessary, to back us up.

"Confirming," I whisper.

Aubrey has been tailing Mr. Holmes for the past few days as he walks home from Davison. As is consistent with his teaching style, he permits himself zero variation in his route: across Seventy-Second to Columbus, down Columbus until it becomes Ninth Avenue, right onto Forty-Eighth Street until he almost hits Eleventh Avenue, and through this alley to Forty-Seventh Street. The alley slashes through two apartment buildings, their glazed brick exteriors staring at each other in an urban challenge. Usually, the alley is empty except for a metal dumpster bolted to the edifice of the eastern building and several black trash bags spilling out beside it, wind tossing the lipstick-stained coffee cups and sauce-coated take-out boxes onto the rough gravel. But today, each of the four fire escapes serves as the landing pad for a girl with a blue hand hidden beneath black gloves, and two more initiates hover just beyond each of the alleyway's mouths.

"He's almost here," Aubrey says. "Turning the corner onto Forty-Eighth."

I make eye contact with Tia, Mai, and Vanessa, who occupy the other three fire escapes. Thanks to the matching black getups and ski masks, bulbous over the night vision goggles, they're mostly interchangeable, except for a few telltale differences: the flash of Vanessa's Van Cleef bracelets between her sleeves and her gloves; the spikes of black hair splaying out from underneath Mai's mask; Tia's patent leather pumps—she insisted that she was so used to the Jimmy Choos that wearing flats would actually make her lose her balance—peeking through the metal slats. I brace my hands on the metal railing of my fire escape to keep myself steady.

"He's past me and Aubrey," Margaret says. "Following him to block the north entrance of the alleyway."

"He's three seconds away from entering," Aubrey says.

I glance at my watch, synchronized with the seven others: three...two...one.

The tips of Mr. Holmes's Merrells emerge from around the corner, leading the rest of him into the alley. His canvas briefcase dangles from between the fingers of his left hand as he stares straight ahead, no earbuds in his ears, marching toward Forty-Seventh Street. Aubrey's and Margaret's silhouettes appear silently behind him.

We've planned our dance to the second, assisted by the digital watches. There are eight of us, plus backup, and one of him. Our faces and voices are obscured. We've scripted our demand so that we're indistinguishable from a team of thieves waiting to jump the balding teacher with the checkered suits who can be counted upon to walk his Rolex through this alley every day at exactly 6:13 p.m.

And, oh my God, I have never been so fucking terrified.

After four more seconds, just before Mr. Holmes passes underneath Mai's fire escape, Chioma and Daphne enter from the south end of the alley. Chioma has padded her frame with three layers of sweatshirts underneath her black jacket, but Daphne doesn't need to do much to take up space besides cross her arms in front of her waffle-knit black sweater.

"Give us your valuables," Daphne says, her voice deepened by the modifier clamped to her mouth beneath her mask. She slides the knife out of her thigh holster and holds it aloft. "Now."

Mr. Holmes's eyes bulge out. His arms shoot out at his sides like a porcupine raising its spikes as his head whips around behind him, then above him, taking in the other six of us for the first time. For half a second, his eyes click with mine, our terror mirroring each other, and a torrent of nausea threatens to launch me out of the fire escape to retch into the dumpster beside him.

"Don't bother calling for help," Aubrey says, filtered through her own modifier. "Briefcase, watch, and wallet."

I can see Mr. Holmes's hands shaking even from twelve feet in the air. His briefcase slides out from between his fingers, whether from conscious decision or from the sweat that must be saturating his skin. The case thuds against the gravel and tips over onto its side. A shuddering exhale wrenches its way out of my throat. Years of internship-matching information should be in there, inside his laptop. Now that he has let go of the bag, the rest of this is for show.

"Good," Chioma says. "Now the other two."

As if in slow motion, his right hand crosses over his left to unclasp his Rolex. He unpeels it from his sweat-sticky wrist, the silver links flashing through the field of my night glasses, and bends down to lay the watch on top of the briefcase.

"Almost done," Daphne says.

Mr. Holmes's mouth opens but doesn't release anything

except air as he begins to fumble in his pocket. He slides out the wallet and drops it next to the watch.

"Good," Daphne says. "Now back away from the pile."

Mr. Holmes nods and takes a step backward, bringing him a foot closer to the tips of Aubrey's and Margaret's knives. Daphne slides her own blade back into her thigh holster and reaches down with both arms, her eyes never leaving Mr. Holmes's, to scoop up the valuables.

And then Mr. Holmes lunges at Daphne, a Taser jutting out from his palm.

CHAPTER 12

According to my watch, it takes exactly one second for the Taser to connect with Daphne's abdomen, the gun separated from her skin only by the thin fabric of her waffle-knit sweater, and then exactly two seconds for her to release an animalistic roar as she sails backward in the alley.

Before I have a chance to react, Mr. Holmes whirls around to Margaret and Aubrey, brandishing the Taser. Margaret screeches as she stretches out her knife farther, farther, closer to Mr. Holmes—despite the blood frothing in my ears, I know that my fear can't come close to hers—and then he ducks underneath the blade and plunges the Taser into the side of her torso, sending her flying toward the opposite end of the alley.

"T-two girls down," I whisper into my earbuds.

Aubrey scrambles forward and snatches up the briefcase, the wallet and watch sliding down to the gravel. I hear a metallic clang as the watch face cracks upon impact. But before Aubrey has managed to run two paces, Mr. Holmes flings himself at her, the Taser landing on her forearm.

He grabs the briefcase as Aubrey's arm jerks back from the shock hurling himself toward the southern mouth of the alley. The only thing in his way is Chioma. And she isn't moving, either away from him or toward him, her knife still affixed to the inside of her thigh.

I can't let him get to her.

I hurtle down the rungs of the fire escape and throw myself through the air, praying that I'll land on Mr. Holmes's back. My legs flail underneath me—oh, fuck, why did I rely on an athleticism that I've never had? I have a fraction of a second before I smash against the ground, so I twist my body forward to distribute the impact as much as possible.

My fingers sink into the back of Mr. Holmes's suit jacket lapel, and as I fall, I claw him down with me.

We both crash, me onto my stomach, him onto his back, a blanket of trash bags separating me from the hard gravel. Still, pain shoots through my rib cage as rice and beans fly out of an open Styrofoam container beneath my chest, guacamole mashing into the fabric of my coat. But there are trash bags breaking Mr. Holmes's fall, too, and he flips onto his stomach, still clutching the briefcase in one hand and the Taser in the other.

His eyes are inches from mine as he raises the hand with the Taser and launches himself at me. I brace myself for the inevitable explosion of pain.

But it doesn't come. Instead Mr. Holmes shouts, something guttural, and his Taser falls out of his hand. I roll to the left and see Mai hunched over his body, her knife buried in the back of his calf.

We agreed that we would do everything in our power to avoid using the blades. We planned to rely on the power of the threat to take what we needed. And now I've forced Mai to commit an act that she'll relive in her nightmares for the rest of her life.

The knife still embedded in his leg, Mr. Holmes grabs at me, the hand that was holding the Taser now grasping the cotton of my ski mask. I long for the mere terror from earlier as I'm overtaken by an emotion so all-consuming that it evades language, certain that my math teacher is about to unveil his assailant as the girl who stayed after class yesterday to ask him to re-explain what it means to raise a number to the power of infinity.

Both my hands shoot to the ski mask, tugging it down as

far as the cotton will stretch, fighting against the pressure of Mr. Holmes's pull. His fingers slip down, yanking a chunk of my hair. The chain of my stupid dangle earring is tangled in the strands—I should never have let my hubris steer me away from my cubic zirconia studs—and I hear myself shriek as my earlobe rips, blood trickling down my neck.

Beyond the struggling mass that is me and Mr. Holmes, Mai seems to have recovered from the shock of using the knife. She lunges for the Taser he dropped while trying to unmask me. Without removing his right hand from the bottom of my ski mask, Mr. Holmes releases the briefcase in his left and stretches out his free arm to snatch the Taser before Mai can reach it, jabbing the stun gun upward into her chest. Maybe even more than the others', Mai's scream sends a jolt of anguish through my body.

Behind us, I'm dimly aware of Vanessa and Tia dragging the bodies of the stunned initiates—Daphne, Margaret, Aubrey, and now Mai—around the corner of the alleyway. Chioma, finally unfrozen, runs toward the briefcase, where it's unguarded for the first time since Mr. Holmes set it down. At the sound of her footfalls, Mr. Holmes releases my mask and spins around, pushing himself into a primitive crawl in Chioma's direction.

Now is my chance to unsheathe my knife. I reach down to my thigh holster, feeling the leather press into my gloved hand.

I need to grab it. One motion and I'll be able to plunge the blade into the back of his neck. Then Chioma can escape with the briefcase, the rest of us following her, leaving Mr. Holmes bleeding out into these trash bags until he has no more blood to lose.

I can't do it.

I pull my hand away from the knife and throw myself onto his back like a turtle shell. Collapsing under my weight, Mai's knife still in his calf, Mr. Holmes tries to buck me off. I hang on, but he succeeds in twisting upward, landing us both on our sides against the gravel. The pain in my ribs jolts through me again upon the impact. He raises the Taser again, and with the pain distracting me, I don't think I'll even be able to swipe at his wrist before he stabs me with the electric shock.

And then a ninth black-clad figure comes hurtling through the alleyway. She leaps over Aubrey's body as Tia and Vanessa begin to drag it away and charges at Mr. Holmes. A single tendril of red hair streaming out from the tail of her ski mask, she winds up her arm and jabs something into his neck.

Instantly, Mr. Holmes's body wilts. Zola brings her hands away from his neck, and I see a needle sticking out of it. This wasn't in our plan. "Wh-what did you do?" I whisper.

"'Thank you' also works," Zola says, her voice hard. "Let's get out of here."

Chioma is still clutching the briefcase. The three of us run around the corner of the south end of the alley, where Tia and Vanessa are now helping Aubrey into a sitting position against the exterior of a walkup, joining the other three girls who are still shuddering from their Taser shocks.

"I've called a driver and a physician," Vanessa says. "They'll be here in a minute."

"Won't they question this?" Mai croaks.

Vanessa snorts. "They've seen worse."

Nausea roils in my stomach. I glance around at the other initiates and Zola, who are all clustered around the four girls on the sidewalk. Inching away from the group, I peer back around the corner into the alleyway.

Mr. Holmes's body writhes on top of the trash bags, his chest shuddering with such force that I can see it from thirty feet away. His limbs thrash from side to side, his right arm slapping against one bag so hard that it splits open, bottles of laundry detergent and rotting banana peels spilling out onto the gravel. His suit is soaked with beer and streaked with a runny brown sludge. This is a man who, I'm almost certain, has been left to die in a pool of excrement.

I feel a presence hovering a step behind me. I don't need to turn around to know it's Zola, but I can't stop myself from looking anyway.

Immediately, I wish I hadn't. There's no forgetting that sick smirk stretched across the lips that have so often kissed mine.

• • • • •

In the body of the van, Vanessa's physician swipes an alcohol pad over my bloodied ear. "Did you have an earring in here?"

My fingers shoot up to brush against my earlobes. My left ear, the intact one, still has the chain in it. My right ear is empty.

I launch myself at the front of the car. "Please! Turn back! I—I left something!"

The driver doesn't acknowledge me. Panic vibrates inside my veins. "Please!"

Zola comes up beside me and brushes her hand against the small of my back, a gesture so subtle that I'm sure the other girls think it's an accident, if they even notice it. "Don't worry. There must be thousands of pounds of trash in that alley. No one will ever notice one bloody earring."

Because I have no other choice, I believe her.

• • • • •

That night, as I nestle my chin into my comforter, the throbbing in my ribs among the many reasons I can't sleep, Mai messages our group chat in Clandestine.

MAI:

Guys we have to get out of this initiation

Chioma writes back right away.

CHIOMA:

I know. I've been thinking the same thing

MAI:

I haven't stopped shaking

None of us were hurt badly enough to need more than what Vanessa's private physician could remedy with his portable medical kit: bandages and topical cream for the Taser burns, a compression sleeve for my rib cage. He also sent us each home with a bottle of anti-anxiety pills. I've taken four pills so far. They haven't quelled my shaking, either.

MARGARET:

You both know we can't leave. They have too much on us

MAI:

Idk it might be worth it. I've been doing some research, and the worst case scenario rn is they turn us in for the crimes we've already committed and we get tried in juvenile court. But I'm going to turn 17 in a few weeks and then I'll be much more likely to be tried as an adult

Two weeks ago, I was reveling in the glow of my first kiss. And tonight alone I've committed multiple felonies. How did I let myself get here?

MARGARET:

Oh God I can't believe this is real

CHIOMA:

Idk about you all, but there's no way I'm getting tried in any court. In case you haven't noticed, I am Black

I wonder if Zola and the other members of the Blue Hand Girls realize the disproportionate risks they've been requiring Chioma to take. I wonder if that factors into their calculus of justice.

MAI:

So you're not going to try to leave?

CHIOMA:

Can't

MAI:

Well I'm not going to ditch this without you guys

MARGARET:

I think we can do more to protect ourselves/ each other within the BHG initiation

MAI:

How?

MARGARET:

I like the overall BHG commitment to righting wrongs, and tbh I'm okay with doing some questionable things to make that happen. And I actually do think that Mr. Holmes deserved to get attacked—had him for calc last year, he was NOT pleased w having a sophomore in his class lol. And, more importantly, I'm 99% sure that we'll find something incriminating about Emily on his laptop based on what was in her permanent record. What I am more worried about is Zola

There's a stab in my ribs. Margaret has no idea how strongly that sentiment has been echoing in my head since we left the alley.

MAI:

Yeah uhhhhhh super bad vibes today

CHIOMA:

You think??

MARGARET:

Do you think she killed him?

I can't keep it inside anymore. I lean over the edge of my bed and heave into the brass wastebasket next to my night table, droplets of what used to be goulash peppering crumpled-up notebook papers and shells of blue ballpoint pens.

CHIOMA:

I don't want to think about it

MAI:

Yeah I think the important thing is that now we know to be careful bc she's a little fucked up

Wiping the cold sweat off my upper lip, I send a message for the first time tonight.

ME:

She's complicated, but I think we should trust her

The Killer has yet to message the general chat. I still have no idea which of the aliases Zola is behind. If and when the

Killer sends their first message, I pray that I won't hear it in her voice.

CHIOMA:

@Kay do you know something we don't?

If only I did.

Putting aside my dearth of knowledge about what Zola did tonight, if I'm going to tell my friends the full extent of my relationship with her, now would be the time. They deserve to know. I'm not sure whether it will change how they feel about her—although it will definitely change how they feel about me—but it's a sliver of information at a time when they need all the information they can get. And after seeing the look on her face as she watched Mr. Holmes writhe, I'm not sure if this is someone I should be protecting, no matter what I promised her in Black Diamond Coffee.

ME:

Believe me, I'm as in the dark as you are. I just have a feeling

• • • • •

The next morning, a Spanish teacher is sitting at Mr. Holmes's oak-wood desk. She slaps a pile of worksheets on Vanessa's table, tells us to pass them around, and props up her phone against Mr. Holmes's computer monitor to watch makeup tutorials on YouTube.

I stare at my worksheet and try to block out everything but the numbers, especially the heat of Zola's eyes on me from across the table. Now I think it's even more likely that he's dead. Earlier in the year, when he called out sick because of pneumonia, he filmed himself in bed wearing a suit jacket and lecturing about derivatives.

When I finish the worksheet, I drop it in front of the Spanish teacher and walk out of class fifteen minutes before the end of the period without asking for her permission. I wait for the familiar rhythm of my chant to reproach me, but it doesn't come.

As I walk down the empty hallway away from the math classroom, with no destination in mind except away from Zola, I hear the door swing open again. There's a patter of footsteps as she catches up to me.

Zola slides her hand into mine, gripping my blue fingers as if she doesn't notice how limp they are in hers. "Kay, I don't understand."

I pull my hand away. "Are you sure about that?"

"I didn't know you had such a weak stomach, baby," Zola says, chuckling lightly, her fingers slipping to my waist. "It's not like I killed him."

My knees buckle from the relief, and I collapse into one of the shallow archways along the side of the hallway. Like the one near the physics classroom, it has a mosaicked Davison crest emblazoned into its tile. Hard chunks of ceramic press into my back as I slide down to sit inside the indent.

Zola sits down next to me and brings an arm around my shoulders, pressing me against her Davison blazer. Her voice now somber, she says, "Baby...you didn't think I killed him, did you?"

I feel like I've had a veil sewn over my eyes for the past fourteen hours, and her words have dissolved it completely. I don't know how I could have let myself jump to such a horrible conclusion. This girl has brewed me tea and wept into my hair. The only response that comes out of my mouth is an ashamed squeak.

"Mr. Holmes will be fine," Zola says, squeezing my shoulder. "He had a nasty few minutes in that alley, but right after we left, he should have woken up with a couple of cuts and a hazy memory of what happened."

"You're sure?" My voice is smaller than I'd like it to be.

"I concocted the poison myself," she says. "I told you I'm good at science, remember?"

When she said that the first time, her knees touching mine on the gingham picnic blanket on the roof, this was not where

I thought we would end up. Even so. The thought of her in her bedroom, pinching an eyedropper over a set of chemicals, is only slightly less sexy than it is frightening.

"But you hurt him," I say. "Zola, it scared me. I'm afraid that this initiation is going too far."

"I know something that will make you feel better," Zola says, leaning in to graze my cheek with a kiss. "Open Clandestine."

Even right now—maybe especially right now—the feeling of her lips on my skin sends a bolt of electricity down my spine. I curse myself again for the way I've betrayed her and bring up the app on my phone screen.

The last pixelated tab has been uncovered. It reads *Origin*. I glance up at Zola. "Is this it?"

She nods. "Just read it."

I tap on the tab. This one is an uneditable page of text, interspersed with images like in a Wikipedia article.

The Clean Hand Girls

Early in the Bohemian Reformation, there was a period in which Czech aristocrats kept indentured servants for the purpose of committing good deeds in order to counteract the aristocrats' sins. These servants, typically young women whose title translated roughly to "Clean Hand Girls," functioned as a private answer to the Catholic Church's indulgences. The aristocrats believed that a well-managed Clean Hand Girl would be able to elevate the goodness of their souls in order to gain them entrance to heaven.

The strength of each Clean Hand Girl's good deeds correlated to the severity of her master's sins. If the master in question only took part in mild debauchery, perhaps some gambling or the errant glance at a woman's ankles, his Clean Hand Girl would then be tasked with baking bread and distributing it to the poor. However, the Bohemian aristocracy was famous for creative takes on sadism, such as the duke who liked to take his boiled eggs with a side of little boys' fingers in place of sausages. So if the master was more partial to this sort of brutality—including, but not limited to, murder—his Clean Hand Girl had to undertake greater deeds to counter his sins. The girls followed fairly standard protocol in the cases of these more severe redemptions. Often, they sought out even more dangerous criminals than their masters and either imprisoned or executed these criminals.

To signify their status within a specialized and respected subcategory of indentured servitude, Clean Hand Girls wore striking blue gloves. The expensive dye indicated the girls' value to their masters while symbolizing a countermeasure to the red of blood.

Between the last two paragraphs, there's an illustration of two figures, pigment saturating a sheet of parchment. It features a blue-gloved young woman kneeling by the body of a bearded man, his head dangling in the viewer's direction, only a flap of skin affixing his head to his neck.

I take a moment to process the article, then look back up at Zola. "So how is this supposed to reassure me?"

"I know what last night looked like: you think that I have a vendetta against Mr. Holmes and that I took the opportunity to punish him," Zola says. "But that's not what happened, so I wanted you to have the full context. The Blue Hand Girls aren't exactly the same as the Clean Hand Girls—fourteenth-century religion doesn't fully translate to the modern day—but the idea is the same. Everything I do in the context of the Blue Hand Girls, I'm doing in order to fulfill the oath I made, committing myself to a tradition that's been around for centuries. It's not an excuse to unleash anything sick inside myself. I promise."

If any part of me still doubted her, it doesn't anymore. After spending the past fourteen hours assuming a level of monstrosity in her that I'm now realizing was more of a projection than an assessment of anything external, she deserves for me to follow my own instructions and trust her. "I know, baby."

"But I'd be lying if I told you that there wasn't a little bit of selfishness motivating me last night," she continues.

Maybe I thought too soon. A chill emanates from where her fingertips rest on my neck. "Yeah?"

"When I decided to use the poison, justice wasn't at the top of my mind," she confesses. "All I was thinking was that I couldn't let him hurt you."

I bury my face in the lapel of her blazer, inhaling her citrus fabric softener. She is solid and clean and mine, her radiance dizzying, all her light packed into the nanometers of space between us. "Hey, Zola?"

"Yeah?" she says.

I tilt my head upward so that I can look into her eyes. "I think I'm in love with you."

And then she presses her lips to mine without even glancing around to make sure the hallway is still empty, whispering to me between kisses, "Kay—oh, my darling—oh, my sweet girl—baby, I love you too."

My heart feels like it lifts into the air the moment she calls me *darling.* I don't know how long we stay kissing, locked in an impermeable trance where everything feels okay. When we finally pull away, panting, and I get to take in the richness of her face again, I can't stop myself from leaning in to kiss her anew. My love.

"Kay?"

Zola wrenches her face back from mine, but of course it's

too late. Mai is frozen at the end of the hallway, hugging her knapsack and staring at me as if my skin has been stripped off. Which, to her, I suppose it has.

• • • • •

Over the course of the next three hours, I text Mai fourteen times.

ME:

I'm so sorry

Please let me explain

Mai?

I realize that last night was the first time I've referred to her as my friend, the first time I've had that thought in two years. I've been arrogant. I never should have assumed that I was done with my penance.

Underneath my desk in English, while Ms. O'Keefe has her red glasses buried in *The Secret History*, my phone finally buzzes. My stomach sears. Despite my begging, I'm not sure if I want to hear what Mai has to say to me after all.

Whether or not it counts as luck, it's a message from Margaret to the general chat in Clandestine.

MARGARET:

I cracked Mr. Holmes's laptop. Meet on the roof at lunch?

• • • • •

Since it's a Thursday, the red brick of the roof is blanketed in canvases. Today they're weighted down with sandbags to keep them from vanishing into the winter sky, wind slashing at my cheeks as I sit cross-legged in a circle with the seven other initiates and Zola. I've positioned myself across from her so that there's no risk of brushing her arm with my fingers. Although I guess it doesn't matter anymore.

Even with the reminder that this is what I deserve after what I did to Emily, my body aches with the resentment that this has to be my experience of love.

"Before Margaret shares her findings, there's something I should be clear about," Zola says evenly. "Kay and I are together."

My skin burns under the heat of seven pairs of eyes. Mai is the only one who isn't looking at me, her stare trained on the brick beneath her.

A choking sound emits from Aubrey's direction. "Are you fucking kidding me?"

God, it probably makes me no better than Aubrey herself, but I can't help feeling a twinge of satisfaction at that.

"I'll get ahead of any questions," Zola says. "First of all, this has nothing to do with the Blue Hand Girls. By coincidence, Kay and I sit at the same math table—Vanessa can confirm;

she's in our class—and we've been getting to know each other over the course of the school year. No, I haven't given her any hints or any advantages in the induction process. Yes, I divulged this information to the other members of the society as soon as our relationship began, and I have recused myself from all conversations surrounding her eligibility."

At her last sentence, my head shoots upward. I study her face: her elegant jawline stoic against the backdrop of gray sky, her bright eyes as unreadable as the agate geodes they resemble. This is the first I'm hearing that she's told anyone. I wonder if it's true.

"That's not really enough?" Tia says. "Like, no matter what you claim, you can't *not* be giving her preferential treatment, obviously."

I force myself to look at Margaret and Chioma. Margaret is wearing her cowl-necked jacket again, and the bottom half of her face is buried in the fabric. I can't figure out what she's thinking, and I don't think I want to. Meanwhile, Chioma's nostrils are flared, and her eyes are narrow. There's no misreading that.

I can't believe I've spent the past few weeks pushing Zola to go public. She was right. And now, because of my impatience and neediness, I've alienated the kinds of girls who would stab a teacher to protect me. I wonder if I should tell Zola that she has chosen to love an idiot.

"So here's the thing," Zola says to Tia. "You don't get to decide what the Blue Hand Girls will accept. And if you have a problem with that, you can open up Clandestine and take it up with any of the BHG members—go on, even the Killer, if that's what you want—but I can assure you that they'll tell you the same thing I have."

Tia rolls her eyes but doesn't say anything.

Zola clears her throat. "Now, if that's all, I'd like for Margaret—"

"Fuck this." Mai's voice is quiet as she pushes herself upward from our circle. "I'm getting out of here."

Between her messages last night and my betrayal this morning, I expected this—honestly, I was surprised that she appeared on the roof at all—but the pain is unbearable anyway.

"And that's your prerogative," Zola says, refusing to break eye contact with Mai. "But I don't know how the others here will feel about that. If and when your conscience begins to insist upon a confession, who will you tell about this group's extracurricular excursion to the file room? Who will you tell about the other black-clad figures in the alleyway with Mr. Holmes?"

Chioma shudders so hard that I can hear her coat rustle, even with its high thread count and smooth fabric. "Mai. Please. Don't do this."

The corners of Zola's mouth curve up into a smile that

doesn't add any softness to her face, still all chiseled bones and stark shadows. I remind myself that I love her.

Mai swallows and wraps her maroon Davison cardigan tighter around herself, today's earrings—peacock feathers, their iridescence glimmering in the midday sun—swinging in the wind. She shuts her eyes. Then she sits back down.

Between Chioma and Mai, I wonder which of them I've hurt more.

"As I was saying," Zola says, "Margaret, please share your findings with us."

Margaret opens Mr. Holmes's laptop where it has been resting on her knees and swivels it around to face the rest of us. "Um. Yeah. So the main thing is that Emily was right. Our applications have almost nothing to do with how the internships are assigned."

On the screen, there's a spreadsheet titled *Fall Internships, Senior Cohorts,* dated with the semester of Emily's death. The leftmost column is a list of six names, each one belonging to a girl who graduated two years ago. Then there's a column for interest area: banking, medicine, politics... The next column is labeled *Connection,* featuring the same fields as in the column before it, although there doesn't seem to be any relationship between the two in each row. Then the fourth column lists the internship placements.

Barrett Hensworthy. Interest: theater production. Connection: corporate law. Placement: Wicked Company Management.

Helene Beaumont. Interest: corporate law. Connection: AI technology. Placement: Garfield & Hobson.

Patricia Liu. Interest: AI technology. Connection: cosmetic surgery. Placement: Hinton Laboratories.

And that's it. Each application is distilled to a handful of characters, nothing in this sheet suggesting that Mr. Holmes, or anyone in the internship program, reads any of our answers beyond a glance at the sites we've ranked. I know that this isn't the point, but my stomach burns as I think about the sheer number of hours I've spent on my applications this semester alone.

"There are pages and pages of these," Margaret says, clicking through tabs at the bottom of the spreadsheet. Each tab is titled with a variation on the same name*Mixer_Subcommittee_1, Mixer_Subcommittee_2* etc.—the numbers climbing as Margaret flashes through the tabs, each one bare except for a new set of six names and those four obnoxiously sparse columns. "They go up to over a hundred, spanning all four grade levels and including more than half the students in the school. And there's a document like this for every season of internships, before and after the one when Emily died."

I force myself to fight through the sting of the revelation. "So we have a few clear pieces of information from this. One is that all the girls' interest areas line up with the connection areas of other girls in their cohorts, rather than with their own connections. So it seems like…the different girls are helping each other to secure their placements?"

"That doesn't make sense, though," Daphne says. "Helene was on the basketball team with me. Yeah, she had a connection to AI; her dad is a researcher, but I know that he worked at a university, not a random laboratory."

Margaret snaps the computer shut. "Hinton Labs is at the forefront of—"

"Not now," Zola says. "Margaret, we have more important things to talk about."

Margaret seethes into her cowl neck but doesn't say anything else. I glance between the two of them, wondering whether I can fool myself into seeing the exchange as a friendly spat between the important people in my life. The fantasy isn't worth the mental contortions.

"What about Parker?" Aubrey leans forward, her eyes unblinking.

Margaret taps her fingers across the closed screen of the laptop. "That's where I checked first, and there was nothing unexpected in her listing. Interested in banking, connected to pharmaceuticals, interned with Goldman Sachs."

"What about Bonum Solutions?" I ask. "Who wound up interning with them that semester?"

"No one of note," Margaret says. "Adora Charles, if you know her. She's a senior now."

"And none of you will doubt my sister anymore," Vanessa says, glaring around the circle.

"If you say so," Aubrey says. "Even without discussing Parker, I'd like to look more into why these tabs are labeled as mixer groups. It's very odd that the parent network is involved with the internships."

"Is it really?" I should stop myself, especially given that half these girls can't even look at me right now, but I suppose that also gives me nothing to lose. "Aubrey, you know that the parents in this school will intervene with anything that has the power to bolster their budding geniuses' college applications."

"Watch yourself," Chioma says, looking at me for the first time. I wish she hadn't.

"Kay, if you're able to put aside your jadedness, none of this makes sense," Margaret says. "I can't figure out the connection between the mixers, the industries of interest, or the industries of connection. And, overarchingly, I don't understand why the school assigns the internships the way that it does. But I think Emily did."

"Do you think she found these documents?" Tia asks.

"It's possible. But I think she found something else, either in addition or instead. There's clearly a missing piece here," Margaret says.

Daphne leans toward the center of our circle. "Oh, like a bug! Maybe the school is bugged, and she somehow found one? That would explain that Google search."

Margaret shrugs. "An alternative is that Mr. Holmes only writes out his important information by hand, like the notes in Emily's permanent records. She could have found something he'd written."

Aubrey twists her lips. "This is all speculation. We need a next step that's rooted in evidence."

For a moment, we sit in silence on the roof, the cold wind burrowing into my skin. As stupid as it feels, something compels me to voice the thought that's seeping through the crevices in my mind. "I wish Emily were here."

Aubrey snorts. "That certainly would resolve things."

Margaret shakes her head. "No. Wait. Kay is right."

"I am?" Even though I'm sure that Margaret's acknowledgment is purely professional, I feel my internal temperature spike a degree or two warmer.

"I mean, Emily may not be able to tell us what Mr. Holmes and the internship department are hiding, but she might have left some notes," Margaret says.

Before I can react to the reality of what she's suggesting, Chioma does it for me. "Absolutely not. No more illegal adventures. We are not breaking into anyone's home, especially not the home of a couple that has lost a daughter."

"It doesn't have to be, like, illegal," Vanessa says, examining Margaret through partially lidded eyes. "Kay, you were close with her, right? Why can't you just pay her parents a visit?"

"I—I can't." The words feel like they're stuck in my throat. "Not after what I did to her."

Margaret glares at me from behind her wire-framed glasses, a harshness I've never seen before twisting her face into right angles. "Don't get in the way of your chance to redeem yourself."

While I have no reason to think she's talking about anything other than Emily's death, it feels much more raw. And so—whether for her, for the Blue Hand Girls, or for Emily—I say, "I'll think about it."

"Excellent, my darling," Zola says, a grin finally breaking up the coldness of her features as her eyes settle upon me. "She'll do it. We have a plan."

I wonder if the truest version of Zola is the girl who cooks me goulash, or whether she's the creature of sinister commands and blue fountain pens that I pictured when the first note appeared in my locker a small lifetime ago. Regardless, she's something otherworldly, channeling all her radiance in my direction as my heart strains toward her, and I hope that whoever she is, her heart is straining back.

CHAPTER 13

As I sling my backpack onto my shoulder in preparation to leave AP Physics a few hours later, someone taps my shoulder. It's Lee, their other hand stuffing the last of their papers into their messenger bag.

"What's up?" I ask.

Lee drags a zipper across the mouth of the messenger bag. "Zola told me that you guys are public now. Congratulations."

My stomach drops. After so many weeks of speculation, I suppose that this is the confirmation I've been too afraid to seek out. Especially after learning that the organization affiliates itself with girlhood, I wasn't sure whether Lee would be eligible, but then again, I know how much the group cares about panache, and Blue Hand Nonmen doesn't quite roll off the tongue.

"Wow, uh, thanks," I say. "So…you've known since our first date?"

Lee removes a pair of leather gloves from the pocket of their oversize Davison blazer. "Zola isn't in my main friend group, and we might not seem like we have a lot in common, but yeah, I mean, we're pretty close. She really likes you, you know."

I feel a smile stretching out my lips. "So I've heard."

"I also wanted to tell you to be careful, though." Lee inserts their right hand into one of the gloves. "Zola can get pretty intense."

I don't allow my smile to falter, focusing on the dent in the wood of our physics table where Ruby dropped a five-thousand-gram block in September. "That's one of the things I like about her."

"Fair enough, but based on what I've learned about you over the course of this year, I wanted to make sure that you're down with some of her more unusual hobbies." Lee slips on their left glove and glances around. The tail of the rest of the class is disappearing out the door of the classroom, and our teacher has retreated into the adjoining office. "She has a weird talent for things like pyrotechnics, which comes in handy for tech theater, but that's definitely not why she learned it. Her dad was a shady guy, it sounds like—I get the impression that he's something like the Czech equivalent of the KGB—and he taught her some pretty advanced forms of self-defense."

I feel my breathing quicken. Lee's words don't come as a surprise, exactly. But they shine a cruel spotlight on the elements of my girlfriend that, until now, I'd been able to relegate to the shadows.

"I can take her." It comes out as a snap. "Sorry. I mean—don't worry about me."

If Lee is a member of the Blue Hand Girls, I can't let them see me as weak. But if they think I need a warning to be careful, it probably means I've failed to impress the group.

Lee gives me an easy smile and ambles toward the door of the Physics classroom. "Hey, I just wanted to make sure."

"Wait." I force my breathing to steady as Lee turns back to look at me over their shoulder. "Are you all really okay with me dating her? It's not...getting in the way?"

Beneath their curls, Lee's forehead crinkles. "Um...why would it?"

• • • • •

After four days of holding Zola's hand as I walk through Davison's palatial hallways, shifting under the weight of my exchange with Lee, and feverishly refreshing my Clandestine chat with Chioma, Mai, and Margaret in hopes of receiving a message that I know will never appear, I no longer have it in me to protest going to Emily's apartment.

I press my back into the trunk of a scrappy tree outside the concrete apartment building where I spent so many afternoons during the fall of freshman year. With one earbud tucked between the strands of my hair, I whisper, "Are you absolutely sure they're in there?"

Inside my earbud, Vanessa says, "Daphne and I have wasted the past, like, two hours on this corner. We saw them both go in."

"But what if they're taking out the trash—"

"They won't be fucking taking out the trash." Aubrey's voice is a low growl. "Stop procrastinating and ring their buzzer."

It's strange to see the rich girls in Crown Heights, their Burberry coats and Hermès scarves stark against the backdrop of crumbling row homes and iron fences with white paint flaking off into gasoline-stained driveways. As I hover in front of the apartment building, the rest of the group is pretending to peruse the bodega around the corner. I wish I were with them, smothering snickers as Vanessa puzzles over how a can of iced tea can cost only a dollar, instead of facing the family of the girl I betrayed.

I brush a hand over the bottle of anti-anxiety pills in the

pocket of my coat and approach the buzzer, steeling my breath as I press the button for apartment 1R. It rings twice. I tug at the flannel underneath my jacket—I never could have come here in my Davison uniform—and try to quell the shaking of my jaw.

"Hello?" Emily's mom sounds so much wearier than I remembered.

"Hi, Alaina," I say. "It's Kay. I was wondering if I could come in."

"Oh, sweetheart." Alaina's voice breaks. "Of course."

The Hendrickses' living room is exactly as I remember it, their leather couch scratched into tatters by their pair of tortoiseshell cats, Cleopatra and Marzipan, and their books spilling out of their shelves and into piles on the hardwood floor. Emily had just adopted the cats the summer before I met her, and the last time I saw them, they were small enough for her to cart one around on each shoulder. Now, as I sit on the Hendrickses' damask rocking chair, Marzipan's body hangs over both sides of my lap as she settles herself across my thighs. I don't deserve her purrs.

"I'm sorry it's taken me so long to visit," I say. "But...I don't know if Emily told you, but I, um, hurt her feelings pretty badly about a month before she passed."

"I'm sure she forgave you," Alaina says, the wrinkles in the corners of her eyes deepening as she talks. Emily's dad, Vaughn, sits next to Alaina on the couch, one arm around her.

"I remember your falling out. She was very upset. But in the days...right before, she told me that she was planning to text you. She said that no one understood her the way you did."

Picturing her text for the millionth time, I feel a knife twist in my heart. "I wish I'd been there."

"Sweetheart, you have no idea how much time I've spent wishing that I had done something different. If I had the resources to challenge the expulsion, if I'd told her to stay home that day—" Alaina shuts her eyes. "But we can't do that."

I hate myself for invading Emily's home, for taking solace in Marzipan's warmth stretched across my lap, for devouring the comfort that Alaina is offering me. More than anything, I hate myself for not coming long ago.

"How have you been for the past two years?" I ask. "Two years this Friday, I know. That's why I came."

Alaina crosses one side of her cardigan over the other like it's a wrap. "I won't pretend that it has been easy. But we have Tommy, you know, so we couldn't fall apart. Can you believe we're looking at high schools for him now?"

"Oh my gosh." Despite myself, I laugh. The last time I saw Tommy, his greatest delight was hurling basketballs at pigeons. "Where is he right now?"

"In his bedroom. Doing homework," Alaina says. "Things are different now."

She smiles at me again, but her eyes are cloudy. I wonder how quickly Tommy grew up after losing his older sister, with her immaculate grades and curated-for-colleges extracurricular list.

I inhale deeply. Now is my opportunity to do what I came to do, what I can tell myself over and over again is for Emily, but that feels like a violation at this point. "Speaking of bedrooms... do you mind if I go take a look at Emily's?"

"Of course not," Alaina says. She pushes herself off the couch, extending a hand to Vaughn as he does the same, his fingers trembling as they interlace with hers. The reminder of his MS sends another pang shooting through my chest. "Come on."

I give Marzipan a final scratch between her ears and set her gently on the rug, then follow Alaina down their hallway, which is lined with art that Emily and Tommy have produced over the years. The most recent addition is an architectural floor plan of a World War II–era battleship, drawn on thick graph paper, the lines of the ship ruler-straight. In the corner, it's signed *Thomas Hendricks, 8th grade*. My heart wrenches when I realize that it's more sophisticated than the last piece signed with Emily's name, a shaky watercolor of a melting candlestick.

When Alaina pushes open the door of Emily's bedroom, her scent rushes out into my nostrils, graphite and cinnamon perfume. The smell immobilizes me. I can't do anything except stand in the doorway, closing my eyes and pretending that she's next to me again.

Alaina places a hand on my shoulder. "Would you like to be alone with her?"

I nod but still can't make myself say anything. This is an ugly, ugly thing that I'm doing.

Her bedroom is exactly the way I remember it. Her tree of glass-bead pendants still sits atop her dresser; her tall bookcase overflows with secondhand copies of Agatha Christie books; and I can barely see the cork of the bulletin board opposite her closet, the board's surface smothered with doodles and Polaroid photos and calligraphed quotes written on scraps of cardstock. A postcard I got her is there—my favorite Salvador Dalí painting, which I bought for seventy-five cents at a thrift store near our tree house, and which she insisted I mail to her, even though she was with me when I purchased it. Suddenly I can't look at the bulletin board anymore.

Even though I know where I should be looking to find any secrets that might still be tucked into this room, I splay myself on the floor like I'm about to make a snow angel in her black shag carpet, my eyes fixed on the map of New York that she taped to her ceiling. She told me once that she memorized the train lines when she couldn't sleep. *The better you know the city, the better you can avoid problems," she said, her ever-moving fingertips dancing closer to mine, but never quite touching me. "Or, depending on your mood, the better you can chase them.*

Now that I'm closer to Emily than I've been since she died, it occurs to me that she would have been pleased to have her death examined by a group like the Blue Hand Girls. Of course, she would rather have been a member of such a group, but I guess that if you can't be the detective, you might as well be the subject.

"Kay, what are you doing in there, resurrecting her?" Aubrey says through my earbud.

"Sorry," I whisper, even though I'm not.

I take one more look at the map on the ceiling and force myself to prowl around the room. Once, around 2:00 a.m., during a sleepover that I thought might have been something...else... she showed me the two spots where she sealed up anything she considered private. At the time, that meant pieces of paper with Aubrey's doodles on them, which Aubrey had cast aside at the end of class and Emily snatched out of trash cans in Aubrey's wake. Now, as I mutter a silent apology to Emily's ghost and pull open the top drawer of her dresser—the first spot—I don't know what I'll find beneath the layer of socks. All the pairs are argyle, cashmere, or both. The memory of our first interaction punches me in the chest. For a moment my blue hand is stuck there, submerged in the balls of soft fabric.

But when I force my hand to unfreeze, my groping reveals nothing inside the drawer except high-quality socks. I shut the drawer and kneel by the side of Emily's bed, fumbling with the broken slat underneath her mattress, her second hiding spot occupying the gap between the pieces of the beam. My breath feels shaky as I stretch my arm deeper underneath the heavy pad until my fingertips reach the end of the slat.

And then they collide with something.

My heart slams as I pinch my fingers around a small wooden box and lift it out to sit on top of the mattress. The box is labeled in Sharpie, Emily's handwriting stark in all capitals: *IF THEY GET ME.*

I was wrong about Emily. She could never just be the subject of a true crime investigation. Even from beyond the grave, she couldn't hold herself back from solving her own murder.

My hands shake as I pull off the lid. When I look inside, I see three tightly folded pieces of loose leaf and a pen engraved with the name *A. Charles.*

I know I should wait for the rest of the group, especially Zola and the three girls who used to be my friends, but I didn't realize until now how much I need to know why they killed Emily. These past two years have felt like moving through sludge. The Blue Hand Girls have been the first beam of sunlight to penetrate the mass that surrounds me, but these papers might be a stick of dynamite.

As soon as I have that thought, I wish that my mind had suggested a different metaphor.

I unfold the first piece of paper. In the familiar jaggedness of her handwriting, far too many angles in her *r*'s and *g*'s, the page is titled *Car Tracking Log.*

Right underneath the title, there's a preface. *I'm starting this on Day 3 (I think) of being tailed by a silver Cadillac with tinted windows. Every time I see the car, I'm going to make a note of the date, time, and location. I'm also going to take down any notes about the car that could help to identify it.*

Below those few lines, she carries out her own instructions. The first date is within a week of her expulsion, and the last is two days before her death. In the notes section, she has only two additions:

- *I got a real look at the front license plate. It's coated with dirt—I think to obscure the numbers—but today I squinted hard and was able to make out an "AT6" at the beginning. I think the driver is a professional at this. They're really good at not letting me see who they are.*
- *They finally messed up. It wasn't much but they got close enough to me that I was able to drag my hand along the side of the car when it passed by. I had a fresh hangnail, so*

I tried to get blood on the car as DNA evidence.

I can almost see her writing this, her pencil scratching feverishly while her knee bounced up and down. She must have been so scared. And instead of being there for her, I was probably doing geometry homework.

I pull my phone out of my pocket and open the Timeline tab of the Clandestine app, reading through the blue-text questions interspersed with the sequence of events that we assembled that night on the roof.

Why was the school so quick to expel Emily?

Why did Emily really stop talking to Mai?

Why did Emily come to Vanessa's party?

Who did Emily think was coming after her? Why did she think that?

What was Emily talking about in her 'I was right' text to Kay?

What brought Emily to Kew Gardens on the day that she died?

What does Tia's car crash have to do with any of this?

The first question now has notes next to it, summarizing our conclusions after reading Emily's file: *The school knew that she was looking into them and got threatened.* There's nothing next to the second, but the third, also, has a note: *Emily was suspicious of Vanessa's sister, but we don't know why.*

As for the fourth question, this car-tracking log makes it pretty clear why Emily thought someone was coming after her: because someone was.

"Seriously, Kay, what's taking you so long?" Vanessa says in my ear.

"Just—just give me a sec," I say. "Still looking."

I unfold the second piece of loose leaf, and a fuchsia Post-it falls out. It's scrawled with an address, a date, and a time in handwriting I don't recognize.

There's nothing familiar about the time, but the date is one that I'll remember for the rest of my life. And the address is deep in Queens.

A wave of nausea crests within my throat, and I feel myself collapse sideways onto her bed. The scent of cinnamon perfume suffocates my nostrils as they press against the thick quilt on top of Emily's mattress. I wanted to find this. Honestly, I think she wanted me to find it, too; I doubt anyone else would have known where to look. Even so, neither she nor I should have assumed I was strong enough to stomach the answers.

I'm pathetic. Emily would be ashamed that this is the best I can do for her.

With one wavering arm, I push myself into a sitting position and grip the second piece of loose leaf, the page crinkling underneath fingertips that are pinching it far tighter than necessary.

When I went to a house party at Parker and Vanessa Hargrove's house, I found this Post-it stuck to the desk in their father's home office. Gregory Hargrove is the CEO of Argenta. After some Google Mapping, I see that the address leads to a storage locker. That must be where they're storing the proof I've been looking for. While I don't know what will happen at that date and time, I can only assume that it's important, especially if the kingpin himself will be there. So I'm going, too.

I want to scream at her, scream that no proof—whatever she's talking about—is enough to hurl herself into an undefined abyss like this. I don't remember her being this brave or this fucking stupid. Maybe the version of her that lives in my memory, single-minded but logical, existed because that's who she was with me. And when I wasn't there, she became overwhelmed by the frenetic energy that always pulsated within her limbs.

But that's disrespectful to her. The fact she left this box makes it very clear that she made her decisions consciously. And if she was this cemented in her choice, I don't think a continent of Kays could have convinced her to do anything else.

I need to keep reading. The third piece of loose leaf is clamped by the pen. When I unfold the page, sickness roiling in my stomach, my mind has enough mercy to override the nausea and absorb her words.

The top of the page features a date during the week before Emily's expulsion. Beneath it, she wrote:

Today I witnessed an exchange that I feel compelled to write down before I forget. I'd gone to Mr. Holmes's office to contest my internship rejection at Bonum Solutions and, while I was waiting outside, I overheard a conversation between Parker Hargrove and Adora Charles, who were also waiting for a meeting. I had earbuds in but wasn't listening to anything—the best way to eavesdrop—so I guess they didn't feel the need to restrict themselves in a hallway that was otherwise empty.

I started listening because Adora had been Bonum's intern over the summer. She presented in this semester's expo, and I spent just enough time at her booth to learn that she couldn't pronounce "micropolymerase." Parker was asking Adora whether she would want to work with Bonum again, and Adora was nodding so hard that I feared her head would fall off. Then Parker reached into her messenger bag and pulled out a very fancy pen. I'm recording their exact dialogue to the best of my memory:

Parker: I told my dad that you wanted this back as, like, a trophy or something, and he said that you could have it.

Adora: What can I say; I got used to writing with it. Did I record everything he needed?

Parker: He said you did good work.

Adora: Cool. It'll still write properly now that it's empty, right?

Parker: Obviously.

At that point, Mr. Holmes called in Parker, and Adora tucked the pen into her backpack. Then Parker headed out, and Adora left her backpack on the bench when she had her meeting, and let's just say that now her backpack is one fancy pen lighter than it was before she went in.

I think it's pretty clear what happened here. When you unscrew the pen, it has a hollow cavity just above the inkwell. And after overhearing that conversation, it doesn't take a genius to infer what used to be in there.

The thing is, I don't know if spying on Bonum was a one-off incident between Adora and Parker's family, or whether it goes deeper. What if the school is in on it? Besides, I don't have any actual proof, so for now the pen is just a pen, albeit a personalized Montblanc pen (!!!). I need to keep looking into things.

I'm not sure if I'm breathing. So this is it.

This is what Emily meant when she texted me that she was right.

Margaret was correct that Emily would have known exactly why Mr. Holmes organized his internship spreadsheets the way he did. The school was—is—definitely in on it. In the internship cohorts, girls weren't interning at the companies with which their peers had direct connections; they were interning at the competitors of those companies. So Adora worked at Bonum, used a bugged pen to record company secrets—that explains Emily's Google search about how small a bug could be—and then passed on the bug to Argenta.

That also explains the new MS drug that Argenta released last year, the expensive one, the one that competed with what Bonum had in the works. The one Bonum had promised to distribute for free.

And based on Mr. Holmes's spreadsheet, something like this is happening in every conceivable industry, in every semester, in every group of rich girls conspiring to keep their families sailing high on seas of blood.

The realizations are hitting me like hail, faster and faster now. Some of the interns, like Adora, clearly know that they're spying on competitor organizations. But Mai and Chioma, both of whom presented at this fall's internship expo, which now seems like a dog whistle for participating in the delivery of secrets, would never be okay with complicity in this kind of scheme. So someone must have bugged them without them realizing and… My eyes pause on the tree of pendants glinting from atop Emily's dresser. Holy shit. It's the missing jewelry. Their parents gave them the pieces at the beginning of the internships and then repossessed the jewelry to remove the bugs, returning the pieces once they were stripped of evidence, like Adora's pen. And Mai and Chioma blamed their own adolescent irresponsibility.

I stuff the papers back into the box and slide it into the pocket of my coat, then stick my arm under Emily's mattress again, groping between the splintered slats. If she found anything else, I need it. I'm not going to let her ghost keep screaming soundlessly in this room.

But there's nothing else under here, which makes sense, since she wouldn't have gone to that fucking storage locker if there were.

"What are you doing underneath my daughter's mattress?"

I yank my arm out and spin around. Alaina is seething in the doorway.

I didn't realize that my heart had stopped pounding, but I definitely feel it start up again, careening around my rib cage so hard that I fear it will burst through the bone. "Alaina, I'm sorry, I just thought—"

"You thought what? What could possibly justify this?"

"I thought I knew why—I wanted to see—"

"Oh God." Alaina's chest heaves. "You're playing detective, aren't you. You think you're the only one in the world who can figure out what happened. You don't think I spent months sleeping in the police station while they looked into the manhole explosion? You don't think I bankrupted myself hiring private investigator after private investigator, certain that one of them would find some kind of answer for why my baby girl died?"

I stare down at Emily's shag carpet so I don't have to see Alaina's face twisted with pain.

"They all said the same thing: it was an accident," Alaina says, her voice quiet but no less full of fury. "There was no reason. God snatched away my baby's life, and He didn't tell me why. And if God can't, neither can you."

"Alaina, I'm so sorry—"

"Get out."

I don't protest. Like the cockroach I am, I scuttle out of Emily's bedroom and through the streets of Crown Heights, clutching her box in my pocket and whispering apologies to a girl who will never be able to accept them.

• • • • •

When I reach the bodega, which is sandwiched between a glass apartment building with a NO-FEE RENTALS AVAILABLE sign and a dilapidated duplex with a porch constructed from wood so rotten that I'm surprised there isn't a hole through the boards, Vanessa's arms are crossed over her Burberry. "Did you learn anything?"

The sight of her silhouette ignites another crest of nausea in my stomach. Her sister knew what the school was doing, despite the innocence that Vanessa claimed on Parker's behalf. And I'm not a strong enough discerner of dishonesty to know whether that feigned innocence extends to Vanessa. "Uh, maybe we should take a night. You know, let things sit."

Zola looks at me strangely. "Absolutely not. Tell us what you found."

I guess I can't start acting cagey right now. Especially not in front of my girlfriend. My girlfriend, whom I love, even as her eyes fill with a hunger that I'm positive is for the intel I have, rather than for me.

"Okay." I sit down on the side of the curb, motioning for the others to join me, and then set the box on my lap.

Eight gasps rush out of the mouths surrounding me. Even Mai is looking right at me for the first time in days. "Kay, what is that?"

Warmth rushes through me at her direct address. Zola, too, beams at me from her seat next to me on the curb, her leg pressing into mine. "You've outdone yourself, my love."

Mai looks away again. But the warmth doesn't dissipate all

the way. I've figured this out. Maybe that means that I don't have to choose between Zola, Emily, or my friends. Maybe I can make them all proud.

As I start to walk them through the documents and my corresponding revelations, hearing myself talking faster as I get closer and closer to a conclusion, a gray van pulls up to the curb. It's probably going to make a delivery to the bodega. I shift my legs so that I'm not in the way of any rolling carts that they unload. "Between Mr. Holmes's laptop and Emily's account of what happened between Adora and Parker, I think there's enough proof to expose the school. The last piece, I think, is the car, since Emily left the DNA evidence. I don't know if it's still there after two years, but if we can locate the car, we might be able to get real proof that they were targeting her."

The door of the van opens, the only other motion on a silent street. Tia squints at me. "Wait, give me the car log? I want to see—"

As I hold out the page to Tia, another hand snatches it out from between my blue fingers. I follow it to its owner's face, horror burning in my chest.

Standing above me, flanked by two hulking security guards, her smile coated in her signature Davison-maroon lipstick, is Principal Ellison.

• • • • •

This is the third time in the past month that I've been inside Davison after hours, but the first that its iron doors have felt like a gateway to a dungeon.

After a silent van ride from Crown Heights to the Upper West Side, Principal Ellison motions for us to sit around the cherrywood conference table in her office. I've only been here once—last year, after winning the schoolwide history essay contest. Principal Ellison invited me in to congratulate me personally. That day, sunlight was pouring through the stained glass of the arched window behind Principal Ellison's desk, warming her bookcase of first editions and the Persian rug that stretches across the room's golden floorboards. Now the office is lit only by a lamp in the middle of the conference table and a fire flickering beside us, which casts harsh shadows across the principal's face as she clasps her hands on top of Emily's box at the head of the conference table.

"It's a real tragedy what happened to that girl," Principal Ellison says. "Even before the horror of her accident, she was clearly suffering all sorts of paranoid delusions about people being out to get her. This box represents the sobering revelation that we didn't realize the extent of her troubles. Remind me where you found this, Ms. Anderson?"

I press my knees together beneath the table and don't respond.

"Underneath Emily's mattress," Vanessa volunteers.

She must have been reporting back to her father from the beginning. That was why it was so easy for her to supply the recalled cough syrup for the heist. If only I had realized sooner that her family was the link between so many clues in our web. I glare at her, and she meets my eyes, cool beneath her thick eyelashes.

"Of course. The mattress," Principal Ellison says. "Now let's see what that poor girl thought was happening to her."

She shuffles the pages from inside Emily's box. I hate watching her fingers trace Emily's handwriting.

"The car…the pen…" She looks up. "Did Emily forget that thievery is strictly prohibited by the Davison code?"

Daphne scratches the back of her neck with her blue hand. "Um, are we in trouble?"

Unlike Vanessa, Daphne must not have been in on it. I scan the table, trying to read the faces of the other girls. Horror surges within me when I realize that I have no idea who I can trust. A few hours ago, I assumed Mai and Margaret were safe because they didn't seem to know their jewelry had been bugged, but what if I'm wrong?

I wonder if I can even trust Zola.

Her face is even more unreadable than the others', although underneath the table next to me, I can feel the motion of her knee wavering from side to side. I move my leg so that it's touching hers. She moves hers away, and my heart grows even colder.

"That's up to you." Principal Ellison smiles again. "After you hear the truth from me. There's a perfectly rational explanation for all of this, of course."

My throat is dry. I try to swallow, but I can't.

Principal Ellison folds up the pages and slots them back into the box. "I'll keep it simple. You all know that, here at Davison, we make it a priority to ensure that families are able to network so that they can achieve their goals. Ms. Anderson says as much in her school tours."

But I had no idea what the parents discussed in their networking sessions. And I certainly had no idea what they were willing to do to prevent those discussions from getting out.

"Now, when families place that kind of trust in us, we have to uphold our end of the bargain and preserve their privacy," Principal Ellison continues. "At this point it wouldn't be prudent of me to claim that Emily was wrong about our internship program. Several of you were already aware of this, and it's no issue to extend the knowledge to the rest of you. But it's unfortunate that Emily couldn't understand the sensitivity of the arrangement. And it's even more unfortunate that she dealt with such severe paranoia and that her demons wound up leading her to the spot of the accident."

"I don't understand," Daphne says, tugging on the sleeves of her sweatshirt until they cover her knuckles. "The only thing leading her to that spot was a pink Post-it she found in Mr. Hargrove's study."

For the first time, it occurs to me how easily Emily found that Post-it. Perhaps it wasn't a coincidence.

"My point is that it was entirely her choice to snoop in the study and then to travel to that address, particularly at that date and time," Principal Ellison says, leaning back in her chair. "There's nothing that any of us could have done."

"I brought her to that party." Daphne slams a fist against the table. All my muscles tense as the vibration travels through the wood and up my arms. "I'm—I'm the reason she's dead."

"Stop being a child," Vanessa snaps.

Mai squeezes Daphne's shoulder as she lifts her hands to cover her face, smothering a sob with her fingers. Daphne, the sturdy, unflappable point guard. I didn't know she could break like this.

I can only imagine what this will do to Margaret.

I swivel my eyes in Margaret's direction. She's a few seats away from me, seemingly transfixed by the fireplace. She must have completely shut down.

"Yeah, about the party," Aubrey says. "Margaret, was Emily in the study when you found her and put her in a cab?"

My eyes land on Margaret again. And that's when I realize that she might not be catatonic. She might just be...unsurprised.

She knew about the Post-it.

She might have even led Emily to it.

Suddenly, several moments in the last few weeks blaze into Technicolor in my memory. Margaret's eyes bulging during our first conversation in the stairwell as we climbed to the roof for our first gathering, when I joked that it was good she hadn't been involved with any murders. Margaret changing the subject in the teahouse when Mai and Chioma brought up the jewelry. Margaret clicking through the tabs in Mr. Holmes's spreadsheet so quickly that we couldn't really read anything except the first page, then shutting the computer and directing the conversation toward what we might find in Emily's apartment. If Margaret had shown us everything notable on that computer, which mixer subcommittee would we have found her name in?

I feel myself starting to choke. Chioma's head whips toward me and follows my eyes toward Margaret. In that moment, I watch Chioma come to the same conclusion I did, her eyelids stretching to reveal the white globes underneath and her lips parting with a sharp pucker. "What did you do?"

Margaret fiddles with her cowl neck. "I hope this doesn't get in the way of our friendship."

Chioma's throat emits a sound somewhere between a tut and a growl. "Are you fucking kidding me?"

"Language," Principal Ellison says. "You're still at school. Besides there's no need to blame Ms. O'Malley for the accident."

"Stop—calling it—an accident," Daphne says, her face still twisted.

"You don't think we would orchestrate the death of a child, do you?" Principal Ellison says. "I will be up-front and concede that the explosion was intentional, not a freak explosion from the sewers. A member of our community did plant a bomb inside the manhole, but our intention was only to dispose of the contents of the storage locker. Our community member was tasked with destroying equipment, not lives."

A twitch of motion cycles around the table as we all shift at Principal Ellison's words. Every pair of eyes is affixed upon the cherrywood of the table. Every pair but Zola's. With her gaze fixed on the fire, eyes unblinking, and her fingers pressed together in front of her lips, Zola whispers, "You're all fucking killers."

Principal Ellison twists her maroon-slathered mouth. "I shouldn't have to ask you girls twice. Keep it civil."

Strangely enough, I had almost forgotten about Zola. My girlfriend. The reason I'm in a room that I have the feeling I might never get to leave. I nudge her thigh with my knee again, and this time she presses back into me, the bone of her kneecap digging into my flesh even through two layers of fabric.

Aubrey leans across the table at the principal. "So, I guess, what still doesn't make sense is why you didn't stop us earlier. If you've known about our investigation the whole time, and you're willing to be up-front about the truth of the internship program, why didn't you prevent us from drugging that security guard? Or attacking Mr. Holmes?"

"An astute question, Ms. Clarke," Principal Ellison says. "Ms. O'Malley, why don't you take that one?"

"Do I have to?" Margaret asks. "They already hate me."

I can't even look at her right now.

"That doesn't matter, dear," Principal Ellison says, glaring at her.

Margaret sighs. "They wanted to treat it as a test of their security system. If you've noticed, that guard hasn't been on duty since the night we broke in. Then, with Mr. Holmes, since he runs the internship program and it's his job to protect all this information, they figured that getting attacked was a natural consequence for letting us piece together so much. They also wanted me to try hacking his laptop for real to see how well he had been encrypting the internship program's information. Not to speak for Principal Ellison, but I'm not sure if Mr. Holmes will still have a job when he gets out of the hospital."

Until tonight, fragility was the predominant characteristic I'd seen behind Margaret's glasses. Now, with the reflection of the flames flickering in her pupils, she looks like the enemy she has been all along.

"But there won't be any threats to that anymore." Principal Ellison tosses the box behind her into the fireplace.

A yelp escapes from Zola's throat as the box vanishes into the flames' embrace. Something ugly within me wonders whether it would elicit as much of a reaction if it were my body that Principal Ellison fed to the fire.

"That doesn't matter," Chioma says. "The car is still out there."

"No, um, it's not?" Tia finally pushes her ringlets out of her face. Like Daphne's, her eyes are red. I had no idea she was crying. "My brother crashed it two years ago."

A shiver encases my body. So that's the final piece.

There's no circle of hell hot enough for Tia's parents—people who could place their own children behind the steering wheel in order to destroy evidence of their involvement with Emily's death. Even if her brother thought he could crash the car without hurting himself, no one insisted that the fourteen-year-old stay out of the car. And she suffered for it.

If I ever go home again, I'm going to hug my mom for an hour.

After a pause, Aubrey asks, "What are you going to do with us?"

"I'm going to give you each a choice," Principal Ellison says. "Now you know the reality of the world your families are in… if you didn't already. You can wash that juvenile blue dye out of your skin, be mature about your newfound knowledge, and tell your parents that you're one of them now, or you can accept an expulsion and understand that, unfortunate as they may be, accidents do sometimes befall those who intend to divulge private information."

Principal Ellison reaches into her purse and pulls out a gray cloth. She unwraps it and lays it on the table. Lying in the center is the earring that Mr. Holmes wrenched out of my ear.

Terror flashes through my stomach. No one can know about that earring. Even if it means betraying both the girls I have loved.

"You can't give us an ultimatum like this," Mai says. She holds her chin aloft. "You know who my mother is. If you expel us, I'll make sure that every newspaper in the country knows what's going on at Davison High."

"Oh, sweetheart," Principal Ellison says. "Why do you think there was only one article published about Emily's death? Perhaps, more importantly, do you remember who encouraged you to reach out to Emily and ask probing questions after her expulsion?"

Mai's face goes pale. "My mom said that Emily needed a friend."

"Well, you know that my dad is the police commissioner," Daphne says, swallowing hard enough that I can see her Adam's apple flicker in her throat. "Even if Emily really did die by accident, blowing up the storage locker is still a crime."

Principal Ellison sighs. "Ms. Fillmore, dear, we do need to work on your powers of extrapolation. Quite similarly, why do you think the police ruled it an accident two years ago, and who suggested that you play ping-pong with Emily two years ago?"

Another sob jerks its way out of Daphne's mouth.

"Now, if we're finished with the Q&A, it's time for you all to make your choices," Principal Ellison says. "If you would like to remain a student at Davison, please rise."

Vanessa and Margaret are the first ones to stand, Vanessa confidently, Margaret with another apologetic glance in my direction. Fucking backstabber. Then Daphne wipes her face and pushes herself up to join them. I'm surprised to see her motion, but this isn't a real choice. Her entire future depends on her position as the point guard of Davison's basketball team. Mai rises next. "I can't let my family down," she whispers, I think mostly to herself.

At this point I can't keep my future dangling off the ledge. I shut my eyes and stand, nausea gurgling in my stomach, tugging up Zola to stand with me. She doesn't resist. When I open my eyes, I see that Chioma, Tia, and Aubrey are now standing, too.

“Oh, hm, I believe I misspoke,” Principal Ellison says, her eyes flitting between me, Zola, and Aubrey. “You don’t all have quite the same choice. For those of you whose families are already quite involved in Davison’s endeavors, it makes sense for you to remain enrolled. But for those who don’t have that same capacity. . .Ms. Anderson, Ms. Wolfe, and Ms. Clarke, I’m afraid that your only option is expulsion. Effective immediately.”

CHAPTER 14

I AM NO LONGER KAY Anderson.

Kay Anderson went to Davison High School. She was a student tour guide. She ruined the curve on AP Physics tests. She was probably going to Northwestern, and if she didn't get in, her safety school was NYU. She didn't have much in common with her peers—maybe because she was a little afraid of them, or rather, she was a little afraid of who she would become if she got too close with them—but it was okay because she only had a year and a half left of high school.

I am no one.

Northwestern wouldn't even deign to read my application at this point, let alone admit me. I'll be lucky if I'm able to go to a state school like my parents. I can't conceive of a version of my future where I can leave this behind. Who wants to hire a criminal to become a criminology professor?

As a final kindness in the burial for the friendship that we never really had, I asked Margaret to delete the email from my parents' inbox informing them of the expulsion so that I could tell them myself. She agreed. And then, when I got home, I couldn't do it. They asked me how school was and whether I accomplished everything I wanted during my group project meeting that I had to stay out so late for, and all I could do was nod and tell them how much I loved them. That's another thing that Kay Anderson had: parents who centered their lives around gifting her a future. I needed to pretend to be Kay Anderson for at least one more night.

So this morning, even though I have nowhere to be, I put on my gray slacks and maroon quarter-zip and leave my apartment at 7:10. "Have a good day at school, honey!" my mom calls from her spot at the kitchen island, a mug of tea clasped between her hands. "Love you!"

I wish I were worthy of her love.

As I walk to the train station, I cross the street at every red light, and I don't check to see whether there are cars coming. I consider waiting for green lights to turn red, too, but decide that would be melodramatic. When I'm on the train going into Manhattan, I watch the sunrise framed by the cold aluminum of the subway window, and I stare at the glowing orb until it's imprinted on the backs of my eyelids when I close my eyes.

I'm on my way to meet Zola. At this point she's the only thing left of Kay Anderson. Although, if I'm being honest, she may be part of the reason why Kay Anderson no longer exists, after spending the past six weeks gnawing on me until all that was left was bone and gristle.

But her hands are warm in mine, and her head nestles perfectly into the crook of my shoulder, and she has such radiant eyes. And if she's going to devour me, at least she does it with pretty teeth.

My phone buzzes as the train pulls into my station. It's a message in the Clandestine general chat. I thought I'd never open Clandestine again, but I can't muster the energy to be surprised.

The names of the six non-expelled initiates have been slashed from the membership list. Now I'm alone with Aubrey and the eight BHG aliases, seven of whom are shielded by an anonymity that I now recognize as cowardice.

The message is from the Killer.

THE KILLER:

THIS ISN'T OVER.

Like hell it isn't, Killer. Speak for yourself.

When I walk into the coffee shop on the Lower East Side—Zola suggested a location that was about as far as possible from Black Diamond, for which I'm grateful—she's curled up in an indigo velvet armchair next to a table with two speckled mugs sitting on it. The blue of the velvet reminds me that, for the first time since just before Halloween, I've forgotten to refresh the ink in my hand. Or maybe I didn't forget. I don't know.

"Here's your chai, darling," Zola says, sliding one of the mugs across the table.

I collapse into the armchair opposite hers and take a sip of the drink. It tastes like detergent. "Thanks."

"Did you get enough sleep?" Unlike me, Zola isn't wearing her Davison uniform. She's clad in the same semi-sheer white blouse she wore the night on the roof, along with a pair of trousers so high-waisted that they almost cover the fragility of her rib cage beneath her shirt.

I take another sip of the chai, hoping it will taste different upon a second pass. It doesn't. "What do you think?"

She places a hand on mine, both of us now cupping the handle of my mug. "I know that this feels like a blow, baby, but last night was a rather extraordinary victory. I mean, I knew that something was off with the school, but to hear Principal Ellison admit it—"

"Zola, what the fuck?" I slip my hand out from underneath

hers and set down my mug on the table. "Were you even there? They *won*. Unequivocally. We don't have a future anymore."

"Then we have nothing to lose, right?" Her voice sparkles.

Lee's warning, delivered from a perspective that may or may not know Zola as well as I do now, echoes in my ears. Has Zola always been unhinged, but I've been too distracted by her radiance to notice? And now, since all that's left is me and her, am I finally seeing her in her fullness?

I do my best to keep my voice even. "Zola…in Clandestine, are you the Killer?"

Zola rolls her eyes. "That's a ridiculous question, Kay."

That means yes. "I want to hear it anyway."

"Sure, fine, whatever. Maybe I'm all of them and none of them," Zola says. "I'm *Zola*. I'm your girlfriend who loves you. Isn't that what matters?"

I don't say anything.

She reaches across the table and takes my hands, both of them this time. Her own mug of coffee sits untouched next to the arm of her chair. "Baby," Zola says. "Do you doubt that I love you?"

A supernova blazes inside her eyes. But the thing about supernovas is that they destroy all life in a twenty-five-light-year radius around them.

"No," I say. For all the things missing from those galaxies, love isn't one of them.

She still looks unsatisfied. "Do you still love me?"

"I. . ." I love the girl who arranged a gingham blanket between graffiti tarps so that we could have a picnic on a roof. I love the girl who made me goulash every time she thought I wasn't eating enough home-cooked meals. I love the girl who cried into my quarter-zip as she told me how much she missed her dad.

I don't know what fraction of Zola that girl makes up, but whatever it is, I'm not sure it's enough.

"You don't." Zola's voice breaks. "You don't love me anymore."

And then she's that girl again, the supernova dimming, a rare flash of youth softening the angles of her face. And she's the girl I promised to protect. Even if she couldn't protect me.

"I—I do," I say. I grip her hands tightly within mine. "But you need to understand. We can't go around trying to make the school pay. We have to pick ourselves up and find another way to be okay."

She tugs away her hands, her voice cold again, the way it is when she speaks to the full group of initiates. "If you loved me, you wouldn't say that."

"Zola!" I hate how plaintive her name sounds coming out of my mouth. "They're going to kill us!"

"This is my world," Zola says, still hollow. "Without the Blue Hand Girls, I have nothing."

"You have me," I say quietly.

Zola squeezes her eyes shut. When she reopens them, the supernova crackles again. "And without the Blue Hand Girls, what's left of you?"

Her words slice me open, my organs screaming as they tumble out from inside my skeleton. But when my hands shoot to my chest cavity to protect my heart from joining the quivering pile at my feet, I find only a hollow cavern, and I remember that long ago, she scooped my heart out of my body and affixed it to her own.

"I'm not a Blue Hand Girl anymore."

I look down at my right hand. The ink has been saturating my skin for so long that it's still a grayish blue, even though it has been at least a full day since I've reapplied. I reach into the back pocket of my slacks to pull out a quarter, then press it into my palm so hard that it hurts the bones in my hand. When I lift it, there's a slight circular indentation in the dye.

"Kay?" Zola's eyes are so frantic that I don't know which part of her is inside them right now.

I slide the coin across the table, the blue-tinted side facing upward. "I think I owe you this."

And then I leave the coffee shop. She doesn't run after me. And I don't turn back.

• • • • •

I allow my feet to take me wherever they want, plunging me down the winding blocks that etch a labyrinth into lower Manhattan. They carry me past tattoo shops that won't open for another six hours, past bookstores with the first wave of holiday tourists weaving in and out of red-trimmed doors, past designer boutiques with oversize parkas drowning the mannequins in the windows. After about an hour of numb movement, I find myself staring up at the black metal gates of a garden I haven't visited for two years. A spike of pain threatens to puncture the opaque mass smothering my mind. Instead of questioning the unconscious wisdom of my feet, I shut my eyes and press my shoulder against the gate's bars, sidling through the barrier and into the garden.

The craggy rock of the path is coated with dry leaves, the echoes of their crunches ricocheting dully against withered tree trunks and splattering ponds. This is where I belong. Like everything else straining to survive as December stretches its maw around us, I am a whisper of something that used to be. A canopy of entangled branches blocks out the high-rises and the sunlight as I drag myself deeper into the garden.

I know what looms at the end of the path, but the opaque cloud shudders again when I arrive at the foot of the dry wooden steps of the tree house. I'm certain, though, that I have no option other than to climb.

The interior of the tree house is unchanged from the last time I saw it, olive cushions lining a slatted bench that cups two out of the four walls, and bookshelves stacked with encyclopedic volumes swarming the space between the top of the bench and the black-beamed ceiling. I tuck myself onto a cushion pulling my coat tight around me. The walls of the tree house barely block out the wind. But I deserve the lashes in my skin. What matters is that I'm alone.

I concentrate on the vibrations of my chest, which hasn't stopped heaving since I left the coffee shop. I can cry now. I'm allowed.

The tears don't come out.

I squeeze my eyes shut and open them again, gulping air and pushing it back out. I hunch over the bench as if the buildup of liquid requires gravity to spill out of me. I open my mouth, feeling the smoothness of my tongue along my teeth, and count the knots in the wood beams of the tree house floor, pretending that they compose a constellation.

I try the words out loud. "I don't love Zola Wolfe."

That's what breaks the dam.

I let my body shake until it can't move anymore. This morning, I had lost everything except the girl. Now I've simply lost everything.

I shouldn't be here. I should be banging on Davison's iron

door, begging them to take me back, or hauling myself to every decent public school in the city, hurling copies of my résumé on their admissions directors' desks. Even though Kay Anderson is dead, I am inside her body, and she would want me to keep operating it.

Whether in an attempt to placate or punish Kay Anderson, I'm not sure, but I plug in my earbuds and cue up the podcast episode that Emily played for me the first time we sat in this spot two years ago.

"Today, New York may be the city that never sleeps, but the 1920s brought in a whole different wave of creatures of the night." Aretha Colby's voice greets me like an old friend, whispering over the keening of the show's ever-present violin. "Today we'll be examining the history of the black widows who spun their webs in the pubs lining Wall Street..."

Aretha's croon guides me into another era, one in which I don't exist. The episode ends and blurs into another, and another, all from the fall when this tree house was my home. As the sound particles leak out of my earbuds, they reformulate themselves into the ghosts of the two girls who sat back-to-back on these cushions, chests heaving with synchronous breaths, daydreaming about what it would feel like to live big lives.

After about an hour, Aretha segues into an episode about a private school in California, where a college guidance counselor extorted parents in return for falsified athletic records, then colluded with Ivy League coaches to recruit the students. "These were the families honored at the school's gala, whose last names plastered the school hallways," Aretha says. "As it turns out, it's easy to be the star of a fake lacrosse team when your legacy is emblazoned on the donation plaque in the school lobby."

And, all of a sudden, Kay Anderson's ghost rushes back into my limbs.

I knew that the story sounded familiar.

Of all things, why would Zola lie about her initiation last year?

A horrible thought stirs on the floor of my mind, the most horrible one yet. My power of motion restored, I jab at the screen of my phone, silencing Aretha's narration. But it's too late. I can't erase the reality of what she has already whispered to me. And now that I know, I no longer have the privilege of trapping myself in this tree house forever, tucked into a pocket of the universe exempt from time and truth.

Emily's ghost stares at my earbuds as I tuck them into my bag and peel my back away from hers. "I'm sorry it took me so long to visit," I tell her. "I'll be with you again soon."

• • • • •

An hour later, I'm following a sixtysomething woman with wiry copper hair and a thick Eastern European accent as she gesticulates at a tapestry that stretches across almost a full wall in the gallery of the Czech Society of New York.

"The Bohemian Reformation created an outpouring of artistic progress," she says. "In this new age of individualism, Hussite leaders encouraged supporters to create paintings and weavings that reflected their personal interpretations of the church leadership. The more critical, of course, the better."

There are only three other people on this tour: a young mother and her toddler, who is clad in a snowsuit puffy enough to render him about as wide as he is tall, and a man who I can only assume has been around since the Bohemian Reformation himself. The man clears his throat, phlegm rattling in his dusty esophagus. "Lots of scenes about martyrdom, then?"

"Yes," the tour guide says, waving her hand in front of a tapestry section that features several peasants weeping underneath a cross. "That appears as a common theme throughout many of our relics from this period."

"How about the Clean Hand Girls?" I ask. "Were they at all influenced by that part of the culture?"

The young mother peers at me, as does the tour guide. I imagine myself through their eyes: a uniformed teenager, who should almost certainly be in school right now, with hair several shades too dark and cheekbones several degrees too soft to be perceived as ethnically Czech. But twenty dollars of my tutoring money is tucked into the clear box atop the admissions desk at the front of the Czech Society—a suggested donation that, I felt, served as a necessary toll for the information I came here seeking—and I suppose that's enough for the tour guide to keep her questions to herself.

"Martyrdom was a core part of the Clean Hand Girls' ethos," the tour guide says. She gestures to a painting on the wall opposite the tapestry. The painting features the body of a pale young woman floating in a creek, blue-gloved hands clasped over her chest. "In most cases, the Clean Hand Girls served roles similar to those of modern-day vigilantes, but the religious overtones of the era permeated the culture's idea of what justice looked like. So when a Clean Hand Girl's master committed a crime that was considered unforgivable, like murdering a child, the Clean Hand Girl typically committed suicide in accordance with the cultural belief that an intentionally martyred soul was the only universal cure for evil."

Even though heat is hissing out of the radiator next to me, a shiver shoots down my neck. I shouldn't have asked that—or, anything, really. I just need to get through the tour as efficiently as possible. It's my entryway into the Czech Society, but fifteenth-century art won't yield the answers I came here to find.

After the tour guide finishes a sermon about the last piece in the gallery, a parchment scroll depicting several papal lackeys bowing to the devil, the other tour participants drift into the community room next door. This is my opportunity. I fall into step with the tour guide, my heart palpitating. "That was really informative," I say. "Thank you."

She smiles and adjusts her cardigan. "It's not often that young people like you come here."

"Well, um, a friend got me into Reformation art," I say, trying not to choke on the word *friend.* "You might have seen her around here, actually. Tall, red hair, uniform like mine?"

"Sorry, dear," she says. "I only started volunteering here a few months ago, and I don't think your friend has come in recently."

Holding back a string of swears, I ask, "Is there anyone else who might know her? I'm looking to, uh, learn a bit more about her taste in preparation for...a birthday gift."

"I'm the only one on duty right now," the tour guide says. "You know, you caught us on a busy day. The Czech Society isn't usually this packed."

I glance through the doorway into the community room, empty except for the three other patrons. The toddler is tugging his mother toward a leather sofa bench, and the old man is scribbling a note in the guest book, which is splayed open on a podium next to the front desk.

"Thanks anyway. I...really enjoyed the tour." My twenty dollars failed to buy me admission to Zola's mind. I don't know where else I might find a doorway. Maybe I could ask Lee, but based on our last conversation, I'm not sure that they would know the kinds of secrets that would clarify just how deep her lies go.

As I turn toward the community room, my eyes fall on the young mother again, and I feel a jolt in my mind. There's something familiar about the fluidity of her movement as she allows herself to fall onto the bench. "Wait, sorry, one more question."

The tour guide tightens the knot on the embroidered scarf around her neck. "Yes?"

"The Czech Society didn't have a section in the Halloween parade, did you?"

"Oh, yes!" The tour guide gestures at the young mother. "Jana here represented us as part of a lovely traditional dance routine. They all dressed as Clean Hand Girls."

My stomach lurches. I mutter a final thank-you and rush into the community room toward Jana, her toddler now nestled on her lap.

"Sorry, hey, I know this is a little odd, but do you know a girl named Zola Wolfe?" I ask, hovering at the side of the bench.

Jana bounces the toddler from side to side. "She used to come in pretty often. Not so much anymore. Why do you ask?"

I search for an excuse, but this time my mind remains an abyss, blank except for the truth. "I've realized that I don't know her as well as I thought I did. I hoped that coming here would fix that."

Jana puffs out a breath, sandy hair fluttering around her face in the burst of air. "If you ask me, that's a futile quest. She barely talked to anyone during the months she spent skulking around this place."

The desire to defend Zola surges within me, but I ignore it. "So she was...always alone here? She never brought any friends to the society? She wouldn't have come here with a group of, say, seven other girls, all probably wearing maroon sweaters, right?"

Jana snorts. "I doubt she knew seven other girls, and I've only seen that uniform on the two of you."

Panic bubbles in my stomach as the most frightening possibility dawns on me.

To my right, the old man finishes his note in the guest book and ambles toward the front door. I nod at Jana, then move to brace myself on the podium, hunching over the guest book and trying to push down the nausea thrusting in my stomach. I shove my hand into my pocket and pull out my phone, staring at the aliases in Clandestine. The odds are incredibly low—maybe nonexistent—that none of the other Blue Hand Girls would have visited the Czech Society. But that would mean something I can't allow myself to believe.

The old man's message peeks out from beneath my phone. *Thank you for preserving the art of our forefathers.* It's the fourth sentence on the page, all expressing similar sentiments through different handwriting, underneath a heading titled *December.*

The book is thick, open to a page about three-quarters of the way through the volume. I set my phone next to the book, my heart slamming. What if...?

I flip back through the pages. January of this year, July of last... I don't know whether I should be looking for the careful print of the letters that arrived in my locker or the messy scrawl of Zola's calc notes. But, as it turns out, it's very clear which message I want. On the page with notes from two Decembers ago, in dark blue ink that bleeds just a bit around the corners of the pen strokes, there's a line that's an unmistakable blend of the two. It begins with neatly formed letters and then devolves into messier and messier handwriting, words blurring into each other toward the end of the sentence:

If my dad had a Clean Hand Girl, maybe he wouldn't have had to run.

And then all the horrible possibilities click together into one horrible truth.

Long before I fell in love with her, Zola Wolfe ceased to exist. If AP Physics has taught me anything, it's that any supernova happens light-years before it becomes visible from Earth. The girl I thought I loved was either a walking memory or a composite of Zola's fragments, like broken shards of a mirror impersonating a single sheet of glass. Given what I've learned today, it seems more apt to picture her as the fragments. Eight fragments, to be specific.

Either way, Emily wasn't the only girl who exploded two years ago.

The nausea pins me to the podium, where I remain collapsed over the guest book until I can muster the wherewithal to drag my phone to the center of the pages. My fingers shaking, I open a group text with Chioma and Mai, Clandestine be damned.

ME:

I need your help

Mai responds almost immediately.

MAI:

I'm sorry, Kay. I'm not mad at you anymore, or anything, but I think we should all stay away from each other right now

CHIOMA:

Me too, I wish things were different

I thought I left my heart in the coffee shop with Zola, or in the tree house with Emily's ghost. But now, I realize that there are at least two chunks squelching through the Davison hallways, their hosts pretending they are still wholly themselves after last night. Their hosts are wrong.

There's only one more thing I can do right now, I think. Kay Anderson would hate me for it. But it's the only thing that I can imagine giving me some whisper of peace inside the thick dark air.

My fingers numb, I open my messages again and text Aubrey Clarke.

• • • • •

"Now this wasn't on my Blue Hand Girls bingo card," Aubrey says, her legs stretched out across two chairs in the reading section of a branch library in Midtown. "Kay Anderson asking me for help."

"Don't be arrogant about it," I say, draping my backpack across the back of my own chair.

Unlike the last time I met Aubrey at a library, in the Rose Reading Room of the Schwarzman Building, this space is small to the point of being cramped. Simple wooden chairs and brown leather couches cram into the community room, bookshelves lining three of its walls and unadorned rectangular windows lining its fourth. Despite the place having too much furniture for its square footage, it feels like there's room to exhale here.

"So you've learned something?" Aubrey hunches forward onto the table that separates the two of us, a book titled *The Student's Rights: New York* face down in front of her.

I nod. "Brace yourself. It'll be worse than you think."

Aubrey twists the silver ring around her right index finger. "I'm not sure if that's possible."

I lean across the table toward her, speaking quietly, even though we're the only ones in this corner of the room. As I talk, the words trip over themselves, desperate to spill out of my mouth. Aubrey clamps her fingers around the book in front of her, the skin stretching tighter and tighter over her knuckles as my explanation continues.

When I finish, she stares at me for a moment before opening her mouth. When she does, it's to mutter, "Motherfucker."

"Yeah."

"I'm taking this to Davison." She snaps the covers of the book shut. "They expelled us because they don't think we can offer anything valuable to them, but if we bring this to the administration, they'll be groveling with gratitude. And they're sure as shit going to let us—"

"No." I reach my blue hand—God, I wish it weren't blue anymore—across the table and rest it on top of Aubrey's forearm. "Those people don't negotiate. Forget Davison; we need to stop the monster we helped unleash before it causes another tragedy."

Aubrey removes her arm from beneath my fingers, but collapses back in her chair. "You're talking about the message in Clandestine this morning, I assume?"

The sick feeling rears itself again in my stomach. "Yes."

"I think we both know what the Killer will consider to be the ultimate reciprocation of justice," Aubrey says. "And given that the next Davison family mixer is in three days, I think it's safe to bet that's the setting of her big finale."

"And we have to stop it." I'm surprised by how unwaveringly the words come out. "It's our responsibility, no matter the cost."

Aubrey runs a hand through her hair. Maybe the room is humid; like that day in the rain, it stays out of her face this time. Underneath her bangs, Aubrey's expression is softer than I expected. "You know, I'm surprised you're able to approach the situation with this much clarity. I know you're in love with Zola."

I don't say anything, but my face must answer for me.

"Oh, man," Aubrey says. "Well...good for you."

"Why are you being so nice to me?" I sound pathetic, I'm sure, but I can't stop myself. "I've been a shitty coconspirator every time you've asked for my help."

Aubrey shrugs. "I think you fundamentally misunderstand who I am. In freshman year, you got it into your head that I'm your enemy. As I've told you before, I didn't mind; I needed you out of my way when I was starting to look into Emily's death. But I've always wanted the same thing: to know as much as possible about everyone around me while giving away as little as possible about myself. And in every situation, I make a new calculation about whether a relationship will be helpful in achieving my goals. What you don't seem to get is that, since the beginning of this year, the majority of my calculations have selected you as my most natural ally."

She's telling me what I've known all along: that she's a snake. But because she doesn't hide her scales, she might be more honest than any of the girls I've wanted so badly to call my friends.

I pull at the zipper of my quarter-zip. "What about Emily? And the day in the park with Zola?"

"I also like getting the girl. You got it right that we tend to be on opposite sides in those situations. But I can admit when I'm beat, and in the case of Zola...you won," Aubrey says, twisting her ring again. "Of course, she turned out to be a psycho. So that's not a great look for you."

"She's complicated," I say. It's the same justification I used with Mai, Chioma, and Margaret. I can't believe that was only last week. I can't believe I'm still using that defense. I tell myself that this will be the last time I do.

"Sure she is," Aubrey says. "Let's figure out how to take her down."

CHAPTER 15

On Friday I leave my apartment at 7:10 a.m. and spend the day walking to Davison. I'm already dressed for the mixer: my Docs and a suit that I found at the thrift store near my apartment yesterday after a three-hour block of tutoring the fourth grader upstairs. The suit was in a pile between a folded-up brocade curtain and a tulle monstrosity that almost smothered the pin-striped fabric beneath it, but when I tugged on the black lapel poking out from beneath the skirt, the suit came tumbling out, and I knew it was meant to be mine. It doesn't fit perfectly, but it's close enough that some hem tape makes it look like it does. I considered dressing in all black for the sake of emulating spyhood à la Blue Hand Girls or wearing my Davison uniform to signal that I'm a part of the school whether Principal Ellison likes it or not, but neither of those entities gets to claim me tonight.

Kay Anderson remains on hospice inside me as I walk her closer and closer to Davison. I'm almost positive that she's going to die today. Whether I'll die with her remains to be seen, but the odds are high. On the off chance that I survive, I'll still have to unhook Kay Anderson's life support from her heart, kiss her on the forehead, and wish her a good night.

So as I walk through the city—first Bed-Stuy, then Williamsburg, then across the bridge into the Lower East Side—I try to hold up Kay Anderson so that she can see through my eyes. She appreciates that, I think. I take her past the garden with the tree house, where we pay another brief visit to Emily's ghost, and past the Greenwich Village walk-up with Dorothy's tucked behind the beaded curtain on its second floor. I realize that several teardrops are nestled in the neck of my winter coat, and I don't know which part of me has been crying.

The city seems to know that it's hosting a funeral. The bare trees in Union Square Park bow as I walk past them, their branches scraping the sky mournfully. This is where I went after my first tutoring session with the fourth grader, when I gifted myself figs and brie from the artisanal deli a block away and had a picnic against one of the tree trunks on the west lawn. I continue north, past the holiday shops at Bryant Park, where I bought my first leather notebook in middle school, and past the Nordstrom on Broadway, where I bought my first pair of wool socks in freshman year. When I reach the fountain in Columbus Circle, which is dry for the winter, I see a crow hopping in and out of the stone basin, flailing its feet for a splash that won't come. "Hey, buddy," I whisper to it. "You might have more luck if you sneak into the Whole Foods. I bet you can take a bath in one of the pickle barrels."

The crow tilts its head and hops closer to me. It's a rather regal-looking crow, with sleek feathers and a sharp beak. In the sunlight, there's a streak of sandy-brown feathers across its right temple. I take a photo of the crow and text it to Aunt Shell; the promise I made to myself no longer applies, since this might be my last night.

ME:

This guy reminds me of you. I hope you're doing okay

Kay Anderson would appreciate that.

By the time I'm passing the brownstones of the Upper West Side, there are still several hours between now and the start of the mixer. I turn into a tiny coffee shop that's far enough from Davison that I can probably count on solitude, and I use the last of this week's tutoring money to buy a large chai. Inhaling the tangled scents of cinnamon and cardamom, I situate myself on one of the three seats in the shop, all of which face the wooden countertop that protrudes from the inside of the window. The paper cup warms my hands as I take a sip. It must be a house blend, a flavor even more multilayered than those of the twenty-four-hour teahouse. Closing my eyes and squeezing the cup between my hands, I can almost forget what I'm about to do.

From the inside of my chest, Kay Anderson wraps her frail hands around the bars of my rib cage and says, *You owe me.*

I've tried to pin and tuck and scrub my body into a version of itself that Kay Anderson would recognize. Last night I spent about half an hour scouring my palm in an attempt to banish the rest of the blue ink. But after so many weeks of inviting the ink into my skin, the blue is woven into my cells, tinting my hand a blueish gray that I don't know will ever leave me completely. Kay Anderson still wouldn't recognize the hand as hers.

In a final attempt to placate her, I take out my phone and open Northwestern's website, as if shoving an iPad in front of a toddler. The website's home page glows a familiar blueberry purple, a balm from the Davison maroon. Inside me, Kay Anderson smiles. As the page finishes loading, a silver banner flashes across the top of the screen: *Applications now open for our summer pre-college program!*

Kay Anderson musters all her remaining might to shake the bones of my rib cage. *Apply. Apply.*

I wonder if she knows that she's terminally ill. I wonder if that would stop her.

I have about ninety minutes left of Kay Anderson, and I suppose that the least I can do for her is make sure that Northwestern knows that she exists.

I tap the link. There's an option to specialize in the social sciences, including a course in criminology. Coughing and collapsed back into her hospital bed inside my chest, Kay Anderson begins to dictate an application, a modified version of the essay that she wrote and rewrote for her futile applications to the Quinn Center for Justice.

What are the issues that motivate you to study people, hierarchies, and societies?

Kay Anderson's voice blends with my own as I tell Northwestern that I have no idea what motivates the wealthy to go to such lengths to expand their hoards. I've seen the depth of it now. Maybe there's some degree to which I can empathize with a family like Mai's, one that might orchestrate media cover-ups and even commit murder in order to clear a path for their children. But parents like Tia's, who are willing to turn their own children into casualties, remain utterly opaque to me.

Part of me hopes that I never understand them, but a bigger part of me is still desperate to know. And with that, I make up my mind: if I survive tonight, I will not allow Davison to castrate me. I'll wrestle through public school and claw my way into Northwestern. Once I'm a criminology professor—and I *will* be a criminology professor—I'll study until I understand how a school like this can come to be. And somehow, when I get it, I'll do my best to dismantle this place. No more Emilys.

A text from Aubrey buzzes at the top of my screen.

AUBREY:

All good to meet in 10?

ME:

Yeah. Remember: I don't want to hurt her

AUBREY:

I agreed to that four times already. See you in a few.

I toggle back to the Northwestern website, hit Submit, and slip my phone into my pocket, maybe for the last time.

• • • • •

It isn't hard to blend into the black-jacketed tidal wave of families sailing between Davison's iron doors. Maybe no one else is wearing a pin-striped suit beneath their coat, but there's enough variety in the formal wear that the security guards won't identify me as a threat. It makes me sick to know that, even though Davison doesn't want me here, it's them I'm here to protect: the school that has cast me off like a stained pair of socks.

As we dragged ourselves out of Davison on Monday night, Aubrey overheard Vanessa tell Chioma that she would see her in Subcommittee Eight, and Aubrey is almost certain that Zola overheard as well. And, according to the chart posted on the lobby wall, Subcommittee Eight is meeting in the tenth-grade English classroom behind the atrium. Popping my jacket collar so that it blocks as much of my face as possible without looking like I'm trying to hide, I weave between three navy-vested tech-bro dads and a gaggle of freshmen in tinselly holiday dresses, training my eyes on the linoleum floor of the lobby. After rounding the corner into one of the hallways next to the atrium, I'm alone. I try to minimize the squeaking of my oxfords as I jog until I reach the classroom door.

Aubrey is already inside, her work boots planted on the teacher's mahogany desk as she rifles through the cupboard behind it. She glances toward me when I open the door. "I got in earlier than I expected, and I already covered most of this wall. Nothing planted. You get the back wall."

It's a typical Davison classroom, with the student desks pushed together into oaken clusters and lanterns dangling from the ceiling, illuminating the space when sunlight isn't rushing through the tall windows. Aubrey and I didn't have much trouble agreeing on what we needed to look for. Lee told me outright that Zola's father had taught her how to create explosives. And when you consider how Emily was killed and factor in the knowledge that everyone who orchestrated her death will be gathering in a single room, it doesn't take a lot of critical thinking to figure out how the Blue Hand Girls, or at least Zola, intend to serve justice. Or to guess what's hidden somewhere in these cabinets.

Aubrey and I are both wearing the precise digital watches from the assault-and-battery goodie bags Tia gave us before we attacked Mr. Holmes. Once again, I'm reminded that the Blue Hand Girls couldn't have designed a better final challenge if they'd tried.

My watch tells me that there are twenty-four minutes to the start time of their meeting, which means that we have roughly nine minutes before an administrator comes to set up. My heartbeat feels like a kick in the chest as I bend down to open the first supply closet on the back wall. Three-foot-high cabinets fill the space between the floor and the windows, a green marble countertop sitting atop them, supporting wooden bins and stacks of books. This closet is packed with copies of *The Great Gatsby*—an interesting choice for this school, I remember thinking when we read it last year—and doesn't seem to have space for anything else.

The next closet over is more jumbled, with stacks of colored pencils and cardstock jammed in at odd angles. My heartbeat quickens. This seems promising. My hands tremble as I turn over the art supplies, all too aware of both the time pressure and the possibility of accidentally pulling the wrong wire. But as I reach the back of the cabinet, all my hands press against is wood. I move down the line, closet by closet, the odds getting higher and higher that the next one will house the bomb I've come here to find. But when I reach the other end of the wall, I have yet to encounter anything more threatening than a pile of rubrics for the class's next literary essay.

By this point we have four minutes left. Aubrey has already covered the wall to the left of the entrance, and the front wall is flat, housing only a floor-to-ceiling collage of illustrations from Lewis Carroll novels. We exchange a look. The tail of Aubrey's white dress shirt is sticking out of her trousers, and the top several buttons are open, revealing two silver chains draped over her clavicle. Her upper lip shines with sweat.

Even in the initiation missions, I don't think I ever saw her look disheveled. Trying to keep my voice strong, I say, "Let's check under the desks. You take the right half of the room; I'll take the left."

The desks pass faster than the cabinets, easier to check with a glance and a shine of a phone flashlight. In another two minutes, we're straightened up again, panting but still empty-handed.

"Fuck," Aubrey says, raking her hair away from her eyes. I can see the skin of her forehead stretch upward from the strength of her tug.

"Okay. Okay," I say. "Let's think logically. We've looked in all directions, including the ground. I don't think we could have missed it. Maybe it's not in the room after all? Or maybe we were wrong?"

Aubrey shakes her head slowly. "We didn't look in all directions."

Wordlessly she points upward. The ceiling is flat, bare except for a few mahogany accent beams and the AC vent.

The AC vent.

"Listen," Aubrey says.

There's nothing remarkable about the vent, either visually or auditorily. It's a square box, maybe a foot by a foot, screwed into the ceiling. It's also dormant at this time of year, so it won't push air into the room for at least another four months. But I can hear something emitting from the ceiling: a slight rhythmic scraping, the sound crawling closer and closer to the vent.

Aubrey and I throw ourselves toward the door. "Do you know where there's an entrance to the vent system?" she asks, yanking on the handle.

I freeze. Of course I don't.

Wait.

"The second-floor supply closet." I race through the door,

checking to make sure that Aubrey is following me, and pull open the door of the stairwell.

But just as the stairwell door shuts behind us, I hear a voice coming from the hallway. One of my arms shoots out to halt Aubrey's footsteps. "Thank you all for joining me tonight, particularly our newest members," Principal Ellison is saying. "And since we have so much to discuss this evening, I appreciate you starting a few minutes early."

Slowly, I raise my face to see through the window in the door. Principal Ellison is leading a procession of Davison families down the hallway toward the English classroom. Two silver-haired men follow directly behind her, one white and wearing a gray vest over a light plaid button-down, one Nigerian and wearing a sharp forest-green suit. Vanessa and Chioma are a half step behind them, Vanessa's mountain of glossy chestnut hair bouncing in rhythm with her Burberry booties and Chioma's fingers twitching as she picks at her nail beds. They're all there. It's not a surprise, but it brings the situation into icy clarity.

"Kay, what are you doing?" Aubrey pulls me up the stairs. "We're losing time."

I push down the thought and hurry after her. The second-floor supply closet is only a few doors away from the stairwell. Based on the fact that we heard the bomb moving, someone must be in the closet right now. As we rush through the second-floor hallway, I send up one final prayer that I'm wrong about the Blue Hand Girls and there will be someone other than Zola inside.

I wonder how they would view me right now if they were able to watch from afar, rather than as the enemy in the closet. Am I acting as a missionary of justice in my quest to prevent the deaths of my peers? Or are they so much the arbiters of righteousness that the act of deviating from their instructions is in itself a sin?

I yank open the handle to the second-floor stairwell door. Ten seconds until I confirm who has been testing me over these past six weeks. Ten seconds until I know whom I'm going to betray tonight.

I run past a stone water fountain, past a mosaic of the Davison crest, past a row of maroon lockers until I reach the door of the second-floor supply closet. Aubrey stops short beside me. For a second I hesitate. Suddenly, the ignorance of what's behind that door feels too sweet to abandon.

But if I don't open the door, Aubrey will, and something in me insists that I have to be the one to confront my fate. So I twist the handle.

Zola squats alone over the open vent in the floor of the supply closet, pushing a long metal rod into the abyss. On the shelf above her, the Clorox containers disappear behind a curlicued gold picture frame surrounding a photo of a broad-nosed man holding a little girl with cascading red hair and intense blue eyes.

And there is no more possibility of uncertainty.

"Aubrey, go wait outside the classroom and evacuate it if necessary. Let me talk to Zola," I say.

Zola stares up at me, shock etched across her face. "Kay, go away. You shouldn't be here—"

"On it." Aubrey vanishes back into the stairwell.

"Please," I whisper to Zola. "You don't want to do this. Take out the bomb."

Zola slides the rod out of the vent. There's nothing attached to it. I recognize the rod now; it usually leans against the corner of the supply closet, a hook on the end waiting to remove items from high shelves. Zola plants it on the patch of floor behind the open vent, the thud reverberating across the floorboards. "Kay. I told you. Get. Out."

I step into the supply closet and pull the door shut behind me. It's just the two of us now, between rusty shelves stacked with Windex and carpet cleaner, underneath the dangling light of the single exposed bulb. Really, it's always been the two of us.

"I won't leave until you turn it off."

Zola lunges at me, scrabbling for the door handle. I shove

my back against the door so that she can't get to it. "Kay, what do you want? I need you to get the fuck out!"

As she presses herself against me, I grab her wrists and wrap my arms around her. The familiarity of her body on mine makes me want to cry. "At least—at least let me talk to you."

She stops struggling in my arms. "But after that, you'll leave."

"If you can convince me, I will. I promise." She goes completely slack, and I allow her to take a step back but don't let go of her wrists. "How long until it goes off?"

She shifts. "Six minutes."

"Okay." My heart is beating faster than it has ever beaten. "First of all, you should know that I know everything."

"That's impossible," Zola says.

"I know that there are no Blue Hand Girls."

I hold my breath, a part of my heart still begging her to tell me I'm wrong.

"Fuck." Zola spits into the vent. "It was my fault, wasn't it? I shouldn't have made that comment about being all and none of the aliases."

She hurls herself at me again, and I pull her into me for a second time.

"Zola, I'm not going to let you win," I say. "I'm not going to let you kill these people."

I want to be furious with her. She deserves it. After the

universe of lies that she spun while telling me that she loved me. But behind the supernova in her eyes, desperate and wild, there's a girl who is too lost to be the object of my hatred.

"I—I don't understand," Zola says. "Why aren't you just evacuating the classroom with Aubrey?"

Even though she's limp again, I don't stop holding her this time. "Because I want you to be the one to end this."

Five minutes until the bomb goes off.

I take in another shuddering breath. "I'm going to tell you what I think happened. If I'm wrong, you can correct me. And if I'm right, you'll hear me out as to why you have to stop the bomb."

"I've made up my mind," Zola says, her voice suddenly hard.

"Then I'll have to remove you by force."

"You wouldn't." Even though she isn't struggling anymore, her face is cold and smug. "You don't have it in you."

I tighten my arms around her. "Maybe I didn't before I met you, Zola."

"Cut the bullshit, and tell me what you think is happening right now," Zola snaps.

Four minutes.

"Okay. Okay," I say, doing my best to keep my voice even. I can't spook her right now. "I know what happened with your dad, Zola. I know what happened right before he left."

Zola's neck twists, and I follow her eyes to the gold picture frame on the shelf behind her. "That's not possible."

"I read your note in the Czech Society guest book," I say quietly.

Zola freezes in my arms but doesn't say anything.

"He killed her, didn't he?" I ask. "Your father killed Emily."

"Fuck." The word is a half sob. Zola leans into my hair, the way she has so many times when she hasn't wanted me to see her face as she confesses something, and my heart sears. "Fuck, Kay."

I'm sure she can feel the banging of my heart against her skin. "Principal Ellison said that it was a member of the Davison community who set the bomb to destroy the locker. And your father left right after Emily died. The timing was too close to be coincidental, and there's no other reason you would be so obsessed with the death of a girl you didn't know."

"That murder was the reason he left," Zola mutters into me. "Someone from the old country read the article in *Kew Gardens Online* and recognized his MO: the manhole bomb. As it turned out, he'd killed like that in Czechia. With his victims' families out for revenge, it was enough for someone to track him down. A hitman came after him. So he disappeared."

Three minutes.

I can't do it. It's not enough time.

It has to be enough time.

"You told me that after he left, it was the first time you learned where your family was from. So that was why you started looking into Czech history and culture, right?" I ask. She nods into me. "And then you learned about the Clean Hand Girls."

"You're good, Kay," she says, laughing bitterly. "Reminds me why I fell in love with you."

Until now I've been pretending that my heart isn't still pinned inside her, but that's not the kind of thing you can take back when you walk out of a coffee shop. It's the same thing I never told the Confiscator—never told Zola—when she asked me whether I was still in love with Emily. Crushed between her body and mine, I can feel the palpitating of that chunk of my heart, gelatinous and raw.

But I can't think about that right now. Not with so little time.

"The Clean Hand Girls resonated with you, then, because you felt so powerless," I continue. "You were unmoored by what you'd learned about your father. But this Clean Hand Girls thing, this idea that you can balance out the evil that those connected to you put into the world—that made it feel a little more surmountable."

"I really gave away all that?" Zola says, I think at least a little bit to herself.

"So you decided to do something to balance out Emily's

murder. You knew that he'd killed her, but you didn't know why, and because of that, you didn't know how to enact justice," I say. "You spent almost two years looking into her death. And when you were almost there, you assembled the girls who could fill in the gaps in the story, and then you directed them to achieve the justice you were so desperate for."

Two minutes.

I picture myself swallowed by an explosion of dust and fire. I've wasted enough time telling Zola what she already knows.

I hold her away from me so that I can study her face. She doesn't protest. And maybe, for the first time, I think I see all of her: the girl with the goulash; the Killer, the Priestess, the Healer, and all the other aliases in Clandestine; the blazing, out-of-control supernova; the daughter who lost her father two years ago, who misses him even though she so bitterly wishes she didn't; and the girl who is terrified of what she has in common with the man who raised her.

"Please, *please* defuse the bomb," I say. "I know you think you're countering your father's sins by killing the people in that room. But I promise it would only be putting more evil into the world. It would make you the same as him."

She twists back as if I've hit her. "Don't you dare say that."

"Zola, please—"

"You're not going to fucking stop me!"

One minute.

I've failed.

Looking at Zola, explosions already spinning inside her eyes, I know that nothing I can say will make her defuse the bomb. I remove one arm from its stranglehold around her to take my phone out of my pocket and text Aubrey to evacuate the room.

With her free arm, Zola swipes at me. I pull my arm back, but not fast enough. I'm not sure if my thumb has connected with the Send button when her hand slaps mine, sending my phone sailing into the open vent in the middle of the closet floor. I hear the device crack against something hard, its screen lighting up in sputtering fuchsias and greens several feet into the hole.

Now there is nothing left for me. I knew that this was the most likely outcome of tonight, either my body or my future consumed by the hunger of the bomb. And if this is how I'm going to go, my final choice is how many lives I can preserve in my place.

I jab the doorknob of the closet with my elbow, pushing open the door behind me. Fluorescent light floods the closet as I fling Zola into the hallway and grab the metal rod with the hook on the end. I shove it into the vent and sweep it across the hollow layer between floors, my panic barely contained enough to prevent me from swinging the rod so violently that when it connects with the bomb, that will be the end. I feel a tap of metal on metal and pull. I don't know whether I believe in God, but if I do, I pray that He won't let my hook catch on the wire that will render my last act insignificant.

Thirty seconds.

I will not be fucking insignificant.

As I bring the collection of wires and batteries through the hole in the floor, the sound of its ticks sending a cold terror crashing over me, Zola barrels through the door of the closet and hurls herself toward the bomb.

"You're not—the one—who's supposed to die!"

And that's when I realize Zola Wolfe did not come here tonight expecting to leave.

So when a Clean Hand Girl's master committed a crime that was considered unforgivable, like murdering a child, the Clean Hand Girl typically committed suicide in accordance with the cultural belief that an intentionally martyred soul was the only universal cure for evil.

Zola rips the bomb off the hook of the rod and dives into the vent. And then I hear a crash. Her body rips through the ceiling and tumbles into the classroom beneath her, still clutching the bomb to her chest.

Fifteen seconds.

I don't think. I leap down after her. The classroom is empty, the door just swinging shut as I plummet to land on top of Zola. I can still grab the bomb—hurl it out one of the windows—push Zola to safety—

Ten seconds.

My body feels like it's reverberating, adrenaline dulling the pain that I'd feel tomorrow, if there were a chance I'd make it to tomorrow, as I grapple for the bomb—

Five seconds.

With a strength I didn't know she had, Zola shoves me off her and hurtles toward the wall of the room, but it isn't the wall with the door, through which she could still throw the bomb at the group, seizing their lives in the last few seconds—it's the wall with the windows—

Three seconds.

I roll across the floor toward her, but from here, there's no way I can traverse the twenty feet to knock the bomb out of her arms—

Two seconds.

Zola leaps onto the countertop below the window panes—

One second.

She looks back at me, the bomb tucked under one of her arms and my heart cradled inside the other, her eyes full of a serenity I've never seen in her before, a single suspended moment before the supernova finally reaches Earth—

And Zola Wolfe explodes.

CHAPTER 16

NINE MONTHS LATER

"I THINK I'M GETTING THE hang of public school," Chioma says, sliding into the coffee shop booth next to me.

"Are you sure about that?" Mai reaches across the table and flicks Chioma's earlobe. Even though Chioma has traded her Chanel jackets for some unbranded denim that she found at a thrift store, she has yet to abandon her stack of Christian Dior earrings.

"Hey, I'm not trying to pretend to be someone I'm not," Chioma says, swatting away Mai's hand.

The coffee shop across the street from HS 244 has become our after-school meeting spot. As I take a sip of my chai, I feel the weight of my backpack pressing into my legs under the table. The bag is heavy with a packet on the college application process, distributed during the twelfth-grade assembly this morning. It's useful information to have, especially after the summer program at Northwestern made it clear that studying criminology isn't nearly as appealing after experiencing it firsthand. The result is that I'm woefully behind on exploring other options.

My phone buzzes on the table. It's a text from Aunt Shell: a photo of the early-fall crop of herbs growing in the garden outside her cottage. Tall stalks of lavender protrude from behind leafy basil. I hold up the photo to the rest of the table. "If she keeps sending me evidence of how idyllic her life is, I might punch her the next time I see her in person."

"You can't do that," Mai says. "Then she'll stop bringing us all fresh herbs when she visits."

I snort and respond.

ME:

Mai wants more lavender

Aunt Shell texts back right away.

AUNT SHELL:

Noted. Also, if you're with your friends rn, no need to text me back right away, but when you have a sec I'd love to hear about the first day of senior year :)

Our text stream has resumed its activity over the past nine months. Aunt Shell hadn't realized how distant she'd become, she told me, and the news that I was in the hospital was about the fastest possible way to remedy that. We're still not as close as we used to be, but I don't think that kind of relationship is what either of us needs anymore.

Aubrey shoots me a side-eye from across the table, a mug of black coffee cupped between her hands. Since she started slicking back her bangs, I've come to learn just how frequently the brigade of judgment marches across her features. "This isn't a good use of time. We should have stayed after school to get to know the new teachers, maybe scope out the way that the locker redistribution has changed hallway social dynamics—"

Mai tucks her sharp bob behind her ears. "Okay, who wants to take a turn at giving Aubrey the lecture on how having friends is 'beneficial to long-term goals'?"

"There's really no need," Aubrey says, taking a long sip of her coffee.

If Mai is this full of zingers, I think it's safe to ask her the question that's been on my mind. "Hey, Mai, have you spoken to your mom, now that there's a date for the trial?"

Mai's shoulders curve downward, closing her into the green leather of the booth. "She still won't talk to me."

Nine months ago, while I was in the supply closet with Zola, begging her to defuse the bomb, Mai and Chioma were in the classroom below us, presenting an ultimatum to their families. They had scheduled an Instagram post that detailed everything: the secret of the internship program, the murder that the parents orchestrated in order to prevent that information from getting out, and the role Davison played in facilitating all of it. Mai and Chioma told the group that they would cancel the post if Principal Ellison agreed to let me back into the school. It's still not clear what would have happened if Aubrey hadn't burst into the room, shouting about a bomb—Mai thinks that my expulsion would have been reversed, Chioma doesn't think I had a chance—but in the chaos of the explosion, the post sent on schedule.

As it turns out, the police commissioner's membership in your conspiracy doesn't protect you when the local chapter of the fire department comes barreling through your school in response to an explosion. And when they find one girl's body strewn in pieces on the back lawn and another girl barely alive, covered in a hail of glass shards from the windowpanes and charred with second-degree burns on the floor of an English classroom, you can't prevent the authorities from chainsawing through the school building until they find your secret file room.

Between those files and the Instagram post, Davison's

network of power couldn't save the families and administrators from experiencing a new side of the justice system. Even putting aside Emily's murder, it's a violation of a number of laws to use teenagers to steal company secrets. Plus, a group of MS patients put together a class action to sue Argenta for taking Bonum's formula and price gouging the treatment, which added another layer to the lawsuits. After the indictments, Principal Ellison shuttered the school—it's rather difficult to uphold your principal duties with an ankle monitor chaining you to your home—and the former Davison families dispersed between other private schools and public options, like HS 244. It's strange to think of Davison ceasing to be. But, man, am I glad it has.

Aubrey places a hand on Mai's shoulder and squeezes it. "You did the right thing, you know."

I suspect Aubrey is thinking the same thing I am: that Mai's mom will be fine. That her mom's lawyers, along with the rest of the barricade defending the Davison families, could convince a jury that Machiavelli's iron fist was simply a style of glove. I don't expect anyone on that stand to experience a higher penalty than a fine—granted, a fine that could pay the college tuition of every student at HS 244, but that's probably just a chip out of their vacation budgets.

However, that doesn't make it any less painful for Chioma

and Mai when their parents refuse to acknowledge them. Chioma is living alone in the mother-in-law apartment of her family's town house—a position that, at first, I struggled to find sympathy for, but the isolation is clearly a prison sentence. Meanwhile, Mai came home one day to find a pile of her belongings tossed onto the sidewalk outside her apartment building, along with a note informing her that she had been formally disowned. She's been living with an aunt, her mother's sister, who became estranged from the rest of the family after a divisive spat while the two of them were in journalism school. Mai isn't sure exactly what happened, but her aunt is a doctor now.

Steam rises from the mug of herbal tea in front of Chioma. "Zola would be way too satisfied with all the lawsuits."

Thinking of Zola still makes my stomach burn. I doubt that will ever change.

"I think about that a lot," Mai says, pulling Chioma's tea toward herself and taking a sip. Chioma rolls her eyes but doesn't comment. "For a society that wasn't real, we really ended up almost becoming Blue Hand Girls."

I glance down at my right hand, the one that spent so long saturated with blue ink last year. It's also the one I used to shield my face during the explosion. The burns and glass cuts covered most of my skin, but my hand was the only part of my body mutilated enough for doctors to need to perform a total reconstruction. I had my third surgery on it a few weeks ago. There are hundreds of colors on my skin, all bleeding into each other: green and purple bruising from the surgery, yellow-white from the skin grafts, black from the stitches, pinks and reds from the blood pulsing right below the skin's surface.

But the blue tinge that I thought would never go away, no matter how many times I scrubbed my hand, isn't one of them.

ACKNOWLEDGMENTS

This book would not exist without the dedication, commitment, and belief of an enormous community to which I'm honored to belong. Thank you to:

My agent, Amelia Appel, for being a champion for me and my writing in even more ways than I thought possible. I'm so grateful to you for your feedback, support, and advocacy. And thank you to everyone else at TriadaUS, particularly Brent Taylor for ensuring that this book is heard as well as read and Uwe Stender for making me feel welcome in Team Triada from the moment I signed.

My editor, Wendy McClure, who utterly transformed this novel. Thank you for falling in love with this book, for recognizing what it wanted to become even before I did, and for guiding me until it was there. And thank you to the entire Sourcebooks team for editing, designing, producing, marketing, and otherwise bringing this book to life: Jenny Lopez, Neha Patel, Jenne Abramowitz, Taylor Geldermann, Thea Voutiritsas, Sarah Brody, Jessica Thelander, Deve McLemore, Karen Masnica, Lia Ferrone, and Delaney Heisterkamp.

To my cover artist, Emily Mahar, thank you for creating the most gorgeous cover I could imagine. It quite literally drips with mystery and intrigue.

My writing mentors and peers in the University of Pennsylvania Creative Writing Department and the Kelly Writers House. Jamie-Lee Josselyn and Al Filreis, thank you for bringing me into Penn's creative writing community. And in particular, Nova Ren Suma, thank you for teaching the young adult fiction class that birthed the first chapter of this novel and for believing in my book enough to take me on for an independent study to finish the draft, even when you were swamped with your own deadlines. Your feedback gave me confidence in my strengths and actionable strategies for improving my weaknesses.

My friends, who have inspired and improved this novel in countless ways. Thank you to Leah Baxter, Sam Kaufmann, Xander Gottfried, and Ian McCormack for starting a secret society and inducting me into it seven years ago; it was very thoughtful of you to support my writing career that way. More recently, thank you to the four of you, together with Quinn Gruber, Milo Roth, and Quentin Wedderburn, for giving feedback on various drafts of the book and for providing insight into topics ranging from the dynamics of private high schools to the Bohemian Reformation. And thank you to the rotating cast of our Creative Writing Peer Pressure Club, including Victoria Garcia, Youseff Jakher, and Emily Paik; it has been a joy to finish this novel alongside you all between our pasta dinners and pots of toffee milk tea.

My fiancée, Penelope. You have made me a better writer and a better person. Your writing inspires and astonishes me; aspiring toward your level has motivated me to make this book the best it could be. You're also, of course, the best muse in the world. There's a piece of you inside all my characters, especially the enigmatic and beautiful ones. Forever with you is happier than any ending I could write.

And finally, my family. Thank you to my aunt Kara Newman and my uncle Robert Silverman for inspiring me with your careers as writers. Thank you to my grandparents Sandra and Alan Silverman for encouraging my writing since I started sending you stories in elementary school. Thank you to my dad, Laurence Miller, for always giving me honest feedback and for reading this manuscript and saying, "Oh, yeah, this is the one."

Thank you to my mom, Joelle Silverman Miller; words can't encompass everything you've done for this book and everything else I've written. On a technical level, you've taught me more about writing than any other person in my life, and on an emotional level, you've always made me feel like a writer. When I was six years old and told you that I'd set a goal to publish a novel, you told me that you knew I could. Above all, that's the reason this book exists.

ABOUT THE AUTHOR

Rowana Miller writes about riddles, goblins, secrets, strange girls, and mischief. After graduating from the University of Pennsylvania in 2022, she moved back to her hometown of New York City, where she lives with her fiancée, Penelope, and two cats, Alice and Jabberwocky. She is the founder and executive director of Cosmic Writers, a nonprofit that provides creative writing education for kids and teenagers. *Secrets of the Blue Hand Girls* is her first novel.